SOMETHING'S ABOUT TO BLOW UP

Sam Blake is a bestselling writer whose books have been shortlisted for Irish Crime Novel of the Year three times. Under her real name, Vanessa Fox O'Loughlin, she is the founder of Writing.ie, The Inkwell Group and Murder One. This is her second YA novel, following *Something Terrible Happened Last Night*, which was shortlisted for the Great Reads Awards and the Teen and YA Book of the Year Award. Follow her on social media at @samblakebooks.

SOMETHING'S ABOUT TO

WHEN CHEMISTRY

BLOW

GETS EXPLOSIVE ...

UP

SAM BLAKE

GILL BOOKS

Gill Books
Hume Avenue
Park West
Dublin 12
www.gillbooks.ie

Gill Books is an imprint of M.H. Gill and Co.

978 07171 9716 3

Designed by Bartek Janczak
Edited by Natasha Mac a'Bháird
Proofread by Esther Ní Dhonnacha
Printed and bound in Great Britain by Clays Ltd, Elcograf S.p.A.
This book is typeset in Minion Pro by Typo•glyphix.

*The paper used in this book comes from the wood pulp of sustainably
managed forests.*

A CIP catalogue record for this book is available from the
British Library.

5 4 3 2 1

For everyone who doesn't feel heard.

MAPS

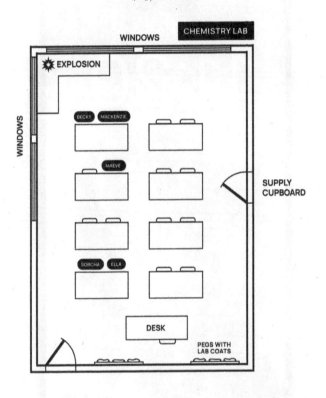

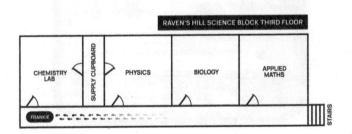

MONDAY

MONDAY

A s Frankie hurried into the Raven's Hill School science building, she had many things on her mind, but getting caught up in the explosive events that were about to unfold wasn't among them. Not even close.

She would have had to have been psychic for that.

And if she *had* been psychic and had had any idea of what might happen in the next 24 hours, she could have saved herself, her friends, her family, her teachers and the Guards a whole lot of drama. To say nothing of public humiliation, life-changing injuries, death threats and prison.

But Frankie *wasn't* psychic, so right now, getting Becky's iPad back to her before Chemistry began was her priority number one. And that was looking increasingly unlikely unless she moved super fast.

Priority number two was making sure everyone had reviewed their group video English project, so she could submit it before the lunchtime deadline. The internet cutting out at home last night had been a major crisis, for her *and* all the guests at the Berwick Castle Hotel, if the irate American at the front desk was to be believed. Her parents, who ran the hotel, had tried to keep everyone, including Frankie, calm. But they couldn't work magic.

Living in a hotel had definite advantages, but some big disadvantages too. At least Frankie had saved the last video edits before the Wi-Fi went down. Becky's ideas for the presentation had been so creative and clever, *everyone* would have killed her if she'd lost them.

Frankie mentally kicked herself as she hitched her backpack higher onto her shoulder with her free hand, holding on tight to the iPad in the other, and pounded up the last flight of stairs.

She was such an idiot for not setting her alarm this morning. And why had she put on her school jumper? Now, the winter sun was streaming through the glass walls that surrounded the architect-designed staircase. It was like a fishbowl. A hot fishbowl, and Frankie was starting to understand how a boiled fish might feel.

If she could just get the iPad back to Becky and get straight on to History she'd only be a few minutes late, and then at least only one of them would be in trouble.

She was just glad she'd pulled her dark hair up in a high ponytail today so at least some air could circulate around her neck. She could feel the sweat running down her back already. And her face had to be at least as bright red as the wool of her jumper.

But she didn't have time to worry about that now.

Getting to the top landing, Frankie paused for a split second and tried to catch her breath. The sprint up just proved her cousin Sorcha was right: she needed to get fit. *Why was the Fifth Year Chemistry lab on the third floor? And who built classrooms six flights up anyway?*

Becky would have full justification to never speak to her again if she didn't get the iPad back before class started. She was having enough problems with Chemistry as it was. And if Frankie landed her in it, after Becky had worked so hard on the project *and* lent her the iPad over the weekend, she knew she'd feel horrible forever.

Becky had only moved to Raven's Hill in third year, and they'd been in different forms lower down the school. When Frankie had first met her, she seemed nervous of everything and just wanted to please everyone. Once she let down her defences enough to trust you, she was an absolute mine of fascinating, random information, and really creative, but it took a long time for her to trust. Ages, actually.

Frankie pushed open the glass doors at the top of the stairs into the bright white tiled hallway and power-walked through them, trying not to run. Teachers had a way of materialising when you were running in the corridor, and she *really* didn't need a detention.

If her little brother Max hadn't dropped Frankie's own iPad none of this would have happened. But then if she hadn't left the group project to the last minute and been up all Sunday night working on it, she wouldn't have overslept and been late this morning in the first place. Maybe her mum was right, and she was spending too much time with Danny. Or 'mooning over Danny', as her mum said. Today was already proving to be the worst Monday on record.

Speed-walking past the Applied Maths room, then the Biology and Physics labs, Frankie glanced in through the glazed panels in the doors. Applied Maths was already underway, and she could see a crowd of girls in white lab coats in Physics, but the other room looked empty. Could she risk running?

Chemistry was in S12 at the very end of what felt like the longest corridor in the school. But the teacher, Mr Murray, always took a few minutes to get everyone settled, so if she stuck her head in the door, Frankie was sure she could hand the iPad to Sorcha to pass back to Becky. If Mr Murray had started already he'd be mad, but at least Sorcha was always at the front. Frankie could just whiz in and whiz out again. And pray he didn't give her a detention for interrupting.

She was almost there. And the door was open, so it looked like the class hadn't started yet.

That was one good thing …

Frankie heard the sound before she felt the impact.

Like a punch to her stomach.

There were probably only microseconds between them, but one moment she was heading for the Chemistry lab door and the next she was falling backwards and hitting the floor. Hard. And the ceiling was coming down on top of her.

And then it all went black.

EARLIER THAT MORNING

THE FIFTH YEAR COMMON ROOM
RAVEN'S HILL SCHOOL
8.30 a.m.
Sorcha

S orcha's dark, bobbed hair was still wet from the pool when she walked into the Fifth Year common room. Jess and Georgia were huddled on the sofa deep in conversation with the new American boarder, Mackenzie, their phones in their hands.

Sorcha mentally did a double-take. Jess's hair was *really* purple. Not even close to black. Jess had sent her pictures over the weekend, delighted with the change and convinced she'd get away with it. Sorcha wasn't so sure.

Jess had moved over from London, where the school she'd been to had been *very* different. She'd only moved to Raven's Hill at the start of this year and her dad had already been in several times to discuss her 'pushing the boundaries' – Jess's air quotes. But then, her dad was a war reporter; pushing boundaries was what he did for a living. In Jess's eyes, life was all about perspective.

Raven's Hill was so focused on 'standards' that it was super strict about uniform. But then, the school's mission was for its girls to be turned into future leaders, so Sorcha supposed it made sense. Even if, as Jess said, it squashed self-expression.

Sorcha wasn't too worried about self-expression. She'd transferred to Raven's Hill so she could board, which meant she could save time on her commute, double up her swim training in the school pool, get into the national squad, *and* ace her Leaving Cert.

Well, that was the plan anyway.

She threw her backpack onto the floor beside the sofa.

'Shunt up. What are you three looking at?'

The girls slid up the sofa to make room for Sorcha. She was tiny, but it was still a tight fit for four. The minute she sat down Sorcha could see they all had Rave-fess, the school confession site, open on their phones. She cocked an eyebrow. 'What's up?'

Closest to her, Georgia pulled a sad face, her brown eyes huge against her sallow complexion. She hooked her long, straight hair behind her ear. 'Jasper Parks, that nerdy guy in Fifth Year in Raven's Park, the one with red glasses, got beaten up on Friday night. There's a post about the Guards looking for witnesses.'

On the other side of Mackenzie, Jess leaned forward abruptly, the dark purple stud in her nose catching the light.

'Squirrel? God, I hope he's okay.' Jess looked shocked. 'He's not nerdy – well, not really, he just has an individual sense of style that involves knitted things. He's the captain of their Model United Nations team. Everyone calls him Squirrel because he's really quick, but he's really shy if he doesn't know you.' Jess hesitated. 'And he's quite cute, actually.'

Sorcha could see that Mackenzie was taking all this in. She was wearing really pretty silver eyeshadow that shimmered on her dark skin, but Sorcha had a feeling that this might go the same way as Jess's new nose stud and have to be removed as soon as the first teacher spotted it. Jess's usual diamanté stud met with disapproving looks, but the purple was like a proclamation. There was a limit to what they could get away with.

Sorcha looked back to Georgia's phone screen, trying to read the post. 'Does he know who jumped him?'

Georgia shook her head. 'He was unconscious when they found him. It would have been pitch dark by the time he left school. It happened at the back of their rugby field. No security cameras.'

That didn't sound good. Sorcha reached for her backpack, jiggling the zip open. Her own phone was inside. 'Someone must have seen.'

Georgia shrugged. 'He'd been in study and was heading for the back gate, apparently – he lives really close. Unless someone was walking their dog on the pitch, there wouldn't be anyone around. But who goes to study on a Friday night?'

'I bet it was someone from his school.' Jess screwed up her face. 'They have a really big issue with bullying at Raven's Park – just ask Viv.' She let out a sharp sigh. They'd all felt very protective of Viv when she'd arrived at Raven's Hill. Transitioning was emotionally stressful enough without the added bonus of an ignorant, ill-informed and vicious pile-on. Jess turned to Mackenzie. 'How's your brother doing – is he settling in at Raven's Park okay?'

Mackenzie hesitated for a split second before she replied. And when she did, she sounded like she was trying to convince herself, as much as them, that he was doing fine.

'He seems good so far. Greg does sorta stand out being so tall and the only African American in the school, but I don't think anyone would mess with him.' Mackenzie let out a sigh. 'His biggest problem right now is missing our dog.'

Keeping half an eye on Georgia, who was scrolling back through the Rave-fess posts, Sorcha leaned forward again to talk across her. 'I heard him in the Music room the other day when I went for my piano lesson. He's unbelievable on that violin.'

Mackenzie flushed. 'I know, he was crazy happy when he found out about the Music centre here, when Mom was looking for schools, and that he could come over for lessons. Music is his life.' She smiled. 'Which is mad given that he's my twin and my musical ability just about gets me through "Chopsticks". I can't even sing in tune.'

'Yikes, Rave-fess just updated.' Sitting between Sorcha and Mackenzie, Georgia waved her phone, interrupting them. 'Wait till you see this ...'

Crammed in on the other side of Mackenzie on the common room sofa, Jess glanced back at her phone to see what Georgia was talking about. Jasper getting beaten up was just awful. She couldn't believe she'd only found out this morning.

Rave-fess, the school's anonymous confession site, had been gossip central since it started during the summer, and, despite pretending to be scandalised, they all loved it. It had grown from confessions to comments to a general bulletin board as more people used it, and they all checked it at least ten times a day. Except Jess, who hadn't been near it all weekend.

Georgia glanced over her shoulder to see who was behind them in the common room, then lowered her voice to a theatrical whisper, her face pure drama.

'See that photo of the roses? "*Some boyfriends are the best.*" I bet you a million pounds that's Ella.'

Still distracted, Jess double-checked to make totally sure that Ella couldn't hear them. There was sometimes a delay on posts hitting Rave-fess because of the admin approval – Ella had probably submitted this one over the weekend – and if Jess knew anything about Ella Diamond, she'd be listening out this morning for everyone's reactions.

Jess leaned forward so she could keep her voice low. 'Why on earth has she put it on the school confession site and not her own Insta?'

'Attention? "*Look at me, I've got the perfect boyfriend.*"' Georgia arched her eyebrows. 'I know that sounds really mean but it's not like we don't all know that she's gorgeous *and* super clever. She doesn't need to put herself into the middle of everything, but somehow it just keeps happening.'

Georgia had a point. The boy seemed very camera shy, but Ella had been all over her private Insta with boyfriend-related photos. And from what they *had* been able to see of him, Jess had to admit he was good-looking. But she wasn't sure he needed to be mentioned in *every* one of Ella's posts.

Jess grimaced, making sure she kept her voice low in response to Sorcha's warning look. 'Ella's just obsessed. Apparently, the relationship is supposed to be top secret for some reason – maybe she doesn't want her parents to know.' She turned to Mackenzie. 'She's dating this guy Tiernan who's in Sixth Year in Raven's Park. He's literally been love-bombing her since day one.'

Sorcha cut in. 'In fairness, Ella *has* improved massively since Ruth left.'

Continuing, Jess quickly filled Mackenzie in. 'Ruth Meaney was what we called in London "the class bitch". Ella was her sidekick in the Mean Girls, but Ruth left at the start of term, and apart from this boyfriend obsession, it's like Ella can finally be herself now.' While she was speaking, Jess had scrolled to the next Rave-fess post. 'Oh heck, what's this one?'

> **Public Service Message: Whoever took intimate photos with their school jumper in the background, they have been shared in a WhatsApp group. They are blackmailing you. We love you, please talk to a friend so they can help. This could happen to any of us.**

'My God, who on earth would do that?' Sorcha leaned in to read the post. 'What WhatsApp group, like a big one? Oh God, I hope not.'

Georgia looked shocked. 'Worst nightmare. Why on earth would you *do* that to someone?'

Jess bit her lip, feeling their collective anxiety manifesting in her stomach. 'And who posted this? How do they know?'

Before anyone could comment, Jess became aware of a girl hovering beside the sofa. Jess leaned forwards to tap Sorcha's knee and Sorcha turned, smiling as she saw who it was. Becky was blushing already, her cheeks almost the same colour as her stunning flame-coloured hair, as if speaking to a group unnerved her.

'Sorry to interrupt you, Sorcha, but have you seen Frankie? She was finishing our video project for English on my iPad at the weekend, and I need it for Chemistry – it's got my homework on it.'

Sorcha swivelled around to face her properly, glancing up at the clock over the common room door. Jess's eyes followed hers. Their free time was almost over; classes started in ten minutes. Where *was* Frankie?

'I'm sure she'll be here any second. She knows you need it. I think she was working on the video late last night to get it finished in time.' Sorcha sounded confident. 'She's normally super reliable.'

Becky bit her lip, the English vowels in her accent almost as strong as Jess's when she was stressed. 'I should have emailed my homework in last week, but it wasn't due till today.' For a moment she looked like she was going to cry.

Jess wanted to give her a hug. Becky had been really badly bullied in her old school. She was Irish but her mum was English, and Frankie reckoned that having a slightly mixed accent had set her apart – her classmates had been *really* horrible about it, apparently. It wasn't until she'd come to Raven's Hill and connected with the international students that she'd started to come out of herself, no longer the odd one out.

Jess secretly thought that another reason Becky's old schoolmates had been mean was because she had a sort of inner glow. She was one of those people who had no clue that everyone turned to look when she walked down the street.

Frankie had told Jess that when she'd met Becky in the library in town to start planning their English project at the start of term, they'd been besieged by the boys from Raven's Park who'd been studying in there. Apparently even the Sixth Years had taken a sudden interest in the local history section that they'd been sitting next to so they could find reasons to talk to Becky. One of them had even asked her out for a coffee afterwards, though Becky had been very shy about who it was when Jess had asked. Jess got the impression that she preferred to be private.

Sorcha's voice cut through Jess's thoughts. 'Frankie will be here, don't worry – she would have texted me if she was sick.' She double-checked her phone to be sure. 'Chemistry's not till after first break. I'm sure she'll be here by then.'

Becky let out a breath, wincing at the same time. 'Mr Murray's going to kill me. I really messed up last week's homework and I was late the week before. I need to check it over.'

Jess felt a surge of compassion at the fear flitting across Becky's face. Jess always seemed to be on catch-up with her homework too. Sorcha obviously spotted Becky's expression as well. 'Can Frankie email it to you? Maybe as a back-up?'

Becky shook her head, her mass of tight curls bouncing like springs. 'No, no, she won't be able to find it, my folders are a mess.'

'Worst case scenario, if she's not here by break, you can copy mine.' Sorcha smiled reassuringly. 'But don't worry, Mr Murray's bark's worse than his bite. Nobody's going to die.'

'**W**hat does your colour guru say today's shade is?'
Leaning on the lockers at the back of the room, Maeve pushed her platinum blonde hair behind her ear as she looked up from her phone at the sound of Tara's voice. She leaned over to give her a kiss. Tara was half Chinese and looked super cute today with her glossy black hair in space buns. Maeve sighed inside; her curls never shone like Tara's hair, no matter how much product she used. There were times, even after so long, when she couldn't believe they were together.

'Blue today – it's good for depression, apparently. You're so late. I was starting to think you weren't coming in.'

Tara rolled her eyes. 'Sorry, I tried to text but the reception was terrible, the bus was late, and I was trying to finish my Maths on the way, plus my flute lesson's been moved to this morning instead of after lunch, so I bet I'm going to be there all first break.' Tara opened her eyes wide at the horror of her morning and, dropping her backpack on the floor, unlocked her locker. She stood for a moment looking at the haphazard pile of sports gear and lesson notes threatening to spill out. 'Oh God. I really hate Mondays.'

Maeve put her arm around Tara's shoulders. Maeve had tied her school jumper around her waist this morning in an effort to start Monday in a positive mood; the honey colour of their blouses was definitely more calming than the angry red of their jumpers. 'You need to bring colour into each day, I keep telling you. It works on your energy. Sunshine yellow is a happy colour; you need to see it the minute you wake up.'

Tara raised her eyebrows, her face sceptical. 'You're obsessed, you know that? Has reorganising your bookshelves into a rainbow made you a better person?'

Grinning, Maeve unwrapped her arm and leaned against the locker next to Tara's. 'Maybe not, but it's very satisfying. Colour has an impact on your emotions, you know – the Egyptians used it. You should follow ColourMeHappy. She's brilliant – and she's got about a million followers on TikTok and Insta, so it's not just me.'

'I reckon half those American influencers buy their followers – they're so fake.'

'She's not fake and she's not American – you can tell from the way she writes her posts. It says "the Universe" on her location. She's spreading happiness and she's not limited by borders or politics.'

Tara pulled a face. 'I can think of someone who's *really* not happy this morning. Did you see the post on Rave-fess about those photos?'

Maeve grimaced as Tara pulled her flute case out from under the pile of sports gear and shoved her locker door closed before everything fell out. It wasn't entirely successful. Tara bent down to rescue her mouthguard as she continued, 'I'd be *dying* inside.'

'It's absolutely your worst nightmare. But God, sending them …'

Tara wrapped her arms around her flute case and rested her chin on it. 'I wonder how bad they are. And who she sent them to. *And* who shared them – what a scumbag.'

Maeve glanced behind her. The rest of the year were busy getting themselves ready for lessons, except Frankie's cousin Sorcha and her friend Jess, who were still on the sofa. They had Georgia and the new girl Mackenzie sandwiched between them and were glued to their phones. In the other corner of the common room Ella and Amber had their heads together, deep in conversation. Maeve couldn't see Viv. She kept her voice low as she spoke.

'They're bad.'

Tara whipped around, her eyes wide open. 'You've seen them? But how?'

'They've been shared around the Raven's Park rugby team …'

Tara interrupted her. 'Like the *whole* team?'

Maeve opened her eyes wide. 'I think so. Enough, anyway.'

'Oh. My. God. That's literally explosive.' Keeping her voice to a whisper, Tara drew the sentence out. 'Did Conan get them too?'

Maeve scowled, thinking about her cousin. There were times when she wished she could divorce her family. 'He thought they were hilarious, sent them to me to see if I knew who it was. Conan said whoever got them told her he'd make them public in the next twenty-four hours if she doesn't go all the way with him. He's already shared loads in their group. It's actually horrific.'

'That's nuts. Why would she ever talk to him again? It's like he's punishing her for not sleeping with him. Could you tell who it was?'

'No, thank God. But she took the photos in her bedroom, and she very obviously didn't expect anyone else to see them.' Maeve was just praying that whoever the girl was would see her post on Rave-fess. It was the only way she had been able to think of to try and show whoever it was that she wasn't on her own.

Tara sighed, shaking her head in horror. 'God, she must be sick. I wouldn't be able to come into school if that was me.'

Maeve closed her eyes for a second, but all she could see was the photos. It was like the girl's humiliation had flooded into her the moment she'd opened Conan's message. It was just too awful.

Posting on Rave-fess had seemed the only way to try and help. Maeve had even thought about adding her name, although the admins would probably have taken it off, and doing that would be likely to alert Conan's friend that he'd shown Maeve the pictures in the first place, which might not end well for either of them. Someone who thought it was funny to do this sort of thing might not stop at blackmail.

Even watching ColourMeHappy posts all the way to school hadn't helped to shift the images from her mind. The girl who ran the account posted videos and memes about a different colour each day with an explanation of its impact. And Tara was right, Maeve *was* a bit obsessed. But it was good obsessed; it was helping her with the stress of the Leaving Cert.

'Is there any way to stop the rugby team forwarding the photos on?' Interrupting Maeve's thoughts, Tara picked her backpack up and pulled it onto her shoulder.

Maeve shrugged. 'She needs to go to the Guards, whoever she is, but she's probably in shock that he'd threaten to share them at all. We need to work out who it is, so we can make sure she's okay and then persuade her to report it.' She sighed. 'Whoever it is, they'll be in SO much trouble, especially if she's under eighteen – it's totally illegal.'

Tara pursed her lips. 'I wonder if they know that. There was that whole ad campaign about how even saying you were going to share images could get you arrested, but maybe they missed it. You should text Conan and tell him.'

Maeve looked at her, one white-blonde eyebrow raised. 'You think that they think the law applies to them? They'll say she sent them to be shared or something.'

Tara sighed. 'They could end up going right around all of Raven's Park if someone doesn't stop them.'

J ess didn't usually sit at the back of class, but she wanted to check the posts on Rave-fess again about Jasper getting beaten up.

And find out the visiting hours for St Anthony's Hospital.

It was only ten minutes from school, and she reckoned she'd have time to go at lunchtime today if she could just find out which ward he was on. She had drama club tonight, and it was the first run-through of the opening scene in *Macbeth*. There was no way she could miss it. *And* she needed to get a load of work done on her Economics project, so this evening would be tricky.

Opening the website, she could see lunchtime wasn't an option. Visiting time was 2–4 p.m. every afternoon – but her last class was a free period. If she called the hospital at first break to find out the ward, and then called her dad to organise a note for her, she was pretty sure she could get back in time for drama.

And hopefully she'd catch up with Frankie at first break too. Jess had been texting her all morning and heard nothing back, but perhaps the battery on Frankie's phone had died. Otherwise Jess was sure Frankie would have texted when she saw the Rave-fess posts – it was all anyone was talking about.

Jess propped her pencil tin in front of her phone; she was pretty sure Ms McNally wouldn't spot it. The sun was really low and streaming in the windows, causing her teacher to squint so much she looked like she needed sunglasses. Even Jess could barely see the whiteboard that filled the wall behind her.

A few rows ahead of her, Georgia turned around and rolled her eyes. Neither of them was brilliant at poetry, and Jess's arm ached from writing the answers to this morning's test. Jess pulled a face. If her friends at home thought A-levels were bad, they were nothing on the Leaving Cert. She'd almost died when she'd found out Maths was compulsory.

At the front of the class, Ms McNally was going through their papers.

'Now girls, I want you to double check the quotes you used this morning. We're going to go back over your notes and see if you missed any or could have used better ones. Please highlight them.'

Ms McNally turned her back to the class to write something on the board and Jess scrolled back through

Rave-fess to find the post about the Garda appeal after Jasper's assault. There was a picture of Jasper, wearing his signature *Doctor Who* scarf. Jess smiled. One of the things that she really liked about Jasper was that he was a total individual: he couldn't care less about what everyone else was wearing or what people thought he should be wearing. He thought there was much more important stuff to worry about – like climate change and the polar ice caps melting.

Jess scrolled back a bit further. Georgia had said she'd seen a post over the weekend that might have had something to do with the attack. She glanced up to check on Ms McNally every few seconds, but there were so many rows between her desk and the front, she reckoned she was pretty safe. Then she spotted it. The first post had appeared on Friday evening. It sounded like it had been made by someone who lived close by.

Ambulance on playing field at RP.
Garda car just arrived.

Going to take the dog out and see
what's occurring. Will update.

Jess shivered. How terrifying must that have been? Jasper wasn't one of the rugby dudes who was used to getting bashed about on a cold, muddy field. And what if it had been more than one person who'd attacked him? Jess felt sick at the thought.

Biting her lip, Jess scrolled on. There was only one more post before the one about the Garda appeal.

Not sure what the story is but over-heard the Guards saying one casualty. Someone got beaten up pretty badly. Gardaí looking for witnesses.

It sounded horrible.

It was scary enough when you thought someone was following you home. That had happened to Jess a few times, her heart beating so loud she was sure everyone could hear it. Had Jasper realised he was being followed across the field? Had he tried to run? Or had he walked into a drug deal or something?

At the front of the room Ms McNally turned around.

'Jessica McKenna, I hope that's not your phone you're looking at. Put it away immediately, please.'

Jess felt the heat of Ms McNally's glare and quickly slipped the phone into her backpack. Meeting Ms McNally's eye, Jess mouthed 'sorry'. The teacher hesitated as if she was about to say more, and then got back to the papers in front of her. *Thank goodness.* She couldn't keep track of Jasper's news if her phone got confiscated.

Part of Jess wished she'd seen the original post on Rave-fess when it had happened. Somehow, she felt like she'd let Jasper down, although she would have had no way of knowing who the victim was back then. Was she being ridiculous? She rarely checked Rave-fess at the weekends – between spending all day Saturday working in the charity shop in the Main Street and revising all Sunday for this poetry test, she'd barely been in touch with anyone.

She just hoped Jasper wasn't too badly hurt.

RAVE-FESS
ONLINE
11 a.m.

Why are sports teachers so competitive?
Not everything in life is a race.

Cannot stop thinking about the post on the
naked photos – who would do that?

> It was definitely someone from RH, I
> heard their jumper was in the back-
> ground of one of the pictures.
>
> It's not the person who took the pic-
> tures we should be talking about, it's
> the scummy lowlife who shared them.
>
> That's blackmail. And it's illegal.
> Whoever she is needs to talk to the
> Guards and report it.

Did you know that breathing lavender helps with anxiety?

Talent alert: Raven's Park rugby lads incoming x 6. Spotted at 10.45. Looked like they were heading to the drama building. Any update?

> They're coming in to help build the big bits of scenery for Macbeth – heard they're building the castle.

> Wouldn't it be epic if they got some of the boys to actually act in it? It would be so much more authentic.

> Shakespeare didn't use any women actors. If his plays were all single sex, why do we need the boys?

> Eh, hello? Because most of the RP rugby boys are gorgeous.

> Macbeth is a tragedy.

> ????? And? Your point?

If anyone sees a copy of The Great Gatsby, sticker of little ghost on front corner, no name, please take to lost property. It has ALL MY NOTES on it.

Does anyone know the name of the guy from Kilmurray Manor with the broken arm who gets on the No 46 by the pier? He's totally dreamy.

ASK HIM!

Did anyone see that Aston Martin in the car park this morning? Are we getting celebs now?

That belongs to Hailey de Búrca's dad. She was here for a meeting with Ms Ashworth and Mr Murray last week. Had to take her on a tour of the Science Block and Music building with her dad. They must be here for another meeting.

Didn't she get expelled from Ardmore Wood in Wicklow? My cousin said she punched someone in the lunchroom!!!

Thought she was suspended for smoking in the bathroom???!

She said she was leaving Ardmore Wood and wants to move here. Didn't mention getting expelled. She said she wants to do engineering or something, needs a good science school.

Didn't Ardmore Wood burn down? I heard it was the same day she left.

Big coincidence if she didn't burn down the school LMAO. I heard she's psychotic, we DEFINITELY don't want her here!!! Who goes around punching people?

Does she have long dark hair? Saw her going into the Science Block wearing black suede Louboutin sneakers, the ones with the spikes (WANT)

Literally half of Ardmore Wood School burnt down, it was on the news – bet we'll get loads of applications for Fifth and Sixth year.

I thought this was supposed to be a confession site?

Admin – I just post what people submit. It's your site not mine!

THE MUSIC CENTRE
RAVEN'S HILL SCHOOL
11.03 a.m.
Maeve

Maeve tried to catch her breath as she peered in through the glass door of the Music room. She'd run straight here from Art as soon as the bell had gone, but Tara was still in her flute lesson. The flute teacher tried to pack everyone in and always ran through break if you were unlucky enough to get the 10.40 lesson. Maeve just prayed they'd started on time.

Maeve could feel her chest tightening as anxiety and anger swirled around her stomach. Could she interrupt? The teacher would kill her, but she *really* needed to talk to Tara. She looked at the clock on the corridor wall. If Tara came out quickly, she'd have a few minutes to tell her what she'd discovered about the photos.

Had she done the right thing, texting Conan?

If she couldn't talk to her now, Maeve needed Tara to meet her as soon as Chemistry was over so they could discuss it. She'd texted her already, but this really couldn't wait.

Maeve let out a sharp breath. She'd stay here as long as she could, which would probably be the whole of break, but she couldn't be late for Chemistry. She'd have to text Tara again if her flute lesson wasn't finished in time, but Mr Murray was like a hawk with phones, so there would be no chance to explain until lunchtime.

Maeve sat down on one of the chairs pushed up in a row against the wall, the pleats in her brown and red tartan kilt jumping as her knee bounced with nervous energy. The other practice rooms were empty now break had started, so at least she was on her own. She didn't think she could make polite conversation right now, or any sort of conversation. Her head was whirling.

She checked her phone again. Conan still hadn't replied. She'd messaged him right before Art had started and sent him a link to the page she'd found on the Garda website about sharing intimate images.

She'd been pretending to pay attention to the new Art teacher, but had actually been anxiety-scrolling through old ColourMeHappy posts under the table when Conan had come back with a row of laughing emojis.

She hadn't even heard what they were supposed to be doing in class, she was so angry. *#ColourMeFurious.*

How could he find this whole thing funny? Like it wasn't serious? Did he have *any* idea how something like this could push someone into a really bad place, into maybe doing something really drastic?

Even Tara had said that she'd feel like dying if it was her.

Whoever had taken the photos must have thought that the boy who wanted them was serious about her. She'd probably been pressurised into sending them, just like the advice website she'd looked at had said, 'manipulated and coerced'. Maybe she thought the boy was in love with her; maybe the girl was in love with him.

And as if being utterly humiliated by everyone looking at the photos wasn't enough, the girl would have realised now that she'd been conned, that this relationship wasn't real at all. That was utterly devastating multi-level shit.

Like being broken up with times 50.

Sitting in the Art room, incensed by Conan's text, Maeve had put her hand up.

'Miss, can I just pop to the bathroom?'

The new Art teacher had looked at her, unimpressed. 'Maeve, we're fifteen minutes into the lesson, can you go before we start next time?' She'd gestured for her to hurry. 'Be quick, I want you to finish the outlines so we can get started on cutting the lino for your prints.'

Fake-smiling gratefully, Maeve had headed out. She was too mad to concentrate on anything. There was no way the boys were going to get away with this. Conan and his friends could save their laughter for jail.

She'd felt so sick when she'd looked at the photos he'd sent her yesterday. After she'd spoken to Tara, she'd started thinking that there might be something in the pictures that would give her an idea who they were of – and if Maeve could find that out, she could talk to the girl about going to the Guards.

She knew it was someone who went to Raven's Hill. She had very pale skin and lots of freckles. She looked like she had to be at least 15. She had a pure white bedroom.

Once she'd started thinking about it, Maeve had realised there was something nagging at her about the photos. She just needed time to look at them again, somewhere totally private.

Thankfully the bathroom had been unoccupied as Maeve slipped into one of the cubicles and sat down on the lid of the toilet. Tucking her hair behind her ear, Maeve had opened WhatsApp and found the first photo. It was a torso shot, the girl's head thankfully missing from the picture, and she must have put her hair up if it was long because Maeve couldn't even see a wisp.

Angling the phone to catch the light from above her, Maeve had enlarged it with her fingers, trying to see into every corner. There had to be something … She flicked to the next photo and winced. Whoever had got her to take these images must have told her how to pose.

This photo showed her pillows and … Maeve almost dropped the phone. She knew something had been pulling at her memory and now she could see it.

On the girl's bedside locker was a box of anxiety medication. The same brand Maeve used.

The girl's elbow was blocking the corner of the photo, but Maeve enlarged it more. She could just make out the last few letters of the name on the label where it wrapped around the side of the box. And, on the next line, what had to be the end of an address. GAN and OINT. The girl's name must end in 'gan', and the address had to be somewhere in Kilmurray Point.

But she needed more than the last three letters of a name. Or did she? If she went through the register for Fourth, Fifth and Sixth Year, she could narrow down the girls whose surname ended in 'gan'. But there were plenty of those: Finnegan, Mulligan, Egan, Vishagan, Sagan – and those were just the ones she could think of off the top of her head.

At that moment Maeve had realised something else – there was another place that she'd seen a box of medication like this.

And she was sure it had been in the same room.

Maeve enlarged the photo. The bedside locker looked familiar, but they all had lockers from IKEA. She made the photo bigger. Lying on the floor in the background was the corner of a book that she was sure she recognised.

In the other picture she'd seen, the book had been in the centre of the image, the end of the box of medication only just in shot. But she was sure it had been on the same locker, in a plain white room.

Same medication, same book – same room?

In the Music room corridor, Maeve checked the time on her phone again. She really needed Tara to hurry up and finish her Music lesson. She stood up and peered in through the glass door. Tara still had her flute to her lips, and it was 11.15 a.m. The bell would be going in a second. Maeve let out a sharp sigh as she realised she didn't have time to get to the common room to get her lab coat before Chemistry.

She'd just have to text Tara again. Now she needed to run.

BULLET JOURNAL
Behind Every Successful Woman is Herself

Writing these notes to myself feels a bit weird, but when they make the Netflix docudrama of my life — with Jenna Ortega playing me, obviously — I'm going to need my real-time thoughts. Things are going to get pretty epic, and I want to be able to remember every moment of this.

I mean, honestly, that was way easier than I expected. I could hear my heart beating so hard as I ran up the stairs, the sweat running down my back. The sun was streaming in through those windows on the stairs — that was definitely a sign, I just know it.

I'd really thought this bit would be a challenge, but this place is insane. I just walked right in with it in my bag.

I thought I'd have to pick the lock, but the lab door was open — I fully expected there to be someone in there, but the room was empty. I could hear someone crashing about in the supply room, but they didn't hear me, so I just slipped it into a cupboard at the back of the lab and came right back out again.

Leaving it in the middle of the benches somewhere would have been better, but I didn't want anyone to find it and I only had a few seconds to decide.

It'll work fine.

I'm pretty pleased with the mechanism, and it really didn't take long to put together. Maybe I've discovered a whole new career LOL.

It's small, about the size of my phone. Easy to hide.

I set the timer and just walked away.

I didn't get a chance to test it, but it should be powerful enough to do what I want it to. To give them all a BIG fright. To show who is in control here.

The two of them are in the same class. Handy. Two birds with one stone. And a bit extra for Big Bird. Who does he think he is, anyway? That letter? Just no.

He's a bonus.

It's all going to happen now.

Nobody messes me about.

THE CHEMISTRY LAB
RAVEN'S HILL SCHOOL
11.17 a.m.
Ella

'Right girls, settle down. I want to get started on time today – we've a lot to get through. We'll be doing a key experiment in the second half of the lesson, but first we'll be going in two groups to the Physics lab to watch Mr Fitzgerald's Faraday cage demonstration.' Mr Murray leaned both hands on his desk at the front of the lab like he was about to deliver a sermon. Ella sighed. Her dad had insisted she take all the sciences. For some reason he thought she was going to take over from him and run his chain of chemists when she left university.

Somewhere along the line he had got her desire to study psychology mixed up with pharmacology.

'Ella, where's your lab coat? How many times have I told you not to come in without it? It's a safety issue, not a fashion choice.'

Ella jumped and exchanged glances with Sorcha, who was sitting beside her on the front bench. Everyone thought Mr Murray's Australian accent was super sexy, but when he got annoyed it made everything he said more cutting.

She quickly hid her phone. She'd been about to take a sneaky look to see if there was a text from Tiernan, but she couldn't risk it now.

He'd messaged this morning about some of the boys from the rugby team coming over to help build scenery for *Macbeth*. And then Rave-fess had updated with news that a group of Raven's Park boys had been spotted on their way into Raven's Hill. She'd been waiting for another message from him ever since.

Thankfully Mr Murray was distracted by Maeve bursting through the door, her face flushed from running.

As the teacher turned to glare at her, Ella checked her phone again. Nothing. Disappointment surged inside her.

Ella could see Maeve scanning the room, looking for a space at a bench. It wasn't a big class, but everyone had spread out and the benches were almost all full. Becky sitting at the back had created a wave and everyone was in different places today.

Seeing somewhere to sit, Maeve headed down the centre of the classroom, grimacing at Ella as their eyes met.

Maeve slipped onto the end of a bench in front of Mackenzie and Becky, and put her iPad and phone down on the white worktop. She seemed really worried about something. *Had she and Tara had a row? Had that been what had held her up?* Ella glanced behind her again as Maeve sat down. If something had happened between Tara and Maeve it would be the gossip of the century. The two of them were inseparable.

'Ella, please pay attention!' Ella jumped again as she heard Mr Murray's voice. She threw him a big grin to show him he had her complete focus. He glowered at her for a moment before continuing. 'Now, as I explained on Friday, today we're looking at how alkali metals react with water. These are soft metals, and they are kept under oil because they are *very* reactive. I'm going to show you exactly how they perform.'

Ella peered at the test tubes in the stand on Mr Murray's desk. Each one was corked and had what looked like grey putty inside it. Beside the test tube rack was a flask clamped into a stand, the heavy base designed to keep it still so it didn't jiggle during a reaction. A pile of spatulas and another flask containing water stood ready beside it. Ella liked experiments, mainly because Sorcha was her partner and she *loved* them, so Ella just had to watch while she did them all.

At the front of the class, Mr Murray droned on. 'Today we will be looking at lithium, sodium and potassium. We'll start as soon as you're all back. As I said, these metals react with water *and air*, so I'll be demonstrating: nobody is to touch anything. You've all met our new lab assistant, Ms Ryan – she'll be keeping an eye on you while I'm next door, and it's an immediate detention for anyone who cannot follow instructions. Am I clear?' He looked around the room. 'Settle down, Maeve, please.'

Ella looked over her shoulder, throwing Maeve a sympathetic look. She looked stressed and was scrolling through her iPad as if she was trying to find her notes. God only knew what had Mr Murray in such a bad mood this morning. It wasn't like he even had his period.

At the back of the class Mackenzie was coughing, her hand over her mouth. Beside her, Becky wrinkled up her nose, putting up her hand. 'What's that smell, Mr Murray? It's really strong.'

'It's bleach, girls, nothing to worry about. Ms Ryan was cleaning up a spill from the class before break. You can open a window if the smell is too strong. Now, I'm going to take half of you into the Physics lab. The rest of you please take down the notes on the board and work through the questions on page fifty-three. When we swap over, the same applies. The demonstration won't take long and if we can transit with the minimum of fuss that would be *amazing*.'

Inwardly Ella sighed. *He said it like they made a fuss all the time.*

Mr Murray continued, 'Ms Ryan is just inside the supply cupboard – she'll only be a few minutes.' He gestured with his head, indicating the tiny room that connected the Chemistry and Physics labs. 'And as I said, she'll be watching you while I'm next door.'

As if she'd finally heard her name, a woman with her dark hair dragged back in a ponytail stuck her head out of the supply cupboard door and pushed her glasses up her nose. Mr Murray looked at her pointedly. She grinned in response.

'Right, I'm going to read out the names of the first group. Line up and go through to the Physics lab quickly and quietly, please.'

Ms Ryan disappeared back inside the cupboard as the girls heading out of Chemistry lined up with their iPads in their arms. Ella took another quick look at her phone while Mr Murray was checking them all off. Tiernan hadn't messaged since he'd told her about the scenery building, but he'd sent a row of hearts straight afterwards. Perhaps he'd been too busy to text when he got here. She smiled. He really was perfect, and he was so attentive, always wanting to know what she was doing. She was sure there was a good reason why he hadn't messaged her.

'I hope you're not looking at your phone, Ella.'

She jumped, looking up and smiling again at Mr Murray. 'Just checking the time so I know how long we've got for the questions.'

He threw her a withering look. 'There's a clock on the wall, Ella. Right, let's move out. *Quietly, please*, girls.'

He looked pointedly at those few staying behind in the lab before continuing, 'The doors are open to the supply cupboard, and I *will* be listening.' He put his finger up to his ear and tapped it as if they didn't know what listening meant.

A moment later he'd followed the first group out into the corridor, leaving the door open as he vanished.

'Honestly, sometimes he talks to us like we're in primary school.' Ella turned around to see what was happening at the back of the class. Mackenzie was doodling on a notepad, her hand over her mouth, still coughing. Becky was over by the window, with her back to her.

Maeve pulled on one arm of her lab coat and looked helplessly at Ella. 'I think I got Mr Murray's coat. This is enormous.'

Ella laughed. Maeve was right: it was huge. 'You could get his whole band in there with you.'

Mackenzie looked up, suddenly interested. 'Is he really in a band?'

Maeve sighed, obviously annoyed with the lab coat. 'It's probably an Elvis tribute band.' She pulled the other sleeve on. 'Oh God, this is ridiculous, I need a smaller one. Today just keeps on getting better.' She came out from behind the bench, holding out her arms to show how huge the lab coat was.

Ella held up her phone, taking a photo of Maeve. Letting out an impatient breath, Maeve headed back up the central aisle to the pegs behind Mr Murray's desk that held the spares. She stopped beside Ella on the way. 'Do you need another one?'

'I'm sure this'll be fine. Here, let's get a selfie, the light's really good in here today.' Her focus on her phone, Ella slipped out of her row and stood in front of the bench, gesturing to Maeve to join her.

'Seriously, Ella, how many photos do you take each day?'

Ella grinned at her. 'Not nearly enough. Cheer up, you look stressed. Smile.' Ella switched her phone to video and fluffed up her fringe, flicking her hair over her shoulder as she turned to the side to get a good shot of them both. *Tiernan would love this, he was always asking questions about her friends.* Maeve pulled a big fake grin. As soon as Ella had finished, Maeve headed towards the extra lab coats hanging on the other side of Mr Murray's desk.

Ms Ryan suddenly appeared from the supply cupboard as if she'd just remembered she was supposed to be watching them. 'Now girls, sit down please. You heard Mr Murray – he'll be back at any moment.'

'I'm just getting a lab coat that fits, Ms Ryan, won't be a sec.' Maeve switched on her biggest grin as Ella went reluctantly back around to her stool, hiding her phone behind her back.

'Mr Murray's told you what to do – wait quietly, please.' Ms Ryan was trying hard to sound like she was in charge, but Ella wasn't sure she was quite succeeding.

Ella looked over at Sorcha and rolled her eyes. Sorcha had her backpack on her knee and was searching for something inside, piling the contents onto the bench top. Sorcha glanced up at Ms Ryan as she put a handful of pens on top of the already toppling pile of books.

'Oh, damn ...'

Two novels and Sorcha's fountain pen slid across the bench and onto the floor.

Ella looked over her shoulder, but Ms Ryan had disappeared back into the cupboard. Quickly, she stood up to take another photo, swinging around so the light from the window fell on her cheekbones. Out of the corner of her eye, Ella could see Sorcha dumping her backpack on the stool and moving around the bench to pick everything up. She was about to bend down when Ella heard a fizzing sound somewhere behind her, followed by a crack.

What the ...?

Before Ella could turn around to see what was happening, the force from an enormous explosion threw her sideways. As she hit the edge of the bench, a bolt of pain shot across her chest and Ella screamed.

And then everything went black.

BULLET JOURNAL

Behind Every Successful Woman is Herself

You'd think it would be harder to build a bomb. I mean, really?

I thought at first that it was one of those crazy ideas that comes when you're mad. When you're thinking of all the ways you can hurt, the way you've been hurt. Reimagining the scene with a different middle and a different ending, the one where you're in control and all the shit that's gone on hasn't happened.

When I get upset about something, it doesn't take long before it turns to anger. The deeper the hurt, the bigger the rage.

Anger is powerful.

It's like it takes over.

And this time I'm really raging.

There's just too much.

I really couldn't believe it at the start. I mean, me?

First that letter. That made me want to scream. Nobody has ever said no to me, eh, hello? That's not even a thing.

And then, when I needed support the most, I found the photos. Those were a joke, apparently. Ha ha.

They started me wondering what else I might be missing. That's when I found the texts. All those love hearts.

The same as he'd sent to me.

Those really did it. I mean, just no. Things need to change. Some people need to be taught a lesson. To back off.

I shouldn't have to put up with any of this. Nobody takes what's mine.

Then I had this idea and starting googling, like not seriously to start with, but everything's on the internet, you just need to know where to look.

And it turns out that it was a total flash of inspiration.

See what I did there LOL.

Getting all the pieces, the timer and the explosive itself, wasn't even that difficult. I bet certain online companies weren't thinking about why their customers might need stuff in a hurry when they dreamed up next day delivery. And, actually, building it wasn't too hard either. Like the Lego robot but with more 'impact'.

LOL, I did it again.

Watch this space.

11:25 AM Vodafone

< Messages   **Unknown**

I told you what would happen
if you said anything

I heard you

You've got 24 hrs to delete those
photos or you're next

   iMessage

ROOM 7: HISTORY
RAVEN'S HILL SCHOOL
11.25 a.m.
24 hours remaining
Jess

'**N**ow girls, as I've explained, History deals with the experience of human life in the past, and in order to discover that we must become detectives, developing research skills and evaluating evidence.'

Ms Kerrigan turned to the huge image of a mummified bog body on the interactive whiteboard behind her and Jess winced. It was pretty gross before you even started thinking about how it had got there.

'Today we're looking at—'

A huge bang split the air and Ms Kerrigan stopped abruptly, looking around her as if the ceiling somehow held the answer. 'What on earth was that?'

But Jess wasn't hanging around for an explanation – she was already under the desk with her arms over her head. They'd practised this drill so many times at the international school she'd gone to in Beirut before they'd moved to London – and too often done it for real.

She'd heard enough explosions to know exactly what one sounded like. And the sickening, deathly quiet after it.

A moment later a clamour rose as everyone began talking at once.

At the front of the class Jess heard Ms Kerrigan trying to speak over the rising noise. 'Calm down, girls, there's probably a perfectly logical explanation.' Then Jess heard her name. 'Jessica McKenna, what are you doing under the desk?'

Before Ms Kerrigan quite finished the sentence, the fire alarm went off, the bell reverberating through the classroom. Around her the noise rose once more, everyone talking at once, anxious, excited.

Jess curled up tighter and stayed exactly where she was. She had no intention of moving until she was absolutely sure there wasn't a secondary device. Her mouth dry, Jess could feel her heart pounding, the sound thumping in her ears. No matter how many times they'd practised it in school, when the threat was real it was absolutely terrifying.

'Okay, girls, calm *down*, please. We'll find out what's happened in due course, but we need to leave the building in an orderly fashion. Line up, please, and follow me to the tennis court, where you need to find your year group. Ms Cooke will take the register outside so this is *not* the time to disappear.' The scraping of chairs almost drowned out Ms Kerrigan's next instruction. 'Jessica, come out from under there immediately.'

Jess could hear the sound of feet moving towards the door, then Amber's voice. 'It's okay, Jess, we're all going out. It was probably a lorry out on the road or something.'

Jess unwrapped her arms from her head and looked up. Amber's long, dark hair was falling in curtains around her face as she looked in under the desk.

'Jessica, would you *please* line up?' Ms Kerrigan's exasperation was clear in her voice.

Amber straightened up. 'She's not messing, Ms Kerrigan. Jess used to live in Beirut.'

'Oh. I see. Well, I doubt this is anything to worry about, it's probably just gas or something. Right, file out, girls. Jessica, you can come with me. Help her up, Amber, please.'

As Jess crawled out from under the desk, she could see everyone leaving. Ms Kerrigan glanced over and gave her a searching look as she stood up and reached for her phone. Jess let out a breath, trying to still her heart. She gave Amber a smile that she knew didn't reach her eyes. That had *definitely* been an explosion.

'Come on, we'd better get moving.' Amber pulled an abandoned chair out of their way and weaved between the desks to where Ms Kerrigan was waiting.

'That's it, quickly and quietly, girls, no running.'

Outside on the tennis court, Ms Cooke, the Fifth Year head, was already standing at the top of the line of their year group, her face grim as she checked their names off against the register in her hand.

Jess shivered as she lined up with the others. Although the sun was shining it was chilly in the shadows, the winter air crisp. But she didn't think it was the weather that was making her shake.

Standing in the middle of the line, Jess searched the sea of red sweaters for Frankie and Sorcha, the feeling in her stomach starting to spiral. Frankie had texted right before break to say she was running late but she hadn't shown up for their History lesson – maybe she was sick? Jess closed her eyes for a minute. She'd never wish the vomiting bug that had wiped out almost half of Fourth Year last week on anyone, but right now she really hoped Frankie *was* tucked up in bed.

Jess heard Ms Cooke call Maeve and then Sorcha's name. But neither of them was here.

The spiral in her stomach stepped it up a notch, sending tendrils of panic out from its centre.

Jess scanned the other year groups and then looked back down her own line. Ella wasn't here either, and Becky and Mackenzie were missing too.

What lesson did Sorcha have now?

Chemistry.

With Becky.

And Ella and Maeve were in the same class.

Her stomach began to whir, the tendrils unfurling into full-on waves as Jess stood on her tiptoes and looked up and down the line again. The Science Block was right at the other side of the school so perhaps it was just taking longer for them to get here. She really hoped so. But deep down she knew something was wrong. Really wrong.

Then she saw a line of girls in white lab coats coming along the driveway that swung around the front of the school, heading towards the tennis courts. They were walking two abreast and seemed to be hugging each other, their faces pale, most of them crying. In the middle of them, her red sweater standing out in the haze of white, Jess could see Tara clutching her flute case and her phone. Beside her a woman with dark hair scraped back in a ponytail had her arms tightly folded, her large glasses catching the light. As the group reached the tennis courts, Tara broke away, running over to Ms Cooke, her face streaked with tears.

Jess couldn't hear what she was saying but she could see, even from here, that Tara was starting to hyperventilate. Taking a step back from Ms Cooke, Tara dropped her flute and put her hand on her chest. Ms Cooke frantically gestured to the school nurse, who was standing with a group of teachers at the entrance to the tennis courts. Jess watched, frozen, fear seeping through her. *What had happened?*

She suddenly felt weird, like she was somehow detached from the action; as if the explosion had separated her from everyone else.

The same feeling that had sent Jess under the desk was making her feel sick.

There had definitely been a bang. A big one.

And Jess was sure it had come from the other end of the school, in or near the Science Block, where almost everyone who was missing had been in Chemistry.

The blackness was deep and velvety, but gradually Frankie realised that she could hear voices. Somewhere, far away she thought, a bell was ringing, and then she heard Mr Murray, his Australian accent getting more pronounced as he came closer.

'My God, that's Frankie O'Sullivan. What's she doing here? Is she okay?'

Was she okay? Frankie really wasn't sure. She wasn't even sure where she was. If she was asleep, why could she hear Mr Murray? Why would he be in her room? More voices came to her, urgent, and somewhere further away she could hear crying. And footsteps, lots of footsteps moving away.

Then Frankie heard another sound, a groan, and realised that she'd made the noise herself. The darkness began to recede, like she was waking up from a deep, deep sleep, surfacing through layers, each time becoming more aware. She was in school. She'd been hurrying to the Chemistry lab. A stab of panic shot through her; had she missed the start of class?

'She's bleeding.' Mr Murray again.

Bleeding? Who was bleeding? Now Frankie could feel her whole body aching. Her head hurt and her wrist felt like it was on fire. She was starting to feel like she'd been hit by a truck, but was she bleeding? Oh God. She'd thought this day couldn't get any worse.

Close to her, she heard Ms Rowan, the Biology teacher, her voice taut, her Donegal accent even stronger than usual. 'It looks like a glass cut. Hopefully it's not too deep.'

Glass? The sensation of being thrown backwards came back to Frankie, and the noise. *Had she been hit by glass?*

'How do you know?'

Frankie wanted to shout at him, 'Because she knows things. Just do what she says.' This was typical of Mr Murray. Always questioning. Maybe it was because he was a scientist, but it seemed to Frankie to be a very man thing to say right then.

Ms Rowan ignored the question, her tone showing that she was taking control. 'I'll stay with her. Go and check on the others – can you get past that stuff blocking the door?'

Frankie felt Ms Rowan take her good hand and squeeze it gently, connecting them, giving her strength.

Whatever had happened it would be okay now, Ms Rowan was there. Frankie gripped her teacher's hand. She was feeling so cold and Ms Rowan's hand was so warm …

Sorcha coughed. A retching cough that tore at her stomach muscles and made her fight for breath. Slowly, she opened her eyes.

She was lying on her side, facing the back of the lab bench, her arms over her head, her knees drawn up to her stomach, as if she was jumping into the pool trying to create the biggest splash she could.

But she wasn't anywhere near the pool.

As she became more aware, Sorcha started to stretch, testing her arms and legs before she uncurled. Her shoulder hurt. Closing her eyes again for a moment, she focused on what had to be the worst headache of her life. It intensified, waves of pain engulfing her, magnified by the sound of the fire bell reverberating around the lab, the sound oddly dulled somehow. Her brain felt like it was in a vice.

What the hell had happened?

She was wearing her lab coat, her goggles hanging around her neck. Tentatively, she turned to try and see around her.

The air was thick with some sort of dust that coated her tongue and swirled in clouds, settling like snow on her, on the floor, deadening the sound. But maybe that wasn't just the dust. She couldn't hear properly. No normal school sounds, no chatter or laughter. It was like her ears were plugged with cotton wool.

Moving a fraction more, Sorcha could see a tangle of metal strips that looked like they had fallen from the ceiling, and sheets of something white that lay like tossed playing cards in amongst the rubble. The dust was as thick as fog, but it looked like it was starting to clear.

As she focused, a shower of grit fell from above her.

Had the ceiling fallen in? She began to move, to turn onto her back to get a proper look above her, and then she lurched sideways as a piece of something bigger fell from above, landing centimetres from where her head had just been.

She needed to get out of here. Forcing herself to turn, Sorcha rolled onto her stomach, spitting dust out of her mouth. Levering herself up, she clambered onto all fours, lifting her head, waiting for the room to steady and realising at the same moment that there was someone lying to her left.

Ella. It had to be Ella.

She'd been taking selfies. And then? What had happened then? Sorcha wasn't sure. She had glanced down the lab as she'd bent to pick up her pen and there'd been a flash and a bang. Now all she could hear was a fire alarm ringing. And maybe a siren.

Moving carefully, Sorcha could see Ella was partially covered in bits of white polystyrene, pieces of what looked like – Sorcha glanced up – ceiling tiles.

Ella was lying on her stomach, her arms outstretched, her red sweater and tartan kilt covered in a thick layer of dust.

Sorcha crawled gingerly across the floor. Ella's long, brown hair, normally glossy, was full of dust, her face turned away. Sorcha pulled Ella's hair back and leaned over to look at her. Her eyes were closed, the colour drained from her cheeks. Sorcha fought the feeling of dread that spiked inside her. She couldn't panic. Not now. Panic wouldn't help anyone.

Reaching under her chin, Sorcha gently put her fingers on Ella's neck. There was a pulse, weak and fluttery, but still a pulse.

Sorcha scanned Ella's body. No blood. That was good, wasn't it? But she was lying on her stomach and Sorcha couldn't see what she was lying on. As the thoughts gathered in her head, Sorcha caught a movement out of the corner of her eye. She turned towards the front of the classroom. Across the tangle of ceiling tiles and textbooks scattered between them, she could just make out a figure slumped against the wall near the coat pegs, and a flash of platinum blonde hair.

Maeve?

Where was everyone? Sorcha looked over to the door; it was open, a pile of debris blocking the way out, a lab stool lying sideways across it.

Had something happened to the whole school? Questions began to build in Sorcha's head. *Had there been a gas explosion? Or maybe they'd been hit by a plane? She'd been bending down to pick up her pen and then …*

And then she didn't know what, but another movement by the wall drew her back to Maeve. She needed to see if Maeve was okay.

Leaving Ella, Sorcha began to crawl, pushing bits of metal out of her way. The bookcase that normally stood beside the door had fallen, scattering books and lab equipment everywhere. Petri dishes and the shattered remains of glass flasks littered her path.

Sorcha could see Maeve's head lolling against her chest. Her hair was coated in dust, her blonde fringe dark with blood.

Hauling herself up, clambering over the tangle of stuff between them, Sorcha staggered over to Maeve. Her friend looked like she was bleeding from her side; the white lab coat that she'd been holding was tangled around her now, and soaked bright red.

Sorcha struggled out of her own lab coat, rolling it up, pressing it into Maeve's side where it looked like the blood was coming from.

Something must have hit Maeve, but Sorcha didn't know what.

'Maeve, it's going to be okay. It's me, Sorcha, it's going to be okay.' Her voice sounded loud in her head. 'Sorry if this hurts.'

Sorcha reached for Maeve's hand, rubbing the back of it. Maeve's eyelids fluttered but she was as pale as a porcelain doll. One that had been thrown down the stairs and was lying in pieces at the bottom. Sorcha glanced back at Ella. She hadn't moved. *But she had a pulse, that was good.* And Sorcha couldn't see any blood. *That was also good.* At least, she hoped it was.

Who else was in here? Becky and Mackenzie had been at the back of the class. She could hear Mr Murray's voice in her head: *'Under no circumstances start without me, girls. I'll be back in a second so we can start the experiments. Don't touch anything until I return.'*

Were Becky and Mackenzie on the floor as well? And where was Ms Ryan, the lab technician? She was supposed to be keeping an eye on them.

Sorcha looked down the room. The heavy wooden benches stood like soldiers down each side, covered in the twisted remains of the ceiling. Above them, dark holes gaped where white tiles should have been, tattered strips of shredded insulation spilling out like tentacles. They swayed menacingly as the Venetian blinds rattled and a chill breeze came in through the shattered windows. This lab was right at the corner of the building, so there was a lot of glass.

Sorcha switched her attention back to Maeve. Her hand was getting warm from her friend's blood soaking through the lab coat pressed against her side. This wasn't good. Sorcha looked around, scanning the room for something, anything that could help her. She had no idea where her phone was. With the force of the blast, it was probably in orbit by now. Where was the first aid box?

More importantly, where was help?

He's still out of it

Deserved it. Got off lightly

What about the other one?

Sorted.

Sorcha heard Mr Murray hauling debris from the doorway before she saw him.

It felt like it took him forever, but as he pulled away the last bit of plasterboard blocking the entrance, Sorcha didn't think she'd ever been as pleased to see anyone as she was right now. Framed by the door, his white lab coat hanging open, Mr Murray's face was taut as he assessed the devastation in the lab.

'I'm here – we're here. Maeve needs an ambulance,' Sorcha called.

She saw him look around, obviously trying to locate her voice. She knew it was barely audible over the dull but incessant ringing of the fire alarm bell. There was no fire, *couldn't someone shut it off?*

'Here, by your desk. We need help, quickly.' Sorcha said it again more loudly, and he homed in on her, pushing plasterboard out of his way as he came into the room.

'Sorcha, is that you? Ambulance is on its way, are you hurt?'

'I don't think so, but Maeve's really bad – she's bleeding a lot. I'm applying pressure to try and stop it. Ella's by the bench. She's unconscious. And I don't know where Becky and Mackenzie are.'

Striding through the debris, Mr Murray bent down to Ella. She hadn't moved.

Sorcha coughed, trying to keep the hand holding the blood-soaked lab coat still at the same time. Her lips were dry and cracked but she didn't want to lick them in case she got another mouthful of dust. She spat out a bit that had got into her mouth. 'I checked Ella; she has a pulse – at least she did – I think she's just knocked out.'

Mr Murray deftly checked for himself. 'I can feel it.'

Thank God.

'Can you look for the others? They were at the back on the last bench.'

He turned, shouting out the door to someone else. 'Julia, can you hear me? Sorcha's here – she's helping Maeve. We need the paramedics as soon as they get here. Maeve's badly injured. Ella's unconscious. I'm looking for Rebecca and Mackenzie.'

Sorcha heard Ms Rowan's voice come straight back. 'Sorcha, I've got Frankie here – she's a bit battered but I'm with her. Help's on its way.'

Sorcha felt tears pricking at her eyes. Frankie had finally turned up. *But why was she here?* That was pure Frankie. She always ended up in the middle of everything. It was like she was a disaster magnet.

But why was Ms Rowan staying outside with her? Was she hurt? A sob escaped before Sorcha could hold it back. Mr Murray looked across at her, taking in the blood and Maeve's slumped head.

'Can you hold on there a bit longer, Sorcha? The ambulance is coming. I'll find the others.'

Blinking away the tears, Sorcha nodded rapidly.

The school had a bunch of first aiders, so *where were they?* Why weren't they all in here helping? As the thought ran through her mind, her head started to join the dots. If it was a gas explosion, had they evacuated this end of the school? Was it just them and the two teachers and Frankie? Panic began to seep into her thoughts.

Maybe they thought the building could collapse?

Turning back to Maeve, Sorcha pushed the intrusive thoughts away – she couldn't lose it now. She needed to keep going for Maeve.

A crashing noise made her look over her shoulder. Mr Murray was making his way down the lab, pushing debris out of his path. The central aisle that divided the two rows of benches was blocked with what looked like half the ceiling and what Sorcha realised were lab stools, their metal legs sticking up like spears. A chill gust rattled the blinds again, the breeze carrying with it the sound of sirens. At last.

'Can you see them?' She didn't know if he could hear her over the sound of the alarm. He'd got to the last bench, was tossing away pieces of debris, looking around frantically.

'Mackenzie, Rebecca, can you hear me?'

The last bench was in the corner of the room with windows on two sides overlooking the drive. At least it had had windows. Sorcha could see pieces of jagged glass trapped in the frames where the triple glazing had once been.

'I can't see them.'

She could tell from the wobble in his voice that this was bad. They had to be here somewhere. Unless … Flashes of news reports on the wars in Ukraine and Gaza came to her, terrifying images of bomb blasts and smashed bodies …

They had to be okay.

How had this happened? It had to be gas, surely, but there'd been no smell. This *was* a Chemistry lab, though – were there gas canisters down the back or something?

Becky and Mackenzie had to be all right. Becky was too gentle for something so horrible to have happened to her, and Mackenzie had only just got here from Boston.

How could you survive school in America then come to Ireland and get killed here? That just wasn't a thing.

The sound of Mr Murray digging into the rubble brought Sorcha back to the lab. He bent over and pulled something away from the bench, ducking down to look under it. Suddenly he raised his hand, his voice loud.

'I've got them, they're both here!'

Oh, thank God.

'Are they okay?' Sorcha said, a little too loudly. Someone had turned that awful alarm bell off, but it was still ringing in her head.

Mr Murray didn't answer, but she heard him call the girls' names again before he disappeared from sight.

Sorcha waited, holding her breath.

Mr Murray's face was grim when he reappeared. 'They're both unconscious. Rebecca's taken a nasty knock. We need to get them out of here.'

THE SCIENCE CORRIDOR
RAVEN'S HILL SCHOOL
11.40 a.m.
23 hours 45 minutes remaining
Frankie

rankie felt the vibrations of feet pounding towards her before she heard them. *Something had happened, but what? Had something hit her?* She held tighter to Ms Rowan's hand, her thoughts tumbling, becoming slowly more lucid as she became aware of what was unfolding around her.

She heard Ms Rowan's voice: 'They need you in the lab, at least four badly injured girls. My colleague Rick Murray is with them.'

'Got it.' Two firemen and a pair of green-uniformed paramedics sprinted past, barely pausing as they followed the direction of Ms Rowan's outstretched arm.

Frankie felt someone else crouch beside her.

'Who have we got here?' The woman's voice was warm and calm as she flipped open a medical pack.

'I'm Julia Rowan, Biology. This is Frankie. She's only

just opened her eyes. I didn't want to leave her with that cut on her head.'

'Very sensible. Hello, Frankie, my name's Orlagh. I'm a paramedic and I'm just going to check you over. You've been in a bit of an accident but we're here to help you now.'

An accident? Frankie tried to process what the woman was saying. Her green uniform felt out of place in a corridor where everyone wore red and brown or white lab coats. But she had nice eyes. And she was smiling.

'Are you back with us, Frankie? Does it hurt anywhere?'

Did it hurt? That was a big yes. Sort of all over but the worst was her head and her wrist. Ms Rowan had eased her backpack off her shoulder so at least she was lying flat now, but her wrist really hurt. She couldn't quite find the words, but as she tried to lift it, a stab of pain made her cry out.

'Settle there now, I've got you. Are you allergic to anything, Frankie? I want to give you something to help with the pain. It looks like you've broken your wrist but we're going to take you to hospital to get you checked over properly. You've been unconscious,' she glanced at Ms Rowan for confirmation, 'so we need to keep a close eye on you.'

'Not allergic.' It came out as a croak. Frankie closed her eyes. Everything was getting fuzzy, and she just wanted to go back to sleep.

'Stay with me, Frankie, keep talking.'

Frankie opened her eyes again and, behind Orlagh, she saw more paramedics in green uniforms arriving, some of them carrying bags, others stretchers.

Suddenly it all came together. Something had happened in the Chemistry lab, something big. There had been a bang. And she'd been thrown backwards. She must have hit her head.

'Sorcha, where's Sorcha?' The air was full of dust and Frankie's voice was barely working.

'She's with Mr Murray, Frankie. He said she looks okay. She's helping Maeve.' Ms Rowan's voice sounded confident and strong.

'Is Sorcha your friend?'

'My cousin.' The paramedic had to lean forward to hear her.

'We'll make sure she's okay, don't worry. Can you remember what happened?'

'A bang. There was a bang.' Frankie's lips were dry, her voice little more than a whisper.

'Can I move this? I just want to check you all over.'

Move what? Frankie realised she still had Becky's iPad under her arm. She'd been holding on to it tightly. 'I need it, I have to …'

'Don't worry, I'll keep it safe; it'll stay with you. I just need to make sure you haven't got any other injuries.'

Frankie felt her arm being moved as Orlagh deftly ran her hand down her side.

Frankie took a deep breath. *Sorcha was okay, thank God. But Becky was in the lab with Sorcha.* Frankie prayed she wasn't hurt.

Jess felt an arm encircle her shoulders. Lifting her head off her hands, she found Georgia sitting next to her on one side, and Amber on the other. Leaning on the fence at the back of the tennis courts, her knees pulled up to her chest, Jess had needed some time away from the rest of the year. She'd felt the levels of anxiety rising as the girls who'd been in the Physics lab and Applied Maths had filtered back into their form groups.

Jess took a shaky breath as Georgia leaned in and hugged her again, glancing across at Amber. 'They'll be okay, I'm sure they'll be okay.'

Jess huddled in to Georgia, leaning her head on her shoulder. 'What did Cookie say – did you hear anything new?' Georgia had shot straight over to the year head as soon as the school nurse had calmed Tara.

'No, just that it was definitely in the Chemistry room.'

Crouching beside them, Amber interrupted Georgia, her voice wavering. 'There'll be news soon. My Snapchat and WhatsApp have already gone nuts with theories.'

'Everyone loves a good drama.' Georgia took a breath, her voice practical.

Amber looked across the tennis court. 'The Guards have arrived, but the ambulances are still here. One of them left a few minutes ago but I don't think they've brought anyone else out yet.'

Jess closed her eyes tightly. 'It feels like ages. Do you think that means people are badly injured, that it's taking time to get them stabilised?' *The worst injured always take the longest to get to hospital.* Jess could hear her dad's voice in her head.

Georgia squeezed her shoulder reassuringly. 'Perhaps it's taking a while for the paramedics to get to them. There's a fire engine out the front too, so hopefully it won't be long.'

Jess let her head fall back on her arms. *How could this be happening?* She couldn't lose her best friends. Sorcha and Frankie had become like sisters to her since she'd moved to Kilmurray Point, their friendship completely dissolving any worries she'd had about a new school, or living in a new city. Living in another new country.

Jess looked up, the need to do something finally pushing away the shock. And she suddenly realised that even sitting on the Astroturf, her bum was freezing. 'I have to go over there and see if there's news. I can't just stay here.' She started to get up.

Amber stood up beside her, putting her hand on Jess's arm. 'I think they want to keep us in one place. They'll have to sign each of us out if they need to send us home, make sure everyone can be collected.'

Georgia looked around Jess to answer Amber. 'You're right. And the boarders won't be able to go back to the boarding house until they know what's happened.'

'So, we have to wait outside?' Jess glanced at the sky. It was sort of warmish in the sunshine today and thank goodness it wasn't raining, but none of them had coats. It was November: they couldn't stay out here indefinitely. Around them, scattered across the tennis courts, she could see groups of girls huddled together, most of them shivering, their bright red jumpers standing out like beacons.

But perhaps it was shock that was making them shiver.

Georgia shifted to stand up next to her. 'Let's see if we can get a bit closer and see what the teachers are saying. Tara was coming out of the Music block when it happened and said the windows blew out – there's glass all over the car park.'

Jess let out a shaky breath. 'Is there anything on Rave-fess?'

'Not much.' Amber shook her head, her long hair falling into her face. 'There were a couple of posts and then it stopped updating.'

'I guess the admins don't want to spread panic with misinformation.' Georgia grimaced.

'Have either of you heard from Frankie? I've texted her about twenty times this morning. She texted me to say she'd overslept and was on her way.' Jess frowned. 'But she should be here by now.'

Georgia shook her head. 'I haven't heard. She probably decided to stay at home. I guess she'll get here pretty quick when she hears about Sorcha being in the middle of whatever's happened.' Georgia flipped her hair over her shoulder and linked her arm through Jess's. 'A walk around the tennis court will help us unwind while we wait for news.'

Georgia was right. A walk would help her stretch and warm her up.

As they reached the far side of the tennis court, Jess could see the drive and the main gates. On the other side of Katie's tiny pale pink Fiat, parked across the front of the main entrance to the school and the boarding house, was a row of emergency vehicles. The back doors of each ambulance stood wide open. Beyond them was the Science Block, all new glass and steel, three floors packed with the most up-to-date technology money could buy.

As the three of them reached the edge of the tennis court, they caught the excited chatter of a group of Second Years discussing what they'd heard: 'Basically Issie said that Mr Murray took half the class to the Physics lab, Mr Fitzgerald started the demonstration and there was this huge bang and all the lights went off and the fire alarm triggered. Apparently *everyone* was screaming.'

There was a pause as another voice took up the story: 'Mr Murray and Mr Fitzgerald tried to calm everyone down. Ms Rowan was doing her marking in Biology, and she came running through and sort of took over. She told Mr Fitzgerald to evacuate everyone and then went down with Mr Murray to see what had happened.'

'And they think it was a gas explosion? That's so weird – how did nobody notice the smell?'

The voices Ella could hear really didn't make sense. They were mainly male, for a start, and urgent. She could definitely catch Mr Murray's Australian accent and a strong Dublin one. Who was that?

She'd caught what she thought was Sorcha's voice, but it sounded weird, like she'd got laryngitis or something. It must have been Sorcha, though, because she was talking about Maeve, saying something about Tara and her mum, and that her own parents were away working. And a woman's voice had said something about stabilising something, and then someone else had said Mackenzie should be next.

There was a weird smell in the air, but then she'd caught a waft of Tiernan's aftershave and felt a wave of relief. No matter how bad things were, if he was nearby, everything would be all right. Had he come over with the boys who were building the scenery for the play, and come up to see her after all? She felt a flush of happiness. He'd been the one who had hit the dude who was bothering her at Katie's party. She hadn't even known him then and he'd jumped in to defend her. They'd been dancing beside each other most of the evening, not with each other, but he wasn't exactly invisible.

She'd noticed him from the minute he'd arrived on the dancefloor, his white T-shirt bright, his blond hair cropped short, dark around the sides and lighter where it curled on the top. She'd been watching him over Conor's shoulder while she was dancing, and every now and again their eyes had met. He was the type of guy you noticed, well built, his black Levis a perfect fit.

And then the creep dancing beside her had tried to kiss her and there'd been a scuffle and Tiernan had decked him and then a whole fight had kicked off with Kilmurray Manor's rugby team laying into Raven's Park College. Thank God she'd found Georgia in the hall. She only lived a few minutes away, so they'd gone straight back to hers and followed the drama on the class WhatsApp group.

Ella smiled to herself. The fight and everything that had followed had been absolutely awful, but Tiernan had messaged her on Insta the next day to see if she was okay.

With everything that had happened that night she hadn't even looked at her private message folders for a few days. They were usually full of spam anyway. When she'd finally seen all his messages, they'd met for coffee, and that was that …

The roses had been amazing; she'd just had to post them on Rave-fess. Who had a boyfriend who sent them a dozen roses to say sorry for something that wasn't even a thing? He'd been so upset, but she could see why.

He'd taken her to Eddie Rocket's for an early dinner before a film and her phone had been pinging with texts.

'Who is that? Don't they know you're busy on a Thursday night?' He'd been laughing until he'd picked up her phone and seen the messages.

I'll need to check your hard drive. Saturday @ 4. Come to mine, everyone will be out.

He'd been so mad. He'd grilled her about who had sent it. She could sort of understand why he hadn't believed that it was just a friend of Jess's that she hadn't even met, and that she was going to his house so he could take a look at her laptop because it kept crashing.

He made her text to cancel and said that he'd pay for the laptop to be fixed professionally. They'd met on Saturday afternoon for hot chocolate after he'd collected it. It must have cost him a fortune to get it done so quickly, but it had come back with a new keyboard and working at super speed.

Ella felt herself smiling inside. Tiernan was so amazing; she'd never dated anyone who paid her more attention or looked after her so well. He wanted to know everything about her friends, about who she talked to, where she went. Most of her boyfriends had been more interested in themselves than her. And they hadn't lasted anywhere near this long.

A voice cut through her thoughts. 'Right, Ella, we're going to move you now. We've given you some pain relief so this shouldn't hurt – just relax.'

It wasn't Tiernan's voice, but she caught another waft of his aftershave, so she was sure he was close. She felt herself glowing again.

The roses had arrived on Saturday afternoon on their two-month anniversary; she was really starting to think that he could be the one.

BULLET JOURNAL

Behind Every Successful Woman is Herself

Why hasn't it been on the news
yet?!!!

I feel like I'm checking social
every 30 seconds.

The pictures from the Raven's Hill
girls' feeds make it look really big.
Like REALLY. WAY bigger than
I expected, but I suppose that's the
beauty of it being a chemistry lab.

I just need to find out if it did what
I wanted it to do.

I texted this morning, but he
hasn't texted back. Which is
UNACCEPTABLE.

If I haven't made the point clearly
enough, I might have to finish the job.

I don't share. End of.

And nobody takes what's mine.

'*If you breathe a word, I'll kill you.*' The words floated around her head like torn paper on a warm breeze. Except the breeze wasn't warm. Mackenzie couldn't get a proper breath. She felt like she was suffocating. Each intake of air didn't seem to be quite enough.

Somewhere in the distance there was a bell ringing, sounding an alarm. Like she needed an alarm. Every part of her was ringing right now. She could feel fear rising, darkness beginning to overwhelm her. She just needed more air …

In her head, she saw her brother Greg look at the phone screen and let out a sharp breath.

'*What do we do?*' Her voice had sounded small against the noise of the coffee shop.

He'd looked at her, shaking his head. 'No choice. Keep quiet.'

Greg had kept his voice low. She'd barely been able to hear him over the bunch of pre-schoolers in the corner. Starbucks was always busy on a Saturday, but at least it was right between their two schools and private. Relatively.

Behind them, a mother had arrived at the next table, juggling her coffee and a stroller. Greg had turned the phone face down on the table, and risen out of his seat, swivelling around to help the lady, moving chairs away to give her space. He'd sat back down with a grim look on his face.

Even with the homely clatter of the coffee shop around them, Mackenzie had started to feel sick again right then. Like she didn't feel sick enough already. Fear and worry swirling around in her stomach like a vortex.

More sick than she'd felt when Greg had gone into the witness box that day back in Boston to give evidence against Robbie Monroe. More sick than when Monroe's defence attorney had started to attack Greg, making out that his overprivileged client was just misunderstood, that Greg had been the real reason he'd gone nuts.

That had been the start of it, Monroe's family coming after Greg then. The cops hadn't done anything when they'd tried to intimidate him, instead threatening Greg when he'd tried to defend himself.

Somehow they'd made out that it had been Greg's fault that Robbie Monroe had taken an AK-47 and shot up the high school, killing fourteen of their class-mates. The attorney had started spewing lies about Greg, suggesting he'd egged Monroe on, that he'd been the reason it had all happened.

No mention of the fact that Greg hustled a bunch of kids into the bathroom and saved their lives.

It was all on video, the cops closing in to arrest Monroe rather than shooting him, like they would have done anyone else. They knew his family; his father was the local football coach. 'He wasn't an incel, he'd just been led astray,' they'd said.

Greg had sat next to Monroe in Math, barely spoken to him, but he'd been called by the prosecution because he'd seen the doodles in Monroe's notebook, had listened to his bragging and vitriol. The cops had berated him when they'd questioned him afterwards, and then the defence had tried to destroy him.

When anyone asked her why they'd moved schools halfway across the world she always said it was their dad's job. It was half true.

Their dad was the high school principal.

'But what about the photos – and the video? It says twenty-four hours.'

Greg had shaken his head. 'We can't say anything. It's too risky.' He'd reached for her hand. 'Just say a prayer.'

Mackenzie had done that before. Lots. And it hadn't made any difference.

A man's voice cut through her thoughts, making her jump. Had he been listening? *The photos – had he heard her say something about the photos?*

'Can you hear me, Mackenzie? I'm a paramedic. There's been a bit of an accident, and we need to move some stuff to help you. It's going to be a bit noisy for a few minutes.' He moved beside her. 'I'm going to put an oxygen mask over your face – it'll help you breathe.'

'If you breathe a word, I'll kill you.'

Mackenzie couldn't tell what was inside her head and what was outside. 'Can you feel me holding your hand? I'm right here. Squeeze my hand if you can hear me.'

The one thing Ollie's girlfriend, Aoife, had told Frankie about the cubicles in the Emergency Department was that everyone forgot they weren't sound-proofed. They were separated by curtains. Pink curtains. And everything that was said on the other side of them could be heard by the patient in the next cubicle. Like *everything*.

Which was what Frankie was relying on at that moment, to give her some answers. She'd been listening hard to every snatch of conversation she could pick up, trying to find out something, anything, that would give her a clue as to what had happened that morning. So far she'd gathered that there were two side wards off the Emergency Department. This and another one set up for serious injuries.

Which was scaring her even more.

She hadn't come in through the main entrance, but straight into this more private section where she'd been seen immediately. It was a small, specially equipped ward, with cubicles like the one she was in all along one side. From what she could see as she'd been wheeled in, the other beds had been empty, complex equipment idle beside them.

But if the others weren't here, then they must be in the other ward …

Frankie had lost track of time, but it felt like she'd been here for ages. The doctor had seen her and suspected she'd broken her wrist, but she didn't care about that. Her first question had been about her friends.

From the moment she'd realised what had happened, Frankie had felt her fears manifest into a huge black dog that was snapping at her, snarling and baring its teeth, its eyes wild. She'd tried to control it, block it out while she was whizzed into X-ray, but now she was waiting for the results it was growling menacingly again, and it was terrifying.

What if one of them had been killed? The dog snapped at her, pulling on a chain that rattled in her head. Frankie closed her eyes tight, trying to shut it out, fighting a wave of despair. *They all needed positive energy.* If the news was bad, they'd have plenty of time to deal with it.

Grief stayed with you like the best friend you didn't need; she knew all about that.

The doctor who'd looked at her arm hadn't been able to tell her much about the others but had reassured

Frankie that they were all receiving priority care, which had sounded like a very vague catch-all sort of an answer.

Frankie could feel the tears pricking at the back of her eyes again. She guessed the medics needed time to see how everyone was before they could say anything, but she *just needed to know that everyone was okay*. Images of her morning kept swirling around her head, as she replayed everything, looking for signs that a catastrophe of this magnitude was incoming.

After the doctor had been, a nurse gave her another injection for the pain and told her she had to wait to see whether they wanted to keep her in or not.

Now she was feeling exhausted as well as anxious.

As Frankie shifted in her bed she heard a door suck open, footsteps squeaking on the rubber floor, then a conversation start beside her, on the other side of the curtains.

Her ears pricked.

'If any of them say anything at all about what happened, will you call me? My number's on my card. We'll be talking to everyone, but we need to capture as much as we can.' It was a man's voice, low and serious. He sounded about the same age as her dad, and he had a bit of an accent, soft, like he came from Galway, maybe.

'No problem, Detective Inspector. Have you any idea what caused it at this stage?' The nurse's accent was soft too, perhaps Kerry, Frankie thought. She was keeping her own voice down as well.

'At this stage we can't say,' the Detective Inspector answered. 'There've been no reports of a smell, but the gas board are checking the whole building. We've got the technical bureau on the way from Phoenix Park. They should be able to tell us more when they've processed the scene.'

The nurse's voice again: 'Headquarters, is it? So, you're taking it seriously, you don't think it was an accident?'

Frankie heard him clear his throat.

'We can't tell for sure at this stage. But this is a school chemistry lab, not a nuclear testing centre. Like the teachers said, there's very little that could produce a blast of that size in that environment. All the indications are that it *wasn't* an accident.'

Frankie froze. She could imagine the Detective Inspector shaking his head as he continued.

'I don't know what it is with schools at the moment. We had a massive fire to deal with last month.' He sighed. 'We're treating the lab as a crime scene, just like we would any other. There are a couple of blast experts coming down from Belfast right now. If this was deliberate, we need to find out who did it and why, as fast as possible.' He paused. 'Let's just hope it's an isolated incident and not the start of some sort of campaign.'

'But why would anyone blow up a school? That makes no sense.' The nurse sounded incredulous. Almost as incredulous as Frankie felt. She couldn't believe she was hearing this. She strained her ears, listening even more intently. Had it been a bomb? *No way* … and was the fire he was talking about the one in that school near Kilfenora in Wicklow?

'We can't rule anything out. Raven's Hill has security cameras, so we'll be checking those, obviously, finding out who had access to the lab over the weekend and this morning. I don't know, perhaps one of the girls inadvertently brought it in with her.'

'You mean in her bag, like? Someone planted it?' The nurse tutted loudly.

'We'll look at every possibility. We'll be interviewing all the staff, but the girls were right there. They might have seen something and not even realised, so if your staff can be alert to anything they say, that would be extremely helpful.'

'No problem, Detective Inspector. We've got one heading for surgery and one on oxygen. And one who's catatonic, so I'm not sure she'll be saying much. But I know what you're asking.'

'Thanks, Sister. We *really* don't want to find out too late that this could be about to happen somewhere else.'

Frankie heard the nurse draw in a breath. 'That we certainly do not.'

'How are you doing, Frankie?' Frankie jumped at the gentle voice saying her name, turning to see who had crept up on her. It was Aoife, Ollie's girlfriend. Frankie put her finger to her lips and gestured with her head towards the curtain that surrounded her, her eyes wide.

'Thanks, Sister, and I know I don't need to say that everything is confidential at this stage. The press is going to be all over this like flies.'

Frankie felt her eyebrows shoot up. Aoife looked at her, amused, shaking her head.

'Careful listening in – you might hear something you don't want to.' Aoife looked at her pointedly. 'I'm afraid I'm going to have to move you, Frankie. We don't have a bed yet, but I'm going to pop you just outside the ED so I can keep an eye on you. We need to free up this space.'

Did you hear the news, everyone's talking about it?

Which bit of the news are you thinking of?

About the explosion, which bit do you think? It was mega. All the windows have blown out. Where have you been?

I've been busy.

Timing is everything. It'll keep everyone distracted while we get the rest of the photos.

And then what?

Then we're in complete control

📷 Ⓐ iMessage ➤ 🎤

lla groaned, her eyes fluttering open for a second. But she didn't want to see more medical equipment with flashing lights or hear anything else beeping at her. This wasn't how she'd expected her day to go.

She'd woken up in the ambulance expecting Tiernan to be next to her, but it wasn't him at all, it was a paramedic with a beard, who'd grinned at her like a weird long-lost friend.

And her ribs hurt, *so* much.

The pink curtain that was drawn around the bed she was lying on whipped back, and a nurse appeared. *No beard. Good start.*

'Hi, Ella, I'm Aoife. We've called a major incident so we're looking after you and your friends as our top priority.' She flashed a pen light she'd pulled from her top pocket into Ella's eyes. Ella winced and tried to turn away. 'It's good to have you back with us.'

'What happened? My ribs hurt.' Ella's voice didn't sound like her own, and as she spoke, she heard some sort of commotion on the other side of the curtain, in the cubicle to her left – people arriving and, close by, a woman's voice.

'Oh my God, my baby, what's happened to you?'

Ignoring the interruption, Aoife continued as if there was nothing going on in the next cubicle. She smiled, her tone reassuring.

'We think you have a couple of broken ribs, so we're going to get you into X-ray.'

Ella opened her eyes and looked at Aoife properly. She was pretty, her strawberry blonde hair drawn back in a ponytail. She had a capable 'I know what I'm doing' look about her. Ella felt herself relax a bit. Aoife picked up the clipboard at the end of the bed.

'How are the others?' Ella winced. It hurt to speak.

Aoife smiled. 'We're assessing everyone so there's no need to worry about anything. Frankie O'Sullivan's nearby – she was first in and she's waiting for a bed now.'

How had Frankie got caught up in this? She didn't even do Chemistry. But Ella wasn't going to start worrying about that now. Her head hurt and she had more immediate problems to solve.

'Where's my phone? I need my phone.'

'I'll ask the Guards to take a look for it. It didn't come in with you, but I'm sure they'll find it. Can someone bring you a spare one for when you're feeling a bit better?'

Ella opened her mouth to speak again, but suddenly she heard the woman in the cubicle on her left continuing, her voice raised. She sounded like she was on the verge of hysteria.

'How can you tell me she's physically fine when she's like this? Look at her.'

'Please be calm.'

'Calm? How can I be calm? And when, in the history of anything, did telling someone to calm down make them calmer?' Whoever it was sounded like she was getting angry.

'I realise it's very distressing seeing your daughter like this. We've still got more checks to make. What I meant is that Rebecca hasn't got any physical injuries. She doesn't have any broken bones and her airways are all clear.'

'But she's rigid, she's not responding at all – she's just staring into space. She doesn't even know I'm here.'

'If you can tell us about any medication she might be on, that would be very helpful. We believe she may be in a catatonic state – it can be brought on by extreme anxiety, fear or shock.'

Were they talking about Becky? Shock was right; it didn't come much more shocking than this.

'I know what a catatonic state is, I'm a psychotherapist.

What I don't understand is what you are planning to do about it.'

The woman and the nurse moved away, Becky's mum's voice still loud and angry.

Ella closed her eyes. Her mouth was dry, her thoughts circling. How could Tiernan get in touch if she had no phone? He'd get upset if he was texting and she didn't reply – it always made him angry. He said it was because he loved her and silence made him feel like she didn't care. A surge of anxiety began to rise. She had to get a message to him. But his number was in her phone. What could she do? How could she contact him?

Ella felt a tear escape and trickle down her cheek.

JESS'S APARTMENT
LAMBAY HOUSE, MAIN STREET,
KILMURRAY POINT
1.05 p.m.
22 hours 20 minutes remaining
Jess

'Jess, is that you?' As Jess closed the front door behind her, her dad came out of the living room, his glasses on the top of his head, his face puzzled. 'What are you doing home so early?' He took one look at her tear-stained face, crossed the hall and wrapped his arms around her. 'What on earth's happened?'

Jess could feel more tears streaming down her face. She'd held them in until she and Georgia had got outside the school gates and then she hadn't been able to stop. Georgia's mum had pulled up on the pavement and offered her a lift home, but Jess had felt like she needed the walk down to the seafront and home to sort everything out in her head. But it had been freezing, a bitter sea wind cutting into her face, making her ears hurt. And she'd been crying so much she'd been barely able to see most of the way.

'There was an explosion, at school.' She drew in a sobby breath and held him tight.

'What happened, Tiger?' He kissed the top of her head.

'They don't know. They only just let us out of school. Everyone's in hospital.'

'Good God, I've been on Zoom all morning, I haven't even looked at my phone – I had it on silent. Everyone?'

'Everyone who was in the lab. It was the Chemistry lab that blew up.'

'Okay. I've got you. Look, you're safe now. Come and sit down and tell me about it. Let's have a cup of tea.'

Jess pulled off her school sweater as she followed her dad into the kitchen, dumping it on the back of a chair.

His back to her as he filled the kettle, her dad glanced over his shoulder at her as he spoke. 'Want me to see if I can find out what's happening?'

Sitting down, Jess nodded silently, all the energy escaping from her like a split balloon. Her elbows on the kitchen table, she ran her hands over her face.

'That would be great. Ms Cooke did an assembly before they let us go – she was just really vague and said the Guards were looking at everything and not to worry. But you know what they say and what the real story is aren't always the same thing.'

He clicked the kettle on to boil, turning around to look at her properly. 'What's the casualty report?'

Jess took a breath. 'Apparently Maeve's in surgery. Frankie and Sorcha seem to be okay, but Ollie texted to say they think Frankie broke her wrist. The new girl from America, Mackenzie, is in ICU, and I think Becky is too. Someone said Ella's got broken ribs.' She paused. 'I really want to go in and see them.' Jess ran a hand through her hair. 'And one of the guys from Model UN got beaten up at Raven's Park on Friday night. I was planning to go in and see him this afternoon during my free period.'

Her dad grimaced. Leaning back on the counter he crossed his arms. 'When's visiting time?'

'This afternoon between 2 and 4 p.m. and tonight from 6.30 'til 8.30.'

'I think I'd wait until tonight – the girls will all need to be triaged and found beds. And if Maeve's in surgery she won't be up to visitors for a while. I'll get on the phone and see what I can find out from the Guards.'

Her dad was the best. He had contacts everywhere. And he was right about visiting. She just felt so helpless, but cluttering up the hospital while they were trying to sort everyone out wouldn't make things any better.

Jess closed her eyes, the dark cloud of worry threatening to overwhelm her. She hated hospitals. It was like her mum being ill all over again; the sick feeling filling her stomach was exactly the same as when she'd been told that her mum's cancer was back. And look how that had ended.

BULLET JOURNAL
Behind Every Successful Woman is Herself

It's finally on the TV.

I thought I was going to die waiting. I've been checking my phone, changing channel on the TV in my bedroom non-stop. It's just as well no-one's home or they'd all be asking why I was tuned into a news channel.

It's not like I care about the rest of the planet.

I was starting to think there was some sort of news blackout, but there's a reporter outside the gates now. The rolling ribbon thing at the bottom of the screen is giving out an emergency number for anyone who has relatives involved. 'Don't call the school, there's a special helpline ...' He must have been practising his sad face.

'Raven's Hill is an exclusive school for girls aged eleven to eighteen overlooking the seaside town of Kilmurray Point.' Blah blah blah. We know all that, it's on the sign behind you — the one with the school logo in the middle?

'Six girls have been injured, two seriously, in what is thought to have been a gas explosion that occurred just before 11.30 this morning.'

Gas? Well, they've got that wrong for starters. And it was 11.25 a.m. Details are important.

Six injured? I've been so hyped I barely heard him the first time. I was too busy looking in the back of the shot to see what was going on.

There's only two of them that I'm interested in, but six doesn't seem like very many.

He still hasn't replied to my text. I can feel the anger swirling again — like mist thickening as the reporter drones on.

What does 'seriously' mean in news speak anyway?

And, more importantly, who's injured? I've been glued to social but there's barely anything. Lots of photos of girls on the tennis courts, and grainy zoomed-in shots of the shattered windows. But no names.

I need names.

Two specifically.

And there's no mention of the teacher.

'All casualties have been brought to St Anthony's Hospital and their relatives have been informed.'

The news reporter's voice is SO irritating, but ... they are all in St Anthony's.

Okay, I can work with that.

Now we've gone this far, it seems a shame not to finish things properly.

This is in motion now. It needs to be sorted quickly. A lot can happen in 24 hours.

Have the pictures arrived?

Not yet

They better hurry up. We can't afford for this to go wrong

Neither of us can.
Trust me. There's no danger

I think you're wrong there

  iMessage

'I really am fine, Mum, really, don't fuss.'

'Frankie O'Sullivan, you've a broken wrist, you've been knocked out by an explosion, you've probably got a concussion and you're lying on a trolley in a hospital corridor. What part of that is "fine"?'

Frankie's mum had a point. But she also had a face like thunder and must have been in a meeting when she got the news because she was wearing a navy suit, had her highlighted hair clipped up and was wearing her stiletto heels. She usually wore flats to run around managing their hotel, but when she needed to show a bit more authority, she wore heels. They made her about two inches taller, and she was already tall. Frankie's little brother Max called them Mum's-no-messing shoes. When Frankie had heard her coming down the corridor, she'd recognised the sound.

Sometimes her mum in no-messing mode was a good thing, but right now Frankie really didn't want to draw attention to herself. She was still in her school uniform and had a temporary dressing on her head and, according to her brother Ollie, who had gone to find her some chocolate, she had the best black eye he'd seen in a long time.

Right now, she just wanted to know how everyone else was and hide away from all the people passing who thought it was okay to take a good look at her. She wasn't an exhibit in the zoo.

'Mum, I'm fine, really. Apparently a doctor will be here soon and they'll admit me as soon as they have a bed. They're worried about concussion. Can you see if Sorcha's okay?'

'She's my next stop. As soon as Ollie gets back – he's gone to find Aoife. The receptionist couldn't tell me much, but they're keeping Sorcha in tonight as well, so they must be worried about concussion at the very least. I've called her mum and dad. They're getting the next plane home.'

Sorcha's parents were always away at scientific conferences. Sorcha's mum, Liz, was Frankie's mum's sister. While Liz had gone into science, Frankie's mum had trained as an accountant and started working for the company who looked after the Berwick Castle Hotel, where she'd met Frankie's dad, whose family owned it. Now she got to work seven days a week and mind five kids while Liz travelled all over the world. But her mum loved organising things and swore she wouldn't have it any other way. Which was just as well, because despite her potentially creating a massively embarrassing scene, Frankie was very glad her mum was here.

Behind her, Frankie could see the doors further down the corridor start to open as her mum continued. 'I met Ms Rowan outside. She said she'd be back to see you as soon as she can but she's talking to the Guards.'

A trolley appeared through the doors and Frankie's mum leaned into the side of Frankie's trolley as the other one was rolled past by a nurse and a porter. The elderly man on it looked very pale and was hooked up to a drip. Frankie's mum shook her head.

'There's no dignity in this place, is there? The sooner they can get you up to a ward the better.'

Frankie wasn't up to a debate on the merits or otherwise of the Irish medical system.

'Ms Rowan stayed with me the whole time, even in the ambulance.' Frankie suddenly felt very tired. She'd always liked Ms Rowan, but today the teacher had been amazing, holding her hand for ages, keeping her calm. Frankie hadn't been sure that she *could* have let go of her hand when the paramedics had moved her to a stretcher and wheeled her down the corridor to the service lift.

Before her mum could comment, Ollie shouldered his way through the double doors behind her. He was wearing his white shirt with the green and gold Berwick

Park Hotel insignia and smart green trousers. He'd slung a fleece over the top, so he looked a bit less conspicuous, but the uniform was unmistakeable.

'Here we are, hot chocolate and a Crunchie. Aoife's keeping an eye on Sorcha and the others in the ED. I texted Danny – he's going to get snacks on his way over. He wanted to come straight away, but they won't let him see you until you've got a bed.' Ollie put the Crunchie bar down beside her. 'He said he'd be here at evening visiting.'

Frankie snaked her arm out from under the blanket, taking the mug from Ollie. 'He messaged. What did he say about all this? It's a huge story for Kilmurray Point.'

Ollie grinned. 'I think he's more worried about you than his future career in TV news right now, but be ready for lots of questions.'

Her boyfriend Danny's *Breaking News* TikTok was all part of his master career plan – he wanted to get into observational documentary, directing as he got his qualifications. The TikTok had already landed him in his headmaster's office at the start of term, with dire warnings about Earlsbrook Comprehensive featuring in online content. But the events of today were exactly the sort of thing his followers would expect him to cover – and he'd be able to get exclusive first-hand accounts when the girls were feeling a bit better. He'd been remarkably restrained in his messages so far, but Frankie could feel the newshound in him straining at the leash. He was dying to get the details.

Frankie took a sip. 'Thanks, Ol, never has hot chocolate been more appreciated. Where on earth did you get it?'

He grinned. 'Staff room. I promised I'd bring the mug back. One of Aoife's friends let me in.'

Her big brother dating a nurse was proving to have definite advantages. Plus, Aoife was lovely.

'Is Sorcha okay?'

'Aoife said she bashed her shoulder, and they think she's damaged one of her eardrums, so they are keeping her in tonight.'

Frankie's mum frowned. 'I'll go and get her some pyjamas now, and she'll need some books. Has she got her phone?'

Ollie shook his head. 'Aoife said she reckons it's in the rubble somewhere.'

'Can you bring in one of your old ones for her? Or ask the twins? She'll need a charger.' Before Ollie could answer, their mum made a sort of huffing noise.

'Honestly, this is ridiculous – we pay enough for that school. I've called Brian McNamara in Health and Safety. They spend enough time checking our fire exits, it's time they were useful. He said he'd update me when he knows anything, but it all seems to be very secretive.'

Ollie leaned in close to Frankie, gesturing for their mum to lean in too as he kept voice low. 'The Guards don't think it was gas.'

Her mum looked at him, her eyes narrowed. 'So what *do* they think it was? I know it was a chemistry lab but it's a *school* – what could there possibly be that could be explosive enough to destroy the place?'

Frankie took another sip of her hot chocolate. 'I heard the Guards saying they have people coming down from Belfast to look at the lab. They can't see how it could have been an accident.'

Ollie let out a sharp breath. 'That's what Aoife said.' He raised his eyebrows. 'They think it might have been a bomb.'

'*WHAT?*'

You could have heard Frankie's mum out in the car park.

BULLET JOURNAL
Behind Every Successful Woman is Herself

Visiting time started at 2 p.m. I'm
waiting in the main reception. There
are rows and rows of seats full of people.

I'm sitting at the end nearest the
nurses' station so I can hear what
they are saying. I was just going
to ask which wards everyone was
on, but as I slipped into the waiting
area, I heard two girls talking beside
the main doors. One of them was
clutching a feeble-looking bunch of
flowers that looked like it came
from Tesco.

'The nurse said only family at the
moment. I said we were swim team, so
we were like family, but she said we'd
have to wait.'

'You should have said you were her
sister. They aren't likely to ID you, are
they?'

'Doh, if her real family turn up what do we say then?'

One of them was younger — a Third Year maybe — and if they were talking about the swim team, they must have wanted to visit that Sorcha Bennett girl.

But the sister thing is a good idea, once I know who is here for sure. The names have been posted on Instagram but it's too early to get excited – the news stations haven't confirmed them yet.

And I'm not about to expose myself by asking stupid questions.

I reckon if I sit here a bit longer, I'll be able to piece everything together. A lot of things can go wrong when you're in hospital.

You'd have thought it was a safe place.

Sorcha jumped as Ms Rowan's blonde head appeared through a gap in the curtains surrounding her bed, the Biology teacher's face furrowed with worry. Sorcha had been half dozing, glad the curtains had been pulled against the constant bleeping and bustle of the ward that she'd finally been brought up to. She'd been starting to think she was never leaving the Emergency Department.

'Sorcha, love, how are you feeling?'

Sorcha pulled the soft pink waffle blanket and stiff sheet closer to her chin; she was still feeling strange and disorientated. Talking to teachers when you were in bed was just another level of weird.

'A bit sore. I seem to be getting stiffer.' Which didn't bode well for her flexibility, but Sorcha wasn't going to think too much about that now.

'Do you mind if I come in?' Sorcha shook her head as

Ms Rowan slipped through the curtains and pulled out the plastic visitor's chair from beside the bedside locker. She sat down with a sigh. She was still wearing her lab coat over her red blouse and dark trousers, as if she'd forgotten to take it off. 'There's a Guard here who needs to ask you a few questions. Do you feel up to that?'

'Do they know what happened?' Sorcha shifted up in the bed, trying to pull the sheet and blankets with her, but they were tightly tucked in at the end and she didn't have the strength to yank them.

Ms Rowan leaned forwards to help her, unfolding the top of the sheet so Sorcha could fully cover herself. 'Not yet, that's why they need to talk to everyone. I'll stay with you. Ms Ashworth has been in touch with your parents, but I think it's going to take a while for them to get here.'

'They're in Finland. It's hard to get direct flights. My aunt's brought pyjamas and my laptop and a pile of books. We couldn't talk because the doctor was here, and she had to get back to the hotel, but she's going to see if she can come later. And Frankie's brother is going to bring me in a phone.'

'That's great. Hopefully you won't be here too long. The Guards need to talk to Frankie too.'

Taking this in, Sorcha wished Ollie would hurry up with the phone. Lack of communication was seriously killing her. She was desperate to know how everyone was, as well as the latest news. And she was sure Frankie would be gathering as much information as she could, in whatever part of the hospital she was in now.

Ms Rowan smiled reassuringly. 'There's an investigation starting into what happened, and why the ceiling came down.' She hesitated. 'It's the explosion that is very worrying. I'd assumed it was gas, but the Guards are looking at a lot of possibilities. They're taking it very seriously.'

Sorcha felt her eyebrows shoot up. Before she could answer, a Guard in uniform stuck his head through the gap in the curtains. Clean-shaven, he had his hat under one arm and looked older than her dad, his salt-and-pepper hair combed over a bald patch that caught the overhead lights.

Ms Rowan smiled up at him. 'This is Sorcha; she says she feels well enough to have a chat now.' Then, turning back to Sorcha, she continued, 'Tell us everything you can remember – we don't know what is, or isn't, going to be useful at this stage.'

The Guard came in through the curtains and pulled a notebook out of the top pocket of his navy bomber jacket.

'I just need to start with name, age, contact details.'

Sorcha reeled them off.

He wrote down her replies as she answered. 'Can you tell me where you were in the lab when the explosion occurred?'

Sorcha turned to reach for the notepad Frankie's mum had dropped in with the books. She'd started doing a drawing of the lab as soon as she'd arrived on the ward. Everything right now felt like it was tumbling wildly, making Sorcha feel seriously anxious. Drawing a plan, thinking through what had happened, helped her feel a bit more in control. Organisation and routine were such an important part of her life with her swimming, that she'd felt she needed to try and write it all down to get a grip on the order of events.

Ms Rowan realised what she was reaching for and pulled the pad and pen off the top of the pile of books, handing them to her. Sorcha smiled gratefully. Turning the notepad around, she flipped open the cover and showed the Guard the plan she'd drawn. 'Here. I've marked everyone and where they were sitting.'

Leaning over, the Guard scanned the page. 'That's great. Can I take a picture of it?' He pulled out his mobile phone as Sorcha tapped the pad with her pen. 'From the way the stools and bits of ceiling were thrown about, it looked like the explosion came from the back of the lab.'

Sorcha chewed the end of her pen. Now she was properly awake, her brain had got back into gear. This was like a Maths puzzle, an equation where she had part of the information, but needed to fill in the gaps. And one thing she really enjoyed was solving Maths problems.

BULLET JOURNAL

Behind Every Successful Woman is Herself

Finally. I can feel my eyes rolling, it's taken so long.

I've been here over an hour and finally I'm getting some of the information I need. The nurse at the reception desk changed about 15 minutes ago — off to have a quick break, apparently. They thought their handover was whispered, but I could hear them. Only just, but enough.

I heard the nurse say one of the girls from Raven's Hill was on St Joan's Ward, so I'll go there first. Visiting time finishes at 4 p.m., but this trip is for information gathering. The nurse looks friendly. She's got blonde hair pulled back in a ponytail, but she really needs to get her roots done.

Once I know who is here — and where — I can work out the next part of the plan. Something targeted.

There are Guards everywhere, which is very annoying, even here in reception, but I've never had problems with them before. They are all incredibly stupid really, but I need to be aware of them. I want this done fast, with the minimum of fuss, and then he'll know exactly what he's dealing with.

We're the perfect couple and I'm not going to let anything ruin that. He needs to learn to show a bit of respect.

The news online has finally caught up, so now I have the list of names. And it won't be hard to find out who's on which ward.

The minute they tried to take what was mine, our destinies became linked. I don't believe anything happens by accident. There was a reason that I saw those photos and read those text messages.

Ah, I just heard the nurse say that it's Sorcha Bennett who's on

St Joan's Ward, the one who looks like a pixie and swims for her school. That's perfect. It turns out she's Frankie O'Sullivan's cousin, and she's in here somewhere too.

I'm a bit disappointed there were so few people left in the classroom — the damage would have been so much more satisfying if the whole class had been there. But I didn't need all of them. I just wanted two.

The new nurse is dealing with someone now, but I'll wait for a lull and record our conversation on my phone, so I get all the details.

RECORDING

'Hi, I'm Sorcha Bennett's sister. She's on St Joan's Ward, but she's really anxious about her friends — can you tell me which wards they're on so I can check in with them?'

She hesitates for a moment. I keep going, 'selling-in', as my mum calls it.

'It was so terrible. I was in Biology, but I'm in Sixth Year so I was on the next floor down. The bang was so loud.

128

It's just so awful. Honestly, I thought a plane had hit the school.'

'Well ... I shouldn't really ... but who does Sorcha want to know about?'

She's testing me, I can see it in her face.

'All of them, Frankie and Ella ... thank you so much, nobody's got their phones and she just wants me to tell them she's okay and see how they are ...'

Sorcha shifted against her pillows and pointed with the tip of her pen at the plan she'd drawn. The Guard and Ms Rowan leaned in closer to read her neat labels. 'Mackenzie and Becky ended up under the bench at the back. I couldn't see very well but it looked like it collapsed on top of them.'

God, she hoped they were both okay.

The Guard looked at her notepad. 'How are you so sure of the time?'

Sorcha had written the date and '*Explosion in Chemistry Lab, Raven's Hill School, 11.25 a.m.*' at the top of the page.

'I looked at the clock on the lab wall right before the first bang – I'm pretty sure the timing's right.'

'The first bang?' Ms Rowan exchanged glances with the Guard.

Sorcha looked at them both. 'Yes, there were two. There was a sort of fizzing noise and then a bang, and a second later the big bang that knocked me over.'

'Two? Are you sure?' The Guard looked at her, one fuzzy eyebrow raised.

Sorcha screwed up her face, her mind back in the lab. She couldn't remember exactly what had happened, but she was absolutely sure she'd heard two. She bit her lip. 'There was this fizzing noise and a flash of light, I think, like the sun reflecting off a phone screen. That made me look up, that's when I heard the first bang.' Sorcha rubbed her face with her hand. 'There was definitely a smaller one first and then the big one.'

The Guard looked like he was working hard to believe her.

'Are you sure, Sorcha? So far everyone's only mentioned hearing one bang, one big explosion.' Ms Rowan didn't look convinced either.

Sorcha looked at them both, trying to hide her annoyance. *Why didn't they believe her? She was a witness – the only one, by the sounds of things. And she wasn't exactly stupid, she was hardly going to make something like that up …*

The Guard cut into her thoughts: 'Could the second sound have been an echo, perhaps?'

Even more annoyed, Sorcha gave him the impression she was thinking for a minute. 'I don't think so, the second bang was louder, bigger. If it was an echo, it would have been quieter. The others must have heard two noises as well.'

Ms Rowan patted her hand. 'The only other one of you who was in the room and who can talk to us at the moment is Ella, and she didn't mention hearing two.'

Sorcha shrugged, wincing as pain ran through her shoulder. 'Ella was busy with her phone; she might not have noticed.' *How could they not believe her? Surely it would have a huge bearing on their investigation?* This was infuriating; she hated it when adults didn't take her seriously.

The Guard tapped his pen on his notebook. 'It can be hard to get things straight when you've been through something like this, but you're sure it was 11.25? With events occurring as they did, nobody else got an exact fix on the time.'

'Absolutely sure. My sister usually texts at 11.30 for a catch-up when her first lecture is over, so I was keeping an eye on the time in case Mr Murray came back in and heard the text arriving. He was already in a really bad mood. I was looking for my phone to put it on vibrate when I dropped my pen. That's why I was in front of the bench – I was bending down to pick it up when everything went flying.'

Sorcha frowned, thinking hard, running through the order of events. As she'd glanced at the clock, she'd looked down the room. She could remember seeing Mackenzie leaning over the bench, writing something down. Becky had finished her homework – had she been doing something with her phone? Sorcha was sure there had been a flash but it was all a bit hazy. And after the noise of the *two* explosions, she had a big blank.

Normally Mr Murray would have got warmed up and would be in full flow by 11.25 a.m., going over the last lot of homework. Normally the classroom would have been full, but not this time, with half the girls going off to the Physics lab first.

The Guard flipped over the page of his notebook. 'Did you see anything unusual when you arrived for class?'

Sorcha shook her head. 'I went up to the lab a few minutes early with Becky.' Sorcha looked up at him. 'It was already unlocked, which *was* a bit odd. Normally we have to wait outside, but there definitely wasn't anyone in the room then. Becky was wondering whether she could sit at the back in Maeve's usual place, so she could finish off her homework.'

The Guard wrote something in his notebook. 'And did she?'

'Did she what?'

'Did Maeve mind swapping places?'

Sorcha shook her head. She'd known Maeve wouldn't mind – Maeve knew all about trying to catch up with homework at the back of the room. But she wasn't about to say that.

'I texted her to ask, but Maeve was late anyway. I don't remember seeing anything out of place. What do you mean by anything unusual?'

'Anything strange, like a bag that had been left behind, maybe?'

Sorcha bit her lip as she realised what he was saying. A bag? Like a rucksack or something? *Did they think it could have been a bomb?*

'Hey dude, how are you doing?' Greg pulled the chair out that was tucked in beside Jasper's bedside locker and sank into it, peeling off his fleece as he did so. His sister Mackenzie was still unconscious upstairs, so he'd slipped away for ten minutes.

This was turning into the day from hell.

As if worrying about Jasper wasn't enough, then Greg had got the call about Mackenzie and had bolted out of school and run all the way there, before hanging around the ED trying to find out what was happening. Eventually he'd found a nurse who seemed to know and he'd been told Mackenzie was in the ICU.

Greg rubbed his hands over his face. *What the actual hell was going on?*

Jasper turned to look at him, his head swathed in bandages, the only eye visible purple and swollen. He made a croaking sound and reached out for Greg's hand, squeezing it tight.

Greg felt tears hot in his eyes. 'Squeeze once for yes and twice for no?'

Jasper made a movement of his head as if he was trying to nod and then, as if he was processing the instructions, squeezed Greg's hand again.

'Are you hurting? Have they given you enough meds?'

One squeeze. That was good. Jesus, he looked so beaten up, though. Greg had been in fights before, knew what it was like to lie curled up on the floor while someone kicked the hell out of you, and he wouldn't wish that level of fear on anyone. Particularly not Jasper.

Why beat him up? You could yell at Jasper and get the message across. Part of Greg hardened inside. This was about anger, about needing to take out aggression on someone weaker. And that was dangerous.

'I'm sorry it's taken me so long to get here – they were only letting family in at the weekend. I wanted to see you so badly, man. I tried to say you were my brother, but I think they saw through that one.'

A glint in Jasper's eye, a rub and a squeeze. That was something else, not a yes or a no. Jasper rubbed his hand again. That was an okay. Greg felt the tears threatening to fall. He rubbed them away with his free hand.

'You're gonna be okay now, dude, they're going to fix you.' He cleared his throat. 'I brought you a card.' He reached for the envelope in the pocket of his backpack. He'd spent so long choosing it over the weekend, but Greg hadn't been sure he'd have the courage to give it to Jasper. He slipped it onto the bed, realising that Jasper wasn't going to be able to open it. Greg could feel himself blushing.

'Will I put it on your locker so you can open it when you can see properly?'

As if Jasper could sense his discomfort, he gave Greg's hand one squeeze and another rub, and Greg felt they were connected. He squeezed Jasper's hand back.

'Christ, I'm so sorry, man, I got caught by that new sports coach on the way down to the hall. He wants me to join the basketball team, wouldn't let me get away.' Greg could feel his anger balling inside him. He'd been heading to meet Jasper after study so they could walk across the field, have a chat with a bit of privacy, but instead the A-hole of a coach had gone on and on about what an asset he'd be to the Raven's Park basketball squad, about how they were almost at the top of the league, how it would be so good for his college application.

In the end Greg had given up being polite. *'I'm fit and yeah, I'm the right height for basketball, and I'm Black –'* he'd looked at the new coach hard, because that's what this was about, he could see it in his eyes. He was Black so obviously he'd be a natural … '– *but I'm a violin player, sir, and I'm not going to risk breaking my fingers even if you want me for the NBA. Sorry, that's a no.'*

Finally, he'd got away, only to get to the hall to find it empty, disappointment flooding the anger. He'd checked his phone and found a text:

> waited 10 minutes, have to make a move.

That was it, no emojis. And a full stop.

Jasper thought he'd been stood up.

Greg had wanted to punch someone himself right then. His hands on his head, he'd circled the hall trying to work out what to say, whether to call or to text. But what could he say? He needed to talk to Jasper face to face. In that moment he'd sprinted out the door to see if he could catch him up.

'Okay …' Greg took a breath; he had so many questions. 'We're going to have to find a better way to talk than this, aren't we?'

One squeeze. Then Jasper tapped the back of Greg's hand with his thumb and pointed to the bedside locker. It took a moment for Greg to work out what he meant.

'Your phone? You want to try and message?' A squeeze again in reply. Greg picked up Jasper's phone from the top of the locker and passed it to him.

Greg had no idea how Jasper was going to manage this; he slipped the card onto the top of the locker as Jasper struggled with the phone.

With one arm and hand bandaged, Jasper was just about able to hold his mobile up so he could see the screen. His one good eye rolled over to Greg, as if he was smiling under all the layers of gauze and tape. He tapped out a message.

Greg heard his own phone ping as it arrived.

> NT YR FALT

Whatever Jasper thought, Greg knew this *was* his fault. One million percent. And Greg didn't think he could ever forgive himself.

Greg cleared his throat. 'Do you know who it was?'

His phone pinged again.

> MAYB. NO SAY.

Greg took a shaky breath. 'Why not, man? You need to tell the cops, I mean …'

> 2 DANGRUS

Greg gripped his phone. 'They said they'd come back if you told the cops?'

> KILL ME. STAY IN MY LANE.

'Christ.' Overwhelmed, Greg shook his head, the tears threatening to fall again. This was so wrong. And such a damn mess. His phone pinged again.

> NOT ABT ME

Greg's mouth went dry, shock flooding through him. 'About me?'

Christ, had Jasper been beaten up because someone had seen them talking?

> NO NOT YOU
> S KK ♥

It's okay. And a heart.

Greg wished it was that simple.

E lla closed her eyes and concentrated on trying to breathe gently. Even with the drugs they'd given her, the pain was huge, rolling over her with each breath. She'd never realised how many muscles she used for just getting oxygen into her lungs.

Ella slipped her hand inside the sheets and pushed under her bum, trying to shift in the bed, to get a bit more comfortable. All it did was make the pain worse. She winced, gritting her teeth, her eyes filling with tears.

She needed more pillows. Her mum had helped her sit up and thankfully brought her short-sleeved pyjamas that buttoned up, so changing out of the awful gown hadn't been a total nightmare, but it had worn her out. They were cute pink satin PJs with white piping and shorts, so she wasn't totally baking either; it felt as if they had the heating on max here 24/7.

Aoife, the nurse who knew Frankie, had been lovely when she'd first been brought up to the ward. She'd said she'd let the others know Ella was awake, but without her phone Ella couldn't message anyone or even look at Rave-fess to find out what the latest news was.

Part of her couldn't deal with what had happened. Not yet. She was just so overwhelmingly grateful she hadn't lost an eye or a limb, that her face was fine. Ribs would heal, but she couldn't have coped with a life-changing injury.

She couldn't think about what might have happened, about what could still happen if one of them had complications.

It was too awful.

She needed to think about something else. At least focusing on those naked photographs and *that* whole drama filled her head and stopped her thinking about *this* drama.

But without her phone, she didn't know if anyone had more news on the identity of the girl whose photos were being shared. Ella cringed inside. It could so easily have been any of them – and how many had she sent? Ella couldn't imagine that she'd be able to face school if her pictures had been seen by loads of people.

Ella would bet that the boy who had asked for them had been nice up to now, trying to get her into bed, probably. Maybe she'd said no and then he'd got nasty. The

24 hours thing everyone was talking about made it feel like a real threat, though. *What on earth did she have to do in the next 24 hours to stop more pictures being shared?*

Whoever had left the post on Rave-fess about confiding in a friend was right. Ella just hoped the girl wasn't too embarrassed to reach out.

On a normal day that's all they'd be talking about – and the post about Hailey de Búrca and whether she was actually coming to Raven's Hill or not. Amber had been full of it this morning at breaktime. Before Ella had even got her locker open, Amber had waved her phone at her, the Rave-fess post on the screen, her eyes alight.

'*Have you seen this?* I follow her brother on Instagram – he's utterly gorgeous.'

Ella had laughed at Amber's excited face. 'If she comes here, maybe she'll have a party and you can meet him.'

Amber had fallen back against the lockers theatrically, the back of her hand on her forehead. 'This could be my actual future, Amber de Búrca sounds so good, doesn't it? And I can manage the family jet – I mean Majorca could be slumming it a bit, I'm not sure the pool in their villa is *quite* big enough, but I *could* learn to cope.'

'You'd have to brush up on your skiing. St Moritz, isn't it, that they go to?'

'Totally is. I could get lessons, before I meet him. When do you think she's starting?'

Ella had been trying to find her lab coat, realising that she'd forgotten to bring it in again. She pushed the locker door closed and locked it.

'I'm not sure Raven's Hill will take her.'

Amber leaned on the locker, her face serious. 'Why not? The de Búrcas are like the richest family in the country, according to, well, everything.'

Ella had grimaced. Maybe Hailey's dad thought he could buy her a way into Raven's Hill. Tiernan was always saying he never got into any trouble at Raven's Park because his dad had bought the sports building. But from what Ella had heard, Hailey de Búrca might not be an ideal fit for their school. She didn't exactly have a track record for getting on with people, and she had a vindictive streak.

'Don't breathe a word of this ...' Ella had sent Amber a warning look.

Amber quickly drew a cross on her chest with her finger. 'Lips sealed, hope to die.' She pinched her mouth closed, then put her hand on Ella's arm. 'Spill, before I die of anticipation.'

Ella had almost laughed. Amber could be more dramatic than Georgia sometimes.

'One of my cousin's friends was dating this girl from Ardmore Wood. Hailey got expelled for punching her, his girlfriend I mean – Hailey broke her nose.'

Amber's hand shot straight to her own nose, as if she was protecting it. 'Never – why?'

Ella kept her voice down. 'She reported Hailey for smoking in the bathrooms. Apparently Hailey had been right under a smoke detector and deliberately blowing smoke up at it. If she'd set the fire alarm off, the sprinklers would have gone off too, like they did that time at Raven's Park when the whole art room got wrecked.'

'I thought that was an "accident" at Raven's Park?' Ella had raised her eyebrows knowingly in reply as Amber continued. 'But that's not a reason to punch someone – that's terrible.'

'Apparently Hailey got suspended for the smoking thing and on her way out of school went straight up to this girl in the lunchroom and whacked her.'

Amber had rolled her eyes. 'Maybe I need to find another way to meet her delicious brother. I was already looking forward to us sipping Bellinis on the terrace of their place in Tuscany.'

'You know I'd never turn down a Bellini, but maybe you need to revise your marriage plans, just until you've made sure anger issues don't run in the family. You don't want to land in some sort of abusive relationship.'

Suddenly the curtains surrounding Ella's bed twitched open, interrupting her thoughts. A face peeped through the gap. It was Amber, with Georgia peering over her shoulder. It was like she'd conjured up her friend by thinking of her.

'Are you awake? Can we come in?'

Ella felt herself grinning with relief. She'd been worried about how she was going to survive the boredom of the afternoon worrying about every breath and with no phone. At least now she could catch up on the gossip.

Ella looked at Amber, rolling her eyes. 'Obviously.' It came out as a whisper. Speaking used another set of muscles that lifted the pain over the dulling influence of the drugs. 'That's so spooky, I was just thinking about you.'

Like twins with their matching glossy brown hair, padded jackets with pastel hoodies underneath, leggings and hi-tops, Amber and Georgia swished the curtains apart one after the other as if they were coming on stage. Ella smiled but didn't dare laugh. She put her hand around her ribs protectively. 'Come and sit down, but you're not allowed to be funny. Seriously, it hurts too much.'

Amber grinned and came and sat on the edge of the bed as Georgia went around to the visitor's chair.

'Sorry we're so late – our mums said we should wait, that you wouldn't be able for visitors until later. They're a bit hysterical about the whole explosion thing so we had to sneak off and get the bus.'

That explained their exercise gear. They both looked like they were going to the gym.

Wincing, Ella shifted a fraction up on her pillow so she could see them both properly. 'Have you heard anything about how it happened?'

Amber shook her head solemnly. 'Nothing yet. The whole lab's wrecked, though. Jess is sure it was a bomb.'

Amber left the word hanging there and Ella felt some of the brightness at their arrival evaporate. *Who would bomb a school?* It was more than she could cope with right now. It sounded nuts.

As if Georgia realised Ella needed to be distracted, she opened her backpack. 'We bought you magazines, since we weren't sure if you're allowed to have your phone on. Look, *Vogue* and *Cosmopolitan*, and *Psychologies*.' Georgia put the magazines on the bed beside Ella. 'We'll have to go in a minute, but we can come back tomorrow. Frankie has her phone – if you need anything, get a message to her and she can text us.'

'Mum's bringing in a phone for me later; I'll message as soon as I get it. And I'd love to see you tomorrow. These are fantastic.' Ella kept her voice low, fighting the pain as she smiled, emotion welling up inside her. Her friends were the best.

Georgia stood up. 'You're wrecked – we'll go now and see you tomorrow. We just wanted to check you were okay. We've been so worried.'

Suddenly a little overcome, Ella could feel tears pricking. Almost dying made you appreciate your friends. Big time. And they'd be back tomorrow. Perhaps they'd have more news then.

'What time do you want me to collect you?' Jess's dad glanced over to her as he swung his orange Mini into the hospital car park, pools of light from the overhead lamps making the darkness more intense somehow.

'Visiting time finishes at 8.30, so then? I'm super early but I want to find out where everyone is.' Jess looked out at the brightly lit, modern building, grey concrete and lots of glass, her stomach hollow and sick. She *really* hated hospitals: the very smell of them brought all those visits to see her mum before she died right back. And now her friends were here. All of them. She swallowed as her dad pulled up in front of the main doors.

'If you decide to hang out with any of the class afterwards, just text, otherwise I'll meet you here.' Jess felt her dad's eyes on her and turned around and gave him a quick hug. He knew how hard this was, how anxious she felt. It was hard for him too.

'Have you got everything?'

Jess checked the contents of the plastic shopping bag on her knee. Grapes, chocolate and Oreos for Frankie, her favourites. She nodded in response to his question.

'Knock 'em dead, Tiger.'

'*Dad*. That is the most wildly inappropriate thing you could say right now.' Jess threw him a withering look and he smiled. He'd always said that when she was little. On the first day of school. Actually, now she thought about it, on the first day of every new school, and there had been a few. In countries all over the world.

They'd moved around a lot, but Kilmurray Point was home now and a new start. Jess took a breath; deep down a part of her felt that it might be her that was bringing this bad luck to Raven's Hill. There were times when she felt as if disaster followed her like a cloud. She shook the idea away; her anxiety was making her overthink.

Her dad must have felt her hesitation. 'As soon as the Guards know anything, my contact will let me know. The technical bureau should have more of an idea what happened by now, at least in terms of the blast pattern.'

She put her hand on the car door. 'Thanks, Dad.' As she spoke, on the other side of the broad pavement, the hospital's huge glass doors slid open, and she saw Mackenzie's brother Greg coming out. He was still wearing his Raven's Park uniform, the navy V-neck sweater piped in gold and red to match the Raven's Hill uniform. He must have come straight to the hospital when he'd heard what had happened. His backpack over one shoulder, he had his hands in his trouser pockets and was shivering hard. Perhaps he had news.

Jess got out of the car, closing the door behind her. Her heart was already starting to pound at the thought of going inside. None of this was going to be easy.

'Hey, Greg, I'm Jess, from Mackenzie's class. How is she doing?'

Greg looked about as stressed as she'd ever seen anyone ever. 'She's ...' He hesitated, as if he wasn't ready to talk about his twin's health status right then. 'Neat car.'

Jess turned to watch her dad manoeuvre across the car park, the bright orange Mini with its two black stripes on the roof looking like a giant bug. 'Thanks – my dad doesn't use it much, he's away a lot, but he used to rally Minis when he was younger. I think it's a way of recapturing his youth.'

'He's the journalist, right? Mackenzie told me. Pretty awesome job.'

Jess grimaced. 'Sometimes I wish he covered flower shows instead of conflict. Be a bit safer.'

Greg nodded slowly. She could tell from his face that he was preoccupied. 'Mackenzie said you haven't been here long either – was moving tough?'

'Easier this time, but I've moved a lot.' Jess shrugged.

An understanding smile flicked across his face. 'It's hard.'

'That's for sure.' Jess pulled her phone out of her pocket. She suddenly had a feeling that this conversation could get a bit deep; she really wasn't up to that right now. And she needed to text Frankie to tell her she'd arrived.

He shrugged, speaking half to himself. 'We thought Kilmurray Point would be safe and sleepy.'

Jess let out a sigh in response. 'You're not alone there.' She tried again: 'How's Mackenzie doing?'

Greg rubbed his hand over his face. 'She's on oxygen. She's got bad asthma, you know? They can't say if it was the dust or if she inhaled something toxic but she's in pretty bad shape. I've just come out for some air.'

Jess could hear the stress in his voice. 'Are your parents coming over?'

'My mom's on her way.' He sighed. 'I just needed a breather. There are cops everywhere and they make me nervous.' He hitched his backpack up.

Jess could see it in his eyes. 'The Irish police aren't the same as the American police, you know. They're here to help. And they aren't armed – not the uniformed ones, anyway. Detectives are, but you aren't likely to come up against any of them.' She tried to sound as reassuring as she could.

He shivered, shaking visibly as he flicked a glance at her. 'Let's hope they can do a better job than the cops at home – we need to find out what happened.'

Behind him, the huge main doors of the hospital slid open, and a wave of heat swept around them as an older woman slowly walked out, helped by a man who looked like her son.

'That's for sure. They're going to be busy. Do you know Jasper Parks?'

A look Jess couldn't quite read passed over Greg's face. He shrugged. 'Yeah, we've got some classes together.'

'I'm on the Raven's Hill Model United Nations Team, so I know him pretty well from our debates with Raven's Park. I thought Mackenzie said you were thinking of joining?'

Greg shrugged again. 'I'm pretty busy getting to grips with Raven's Park, to be honest.'

Jess suddenly felt like she wanted to give him a hug. *Being so far from home and frightened for your twin was just horrible.* 'You probably heard – Jasper got beaten up on his way home after school on Friday. I'm going to pop in and see him too.'

'Nasty.' Greg winced a bit as he spoke, his eyebrows knitting with concern.

'He's not great from what I can gather, but I'm just going to find out now. Give my love to Mackenzie? I guess it's family only in ICU?'

He nodded, his jaw taut. For a moment she thought he was trying not to cry.

'They'll fix Mackenzie, don't worry, she's in the right place. And I'm sure the Guards will get to the bottom of what happened.'

Sorcha checked the time on the phone Ollie had brought her. Evening visiting time started in 20 minutes and she couldn't wait to see Jess. Frankie had texted earlier to say she still didn't have a bed, but they were definitely keeping her in. She was feeling very fed up with being in the corridor.

Sorcha pursed her lips, thinking. Jess was the only one of them who was mobile and could gather information from the others. Which was what Sorcha really needed right now.

'You didn't see me, I'm not here.' Ollie had slipped into the ward well after visiting time had finished this afternoon, winking as he'd handed her a bag with a phone and charger in it. 'I've factory reset it and put in a new SIM with credit on it – you can switch it to your own number when you get a chance. The battery isn't the best, so you might need to keep it plugged in.'

He turned to leave, then added, 'I gave this new number to Frankie, I've texted it to your mum and Beth, and my mum's got it. The hospital guest Wi-Fi password is in the box. And I put yours and our family numbers into the contacts. Frankie will be able to send you all your friends' contacts.'

Sorcha had grinned. Ollie was the best. As cousins came, she'd scored a clear ten. Even with Max. His adorable moments made up for the more demonic ones.

Pulling the phone out of the bag Ollie had dropped off, Sorcha had plugged it in straight away. She glanced at it now; it had enough battery for her to check the local news to see what was being reported about the blast.

She quickly found what she was looking for.

She'd expected it to be bad, but the photos of the outside of the building were shocking. The picture must have been taken with a zoom from an upstairs window in one of the houses across the road. Somehow the photographer had found a gap in the trees that lined the road in front of the school and got a snap of all the emergency vehicles pulled up around the Science Block. Unless he'd been up one of the trees, of course.

Sorcha scanned the reports. There was nothing that she didn't already know, but there was a good dose of speculation and quotes from locals who had been horrified at the bang.

Not nearly as horrified as she'd been.

There was a casualty report at the end that spelled Mackenzie's name wrong and made it sound like Maeve was fighting for her life.

And then there was a paragraph about Raven's Hill being an international day and boarding school: 'Local councillor Eustace Murphy has become very concerned at the number of places at Raven's Hill School taken up by non-nationals, which, he claims, blocks Irish children from the same privileges. He intends to raise it at the next council meeting.'

Sorcha read it again and then googled the councillor. He was part of an anti-immigration far-right party that had objected to Ireland taking in refugees and asylum-seekers, and actually anyone who wasn't Irish. The very first picture that came up was of him standing on some sort of stage at a street protest. There was a sea of placards in front of him and he was slamming his fist down on a lectern, bright red in the face, anger surrounding him like a cloud. She blinked. If the pictures of the building were shocking, this was somehow worse. The speech he'd made was full of xenophobic and racist undertones.

Sorcha googled again and another report came up. 'Violent Protesters Arrested in Midlands Town.' Murphy was right in the middle of the photograph with a placard behind him that read *Ireland for the Irish.*

Sorcha read on. Apparently the group's plan was 'to stir up fear and mistrust and provoke confrontation'.

The journalist had heard rumours that they had threatened to blow up a hotel – that was just horrible. How on earth did someone like this Murphy character get into local government in Kilmurray Point? It took a few more moments for the pieces to fall into place in her head.

Could the explosion have been caused by far-right fanatics, like this group? The people in this photo looked riled up enough to start a war. Perhaps Kilmurray Point was the next place they wanted to target with their extremism and they were starting with a school known for its international student population.

Sorcha looked at her phone again. She really needed Jess to get here so she could show her the article – maybe her dad could find out from the journalist if the mood had been as bad as it looked in the photos online.

Plus Jess got on really well with Ms Rowan; maybe she'd have more news from the school side.

Sorcha pulled her notepad onto her knee and looked at the plan she'd drawn. Narrowing her eyes, she flipped the page over and wrote *WHAT WE KNOW* at the top.

They needed answers, and if the Guards wouldn't listen to her about something as fundamental and important as how many bangs there had been, she and her friends were going to have to find out what had happened themselves.

Nude photos. Discuss.

If whoever has them publishes them,
isn't that revenge porn? There's a law
about that.

Why did she do it in the first place? I
think she's a total twat ngl.

That's victim blaming, she didn't take
them to be shared OBVIOUSLY. Listen
to yourself.

How can you be thinking about
this when six girls are in hospital???
Perspective, people.

Maybe some of us need to take our minds off our friends being in intensive care?

I bet the person who's in the pictures is focusing on it right now – idk if it was post break-up or if they were blackmailed into sending, but solidarity, sister.

I heard she had to do something in 24 hours or more would be shared???

What? OMG. That's worse.

I think we need to start a campaign – awareness for the younger girls and to support whoever this is. We need to talk to the prefects.

If it's someone's sister or girlfriend who found out about that WhatsApp group, they need to tell the dirtball involved that they're in a LOT of trouble. *We are the granddaughters of the witches you couldn't burn.*

That's SO cringe.

It's *SO TRUE*.

Does anyone have any updates on the explosion? Cannot cope not knowing what's happening.

I heard Maeve was really badly injured and Sorcha basically held her together until the ambulance came. Tara is destroyed. Sending love to both.

Fire brigade and the Guards still at the Science Block. There are forensics people everywhere.

And press. Sick dude trying to take photos. Ms Ashworth ran him off. All hail the principal.

The gas people have been, and the boarding house is back open. School open as usual tomorrow.

HALF THE SCHOOL BLOWS UP AND THEY CAN'T EVEN GIVE US A DAY OFF???

Standing beside the huge circular reception desk just inside the main doors of St Anthony's Hospital, a scribbled list of names and wards in her hand, Jess checked the time on her phone. Evening visiting hours only ran for two hours and she wanted to say hello to Frankie as well as drop in to see Jasper and Sorcha, then double back to Frankie, who she hoped, by then, would be in a bed in an actual ward. The only hitch seemed to be that there was going to be a bit of sprinting between them.

She was early, to give herself a bit of extra time to find her way about, but also because she knew she'd need time to focus on not having an actual panic attack. Jess ran a hand through her hair. This morning she'd known from Sorcha's face that the purple dye was brighter than she'd expected, but they all needed a bit of bright right now.

She suddenly felt a creepy self-conscious feeling, the hairs rising on the back of her neck as if someone was watching her. Weird. She shivered.

In front of the reception desk there were rows of chairs. The people sitting on them looked like they might be waiting for appointments, but they were all facing away from her. She glanced around. The atrium was circular and opened off to corridors going in all directions. Perhaps it was her purple hair that was attracting someone's attention – or maybe it was just her imagination. As she stood in the reception area, the unmistakable hospital smell was already making her feel queasy. *She could do this. She just needed to focus.*

Shaking the creepy feeling, Jess scanned a grey sign detailing the ward names and their floors, arrows pointing in every direction, and worked out her route. Frankie was still in the Emergency Department corridor, but as Jess looked up at the sign again, her phoned pipped with a bunch of texts from her.

They're moving me to St Thomas's Ward.

Should be soon.

> Will let you know as soon as I
> get there.

That was great news. Jess hadn't known if she'd be able to see Frankie in the corridor; she was pretty sure they needed to keep it clear of visitors. She deliberately hadn't asked at Reception; she was hoping to see Ollie's girlfriend Aoife and sneak in.

Jess quickly texted Frankie back. So, Jasper first. He was on the same floor as Sorcha so that was something. Jess looked for the lift.

✗ ✗ ✗

Upstairs, Jess followed the signs to St Brigid's Ward. Crossing the wide corridor and pushing open the door to the ward, Jess hesitated. There was someone in one of the middle beds, covered in bandages. Was that Jasper? Jess winced. He looked even worse than she'd expected.

A nurse in dark blue scrubs was just coming out of the ward. She must have read Jess's confused face. 'Who are you looking for, love?'

'Jasper Parks? He came in on Friday.'

She smiled. 'That's him in the middle there. He was getting bored with his curtains closed.'

That sounded like Jasper.

Jess smiled her thanks.

It was a men's ward and Jess felt a bit conspicuous walking over to his bed, her hi-tops squeaking on the polished rubber floor.

'Hey, Jasper, are you accepting visitors?'

It took a moment for her voice to register, but then he raised his one good hand, gesturing for her to sit in the chair pulled up beside the bed.

Jess was sure his parents would be in any minute and she didn't want to get in the way, but she knew if it was her in a hospital bed, she'd want some contact with her friends and news of the outside world. Well, maybe not if she'd been beaten up like he had, and looked this horrific, but still.

'You're in a bit of a mess. I bought grapes and chocolate, but I don't know how you're going to eat them.' Jess grimaced. 'Maybe you can keep them? I'll put them here, will I?' She leaned in to put one of the brown paper bags onto his bedside locker. The top was already crowded with cards and boxes of chocolates.

Tucked under his red-framed glasses was a card with a big heart on it. She didn't know he was dating anyone.

But then, let's face it, perhaps she didn't know him as well as she thought.

Maybe this was a bit awkward.

But he seemed okay with it, and she really didn't plan to stay long.

Jess slipped off her denim jacket and laid it over her knee as she sat down. When she'd got home that afternoon she'd changed into a black polo neck sweater but she was already regretting that: it was baking in here.

'Did you hear about the explosion at Raven's Hill?' He inclined his head. She took that as a yes. 'The girls who were hurt in it are here too. I have to shoot off in a minute to see them, but *drama*.'

He pointed to something on the bedside locker. It took Jess a moment to work it out. His phone. What did he want that for?

She picked it up, puzzled, and put it in his unbandaged hand. Transferring it to his bandaged hand, holding it with the fingers not completely wrapped up, he lifted it close to his face, as his good thumb flew over the keyboard. A moment later her own phone buzzed with a message. Clever.

Can't talk. Mouth 2 swollen.
Heard gas? All okay?

Jess didn't want to think what had happened to Jasper's face to make it swell. The thought of him being attacked in the dark and left bleeding on a freezing cold, muddy rugby pitch made Jess's heart break, but she hid her reaction. He'd had a bad enough time without her making it worse.

'I think everyone's sort of okay – they're all alive, anyway, which sounds like a bit of a miracle. Maeve Andersson's the worst, I think. She's been in surgery, but I heard they're happy that they've got her almost back together.' Jess took a breath, trying to keep her voice level and upbeat, which felt a bit ridiculous, but Jasper had enough problems. 'She's still in intensive care. Becky's got mainly cuts and bruises, but nothing broken. I haven't heard much about her ... but they're worried about Mackenzie's breathing, which is a bit scary. But it looks like you've had it just as bad. Do you know who it was?'

Jasper reached for his phone,

> No idea. Dark. Behind.

Jess pursed her lips, trying to hide her anger. It had been a pretty emotional day and now this. 'Did they take anything? Was it muggers or junkies or something?'

He reached for his phone again.

> Left bag phone iPad.

Sighing, Jess shook her head; it made no sense. Random attacks happened all the time, but more often in Dublin City.

'Did they say anything? Can you remember?'

He tapped out a message on the phone again:

> Stay in my lane.

'What on earth's that supposed to mean?'

He made a movement that could have been a shrug, then reached for the phone again.

> Guards good. Button on grass.
> Not mine.

'Wow, so they might have a lead? God, I hope so. Maybe someone who lives along the back of the field has security cameras or one of those video doorbells?'

He moved his head slightly, as if he was trying to nod.

Behind her, Jess heard the ward door suck open. She glanced over her shoulder to see a guy in his twenties with a huge box of Ferrero Rocher chocolates under his arm, the gold foil label catching the lights. She needed to get moving: Jasper's parents would be here soon. And maybe whoever had sent him the heart card.

'Look, it must be exhausting having to talk through your phone. Text me if you need anything.'

He reached for the phone again.

> TY, come again?
> Hope friends okay.

Smiling, Jess nodded. 'Thanks, so do I. I'll find a quiz for next time, gotta keep the grey cells oiled so you're all set when you can talk again.'

She said it lightly but inside she was raging. *Who had done this?*

F rankie shifted on the trolley, trying to get comfortable. The rubber mattress felt very narrow, and the sheet was too big, slipping off when she moved. Her dark hair had come out of her ponytail and kept getting in her face, but she couldn't tie it back up with only one hand.

At least she'd tucked Becky's iPad in beside her, close to the wall, just in case she fell asleep. There was no point tempting fate by having it in full view of the passing public. She'd held onto it this long and she wasn't going to let it out of her sight until she could hand it over to Becky personally.

But sleep seemed unlikely with the bright overhead lights and doors constantly sucking open and closed. The corridor was even fuller and busier than when she'd arrived. The sooner she got out of here the better.

When she'd got back from the loo earlier, Frankie had started to feel a bit sick, and things had gone a bit fuzzy, and everyone had started worrying about her head. Then her mum had reappeared to say that there would be a bed around 6.30 p.m. – it was on a different ward to Sorcha and the others, but at least it wasn't in a corridor.

But now time was ticking on, and she was wondering if they had a bed at all. They wanted to keep her overnight to make sure she didn't have a concussion, but she'd sort of thought that meant she wouldn't have to stay in the corridor.

At least visiting time had started – Frankie was desperate to see Jess. Incoming news was a bit limited, even though Sorcha had a phone now. Maybe Jess had heard what was happening.

Frankie checked her own phone again. Rave-fess was quiet, and the year WhatsApp group hadn't updated for ages. She felt like she'd been watching TikTok forever. It sucked up time and was funny, but Frankie felt so cut off down here. She jumped as her phone pinged with a text.

It was from Sorcha.

Perhaps she'd heard something about the explosion.

Frankie opened the message. Sorcha's text linked to a Google doc. She'd typed 'WHAT WE KNOW' at the top of the doc. Frankie grinned. Sorcha's brain just never switched off.

After the list of who was where in the hospital, she'd written:

~~Gas explosion~~
Accident? How?
The Guards don't think it was an accident.
Deliberate? Why?

Frankie sent her a message to say she was reading and then updated the casualty list on the doc with what she knew from Aoife. Maeve was out of surgery now, and they'd moved Ella to St Valentine's Ward. That would be perfect for her when Tiernan arrived. He'd probably come laden with flowers and chocolates.

Aoife was working late tonight covering for a friend and was planning to keep an eye on them all. Frankie had put in a special request for her to try to get a look at the legendary Tiernan and see what he was like in real life. He was on the Raven's Park rugby team, but he was a Sixth Year, so he didn't hang out at Starbucks with the Fifth Years – at least Frankie didn't think she'd ever seen him there.

Ella said he lived close to Dublin city centre, so he hung out in town with a load of ex-Raven's Park guys who had moved to the Institute to take their Leaving Cert. Frankie was going to ask her twin brothers, Cian and Kai, if they knew him. They were Sixth Years and at the Institute too. They were a bit useless when it came to gossip because they were constantly studying, but they might be able to find out more about him. He was definitely mad about Ella.

Thinking of her brothers made her think of Mackenzie and Greg. Twins had such a close bond, and Frankie knew Greg would be worried sick about his sister. Aoife had said he'd been pacing about upstairs close to the ICU waiting to see how Mackenzie was. Their parents had to be crazy worried too – even if they managed to get on a plane straight away, they wouldn't be here for hours.

'Hey, soldier, don't look so worried. How are you doing?' Frankie looked up at the sound of Ollie's voice to see him coming down the corridor, a bag of fish and chips in his hand. All thoughts of sickness gone, she suddenly realised she was starving.

'Very pleased to see you, big brother.' She held up the fresh cast on her wrist. 'They've stuck me back together. Are those for me?'

Ollie rested the warm bag on her blanket and looked surreptitiously up and down the corridor. 'They are indeed. I'm not sure the nurses will approve, but you need to keep your strength up and I don't think they have a full catering service down here.' He indicated her cast. 'Who's going to be the first to sign it?'

Frankie hadn't thought about that yet. Opening the bag and popping a chip into her mouth, she spoke with her mouth full. 'Danny, obviously, then Sorcha and Jess and Katie. I'll see if I can get the whole class on.'

Nodding, Ollie continued, 'And your noble brothers,

I hope. The twins said they'd be in tomorrow if you're still here. Max is desperate to come too, so they're trying to keep him distracted. Any sign of a bed yet?'

Frankie reached for another chip, silently glad her twin brothers were keeping Max out of the hospital. She adored him, but he was a handful on a good day. 'I'm supposed to be on my way to St Thomas's Ward any minute. Someone came to check my stitches as well and shone a light in my eyes for the ten billionth time. But I haven't heard anything about when I might be moving since Mum left.'

Ollie nodded. 'She's gone back to the hotel to check on everything, then she'll try and get back before visiting time's over.'

'Hopefully I'll be upstairs by then. Is there any news on the others?'

Ollie looked thoughtful as he pulled out a chip. 'I popped in to Aoife to say hello when I dropped off Sorcha's phone earlier. Has that brother of Mackenzie's had problems with the police?'

Frankie looked at him, puzzled. 'I don't think so. Mackenzie hasn't said anything. You mean here in Ireland or in America?' Ollie shrugged and reached into the bag again as Frankie continued, 'They've only been here a few months so it's not likely. We'd have heard.' Frankie shook her head. 'All you see on TV is horrible things kicking off in America. Mackenzie was telling me about their active shooter drills in high school. It's horrific – talk about making no sense.'

'Yep, legalising something that can kill your kids, and then having to protect them from it? Eh, hello? I reckon the next generation is going to have massive PTSD.'

'Jess is always talking about that. She wants to do human rights in college. She'll be a brilliant lawyer. She says in a country that has no healthcare, creating your own mental health crisis is a bit short-sighted, and freedom to do anything shouldn't impact another human in a life and death way – that's just not civilised.' Frankie screwed up her nose. 'Why'd you ask, though?'

Ollie reached for an onion ring. 'Oh, just something Aoife said. A Guard came in to see how everyone was doing, they need to question them, and – Greg, is it?' Frankie nodded. 'He totally vanished when he heard the Guard saying he needed to ask a few questions. One of the other nurses was coming back to tell him something and had no idea where he'd gone. The Guard didn't even want to speak to him.'

'Maybe he just went to get a drink or something. Listen, Sorcha's sent me a plan of the room and it looks like Becky and Mackenzie were closest to the explosion – it's a miracle they're still alive.' Frankie paused, her mind catching up with what Ollie had said. 'But why would Greg be worried?'

Ollie shrugged. 'Maybe he just doesn't have a great experience of law enforcement. American cops don't exactly have a brilliant reputation. I'm sure that's all it is.'

Frankie looked at him suspiciously. 'You don't *sound* sure.'

Ollie shook his head. 'It's just the other nurse, Aoife's friend, thought he looked really frightened. I don't know. Why did they move over here?'

'Something to do with their dad's job. But both their parents have big jobs – so they couldn't move over with the twins. It is a bit of a weird time to change schools. They're both eighteen, but apparently the American system is a year behind ours so they couldn't go into Sixth Year.' Frankie shook the bag to get to the chips with the vinegar on them. 'Her mum was brought up in Dublin, and she wanted somewhere safe for them. Mackenzie didn't seem want to talk about it, so I didn't push.'

Ollie smiled wryly. 'That's a funny way of putting it, "safe". Do you think something could have happened before they came here?'

Frankie shrugged. 'Maybe their mum's just anti-gun. I doubt it had anything to do with things blowing up. I think this is a whole new experience for us all.'

Jess was heading down the corridor towards the nurses' station when she spotted Ms Rowan and Mr Murray in what looked like a very deep conversation with a uniformed Guard and a man she guessed was a detective. They were clustered around one end of the nurses' desk, at the corner where two corridors met. Jess looked around quickly. She didn't want them to see her and clam up – not before she'd found out what they were discussing so intently, anyway.

Between her and where they were standing was a small waiting area, like an open-sided room filled with easy chairs. Newspapers and magazines littered pale wood coffee tables between soft blue easy chairs. Jess slipped inside and went to lean on the wall closest to them. She knew she shouldn't be eavesdropping, but they were hardly going to tell her what they were talking about, and from the serious expression on Mr Murray's face it looked like it might be interesting.

Jess peeped around the wall. There were times when having purple hair wasn't the most useful thing in the world. Right now, she just wanted to blend into the background. But the group seemed to be totally absorbed in their conversation and unaware of her presence. And they were speaking just loud enough for her to hear.

Mr Murray had his back to the nurses' desk. His arms folded, he was looking at the ground and rocking on his heels. Ms Rowan was next to him, still wearing her lab coat, grey with patches of dust, her blonde hair tied back in a practical ponytail. She had her hands in her pockets. They both seemed to be listening to the man Jess had guessed was a detective. Her dad always said they had a particular way of standing, with one hand in their trouser pocket, and in Ireland they often wore jackets if they were armed, even when it was hot, because they needed to conceal their guns.

The uniformed Guard beside him had his bomber jacket undone and his hat under his arm; he looked like he was melting.

Jess leaned out just enough so that she could hear. Their conversation was coming in snatches, lost every time someone walked past talking, but she could just about piece it together.

The detective's voice was louder than the others: 'The technical bureau should have most of their work done today but we won't be releasing the scene until tomorrow at the earliest.'

As Jess watched, Mr Murray nodded, his accent distinct as he spoke. 'That's to be expected. We want you to take your time and get to the bottom of this.' He shook his head. 'I still can't believe it.'

The Guard pushed something that looked like his notebook into the top pocket of his jacket. He didn't look much older than Ollie.

'I think you were lucky that the building didn't catch fire. I was up at the incident in Ardmore Wood and the old part of the school was completely devastated.'

Mr Murray pursed his lips. 'We interviewed a girl from there last week. Her parents are very keen for her to come to Raven's Hill. I wasn't so sure she'd fit in, in all honesty. That class have been though a lot already this year.'

The Guard looked concerned. 'That wouldn't be Tony de Búrca's girl by any chance?'

Mr Murray looked surprised. 'It was, actually. She and her father were back this morning for a follow-up meeting.'

The Guard pursed his lips before continuing. 'You know why she was expelled? She assaulted another pupil. We'd only got back to the station after being up there to sort out the assault and then the place went up in smoke.'

'The same day?' Ms Rowan chipped in, the astonishment in her voice obvious, even to Jess.

'Yep. It was bad. Five tenders from Wicklow and two from Arklow.'

'How did it start?' Ms Rowan looked from Mr Murray and back to the Guard.

He shrugged. 'Our fire inspectors are still investigating. The forensics team found faulty wiring, but it looks like the blaze could have started in a toilet block. They think the main accelerant was lighter fuel. Proving who was holding the can is the hard part.'

The detective turned to Mr Murray. 'How did your meeting with Mr de Búrca go?'

Mr Murray grimaced. 'Our principal met them on her own this morning. I was involved with the original discussion. I'd written to tell them that we didn't have a place for Hailey this year but Mr de Búrca insisted on a face-to-face meeting to discuss it. And he brought Hailey with him. I was the one who vetoed the application. She just didn't seem to have the right attitude. It's possible I might have made that a bit too clear in our initial meeting. I don't think Tony de Búrca is used to people saying no to him. He wanted a follow-up without me there.'

Jess felt her mouth drop open. This was real news. Hailey de Búrca and her dad sounded wild.

And Hailey had been in Raven's Hill this morning even though she'd been turned down for a place ...

Moving to sit down in the nearest chair, Jess pulled out her phone to tell the others, but it was too hard to explain by text. She needed to tell them face to face.

Lots of questions being asked

No sweat, all taken care of.

You sure?

Of course

Kk. Can't afford any heat.
You owe me

Chill, all under control

That explosion was a
big one, headline news

What about the photos though?

You worry too much.
Trust me. Won't be long now

    iMessage   ➤ 🎤

WHAT WE KNOW: Explosion in Chemistry Lab,
Raven's Hill School, Kilmurray Point

Six girls in St Anthony's Hospital: Frankie
in St Thomas's Ward, Sorcha in St Joan's
Ward, Ella in St Valentine's Ward, Mackenzie
in ICU, Maeve in St Raphael's Surgical
Recovery Ward, Becky in Emergency
Department side ward.

~~Gas explosion~~

Accident? How? The Guards don't think it was
an accident.

Deliberate – Target?

Sorcha closed her eyes and ran the events of the morning through her head again. She was sure there had been two bangs. Very close together but definitely two. *She was absolutely positive.* But Ms Rowan and that Guard hadn't believed her at all.

'Bang' didn't feel like a very technical term, but it described what she'd heard.

Their reaction had been going around her head all day and was making her feel very cross. She'd been the one who had been there, IN the lab. They'd come to ask her what had happened and then tried to tell her that she'd got it wrong.

She'd read all about how stress could affect people, and how your subconscious could create false memories, but this wasn't false, it was real.

Still annoyed, Sorcha leaned over and checked her texts, looking at the battery life on Ollie's phone at the same time. It had taken forever to get fully charged but it was working now. So at least that was good. And her hearing was getting better, thankfully.

The ward was busy now with visitors milling about, people arriving with books and chocolates. Sorcha wished she could pull her curtains. She felt very exposed lying here on her own, but she couldn't get out of bed without the whole room going into motion and the last nurse who had checked on her had opened them for some mysterious reason.

Her sister Beth was still in Edinburgh Airport, her flight delayed, but her parents were on their way from Helsinki via Frankfurt. They'd all miss tonight's visiting time, but they'd be there in the morning. Which would be great. At times like this Sorcha really missed Beth – they discussed everything, texting every day, but seeing her face to face was totally different.

Jess was on her way now though, thank goodness. And her aunt would be back later.

As Sorcha put the phone back on the locker, a text arrived from Frankie:

> updated doc ... see what you think.

Sorcha opened the Google doc she'd created. As her notes had grown, she'd realised she needed to move off the notepad so she could share her thoughts with the others, and so they could all edit it. She could immediately see Frankie's additions:

~~Accident? How?~~

Deliberate: if so, **who** was the target?

Sorcha did a double-take. *Frankie was right – what if one of them had been the target, rather than the school itself?*

As she was reading, Jess appeared at the end of her bed.

Sorcha reached out to give her a hug, feeling a surge of emotion. For a few seconds earlier today, she'd wondered if she was ever going to see her friends again. Jess hugged her tight and then let her go.

'What's up?'

'Frankie just updated my doc. I've shared it with you too – it's called *WHAT WE KNOW.*' Sorcha paused. 'She's wondering, if this was deliberate, who the intended target could be.'

Jess put her jacket over the back of Sorcha's visitor's chair and sat down heavily. Putting her elbows on the bed, she ran her hands over her face. Sorcha could see Jess thinking hard. Perhaps she should be making small talk before plunging Jess into Frankie's thoughts on the document, but this was important and Jess knew that Sorcha didn't like sitting around doing nothing.

'That is actually a *very* good question,' Jess said, obviously preoccupied with something. 'It could be Mr Murray.'

Sorcha looked at her quizzically. 'Mr Murray?' She gestured with her hand, encouraging Jess to elaborate. 'Theory? Let's hear it.'

'I was just down seeing Jasper, and I heard Mr Murray and Ms Rowan talking to a couple of Guards.'

Jess stopped speaking for a moment, trying to organise the information in her mind. 'You won't believe this, but Mr Murray interviewed Hailey de Búrca last week for a place at Raven's Hill – there was a post on Rave-fess this morning about her dad's car being parked outside the Science Block. Anyhow, Mr Murray didn't think she'd fit in Fifth Year, and he said he made it quite clear. Turns out Hailey was expelled from Ardmore Wood for punching someone.'

Sorcha's eyebrows shot up. 'Well, I'm glad she's not coming into Fifth Year, so.'

'That's not all; apparently the same day she got expelled, someone set fire to her school.'

'Yikes.' Sorcha paused. 'But how does that fit with our bomb?'

Jess raised her eyebrows. 'Could it have been Hailey, getting back at Raven's Hill because she didn't get a place?'

Sorcha wasn't convinced. 'That's a bit extreme. And the Ardmore Wood fire could have been an accident. It was an old building, wasn't it?'

Jess shrugged. 'It just seems a bit of a coincidence to me. If she was mad because she wasn't allowed to come to Raven's Hill, and she thought it was to do with Mr Murray – perhaps she decided to give him a fright?'

'Maybe ...' Sorcha shifted against her pillows. 'Tell me if this sounds a bit crazy, but I saw something in the newspaper earlier about a local councillor – Murphy,

I think his name was – commenting on the news and objecting to non-nationals going to Raven's Hill. He's in this party called Ireland for the Irish. Do you think they could have anything to do with the explosion?'

Jess's eyebrows met as she thought about it. 'It *does* seem a bit strange to focus on that when a load of people could have been killed. Talk about insensitive.'

'He sounded really xenophobic. It made me wonder if it could have been some sort of racist attack. His group have been involved with other stuff, and that riot in Dublin proved there are people out there who think violence is the way to protest against immigration. Mackenzie was the only international student in the lab when the explosion occurred, but that's only because half the class had gone next door.'

Jess played with her necklace for a moment, clearly considering it. 'It's one way to draw attention to your cause. People have been blowing things up to make political points for a very long time. I think we need more evidence, but put it in your document as a possibility. It's as strong as any of the other theories we don't have right now.' She scrunched up her face, thinking, the purple stone in her nose glinting as she moved. 'But do you think it *could* have been Hailey getting back at Mr Murray?'

Sorcha could see that Jess was still worried by what she'd overheard.

'A political motive feels more likely, honestly, but we have to include everything. I'll add Mr Murray to our list of possible targets, with revenge as the motive.' Sorcha pushed her dark hair behind her ear. 'Really, it *could* be something to do with Mackenzie. She and Becky were right beside where it went off.'

Jess rubbed her face again. 'I think we have to look at every possibility until we can definitely exclude it. If this *was* a bomb, there has to be a reason for it.'

Sorcha picked up her phone and added their notes to the document.

Theory #1: Mackenzie/International girls – racist attack?

Theory #2: Revenge against Mr Murray?

Sorcha put her head on one side. 'Wouldn't there be some sort of statement to the media, if it was a political group that planted it? There's no point in blowing somewhere up and *not* claiming responsibility.'

Jess nodded slowly. 'You'd think so. My dad might know if there was and if the media is keeping it quiet for some reason, or Beth might be able to find out – didn't you say she interned with the *Irish Times*? She might be able to get an off-the-record answer from someone there.'

'She's still in Edinburgh Airport, her plane's been delayed, but I'll ask.'

Jess looked at her, surprised. 'Oh, I thought she was already here. I heard one of the nurses say something about your sister asking which wards everyone was on.'

'There you go.' Ella's mum screwed the lid of her mascara back on. 'I don't know how you're going to take it off properly, but I picked up wipes on the way over. They'll do until you can get to the bathroom to wash your face. They're in your bag with fresh pyjamas and your toothbrush. I've popped some snacks in there too, just in case.'

Ella smiled, shifting against her pillows as she tried to get comfortable. Her mum had put on her foundation for her, but even the slightest movement was painful, and she was paying for it now. 'Thanks, Mum, but you know chocolate gives me spots.'

'It's not chocolate, love, obviously.' Her mum raised her eyebrows. She looked like she'd come straight from walking the dogs; she was wearing her grey cashmere sweater and had her hair pulled up in a ponytail. 'I went to that health food place in the shopping centre and got dried apricots and mango. You can give yourself a little treat – this isn't the time to worry about your diet.'

Ella smiled weakly. 'Not much chance of that; if dinner was anything to go by, the food in here is pretty grim.'

'Hopefully you'll be home tomorrow, and if not, we'll get you transferred to the private floor. At least you'll have your own room there.' Ella's mum zipped up her make-up bag and slipped it back into the soft overnight bag she'd brought with her. *The bag looked new; she must have been worry-shopping.* 'There's a new phone in here too, it's fully charged, and I've had your number transferred to it. You'll have to log into your apps, but the man in the shop installed the ones he thought you'd be most likely to use. Text me before you go to sleep, okay? I'll have my phone next to my bed, so if you need anything, just call or text.'

Ella's mum reached into the bag and pulled out a new iPhone for her.

'Can you get the lid off the box? I don't think I can manage that.' Ella sighed; even with the painkillers she'd been given her ribs were impossibly sore.

Her mum eased off the lid. 'Let's get the fingerprint thing set up and then it'll be easier to use.'

Ella's mum deftly set up the biometric access, then held it out for her. 'Check it quickly now and log in to WhatsApp and then you need to rest. Don't be up all night chatting to people.'

Ella fake-yawned. 'I won't. I'm really sleepy now.'

Ella's mum sat down again but didn't look like she was going anywhere. Ella glanced at the time on the phone screen. After logging into the Dashlane account that held all her passwords, she opened WhatsApp. She could see a pile of notifications had come in, over a hundred messages in the year group chat.

Ella's mum reached out and touched her arm. 'Did you see Ms Cooke this morning, before this happened?'

Puzzled, Ella shook her head. Why would she have needed to see Ms Cooke? What had she missed here? There was something about the frown on her mum's face …

'You really don't need this on top of everything else, but a court date's been set. They'll be wanting to talk to witnesses, I'd imagine.'

It took a moment for Ella to catch up. 'Oh my God. About Katie's party?' Anxiety gripped Ella's stomach like someone had reached in and grabbed her. Her mum rubbed the back of her hand as Ella continued, 'Will I have to be a witness?'

'It's quite likely; they may want to ask you about that fight and what happened. I'd imagine it could be part of the defence.'

Ella's mum had her professional voice on. When she wasn't worrying about Ella and her brother, or walking the dogs, she was a corporate lawyer, dealing with very big but – her words – very boring insurance cases.

'I really don't want to have to go into court.' Ella's mind went back to that night. Katie's 17th birthday party. When she'd left Katie's house, she'd thought the fight had been a disaster, but that was nothing to what they'd found out the next day...

'I won't have to go in if I'm sick, will I? I mean, broken ribs?'

'We'll have to see; it's not for ages yet. I only found out this morning after you'd left for school, so I haven't had a chance to discuss it with anyone. You left after the fight, so I can't see that you can shed any light on subsequent events.' She looked serious. 'But just in case the press come sniffing around or anyone asks, just ...'

'No comment.' They said it in unison.

'That's my girl.' Ella's mum squeezed her hand. 'Let's concentrate on getting you better. But that school has some questions to answer. We're paying for you to be kept safe, not for this sort of thing to happen. I saw your Biology teacher outside; she was talking to the Guards.'

'Mum, I don't know what it was, but it wasn't the school's fault.'

Her mum pursed her lips. 'We don't know that yet. You father's made an appointment to see the principal later in the week, so we'll see if we can get some answers.'

Ella yawned again. 'What time can you come back tomorrow?'

Her mum smiled. 'I can come in the afternoon and your father will be here tomorrow evening.'

Ella rubbed her face. 'Amber and Georgia said they'd come in tomorrow afternoon as well. Can you see if Dad can come after lunch too? By tomorrow evening I think I'm going to be exhausted.' She pouted as she said it. If she could get them to come in the afternoon, then evening visiting time would be free. 'It would be great if you did that. I'll text if breakfast's terrible and I need supplies. Gosh, I'm really sleepy now. I think it's all the drugs.'

'Do you hurt anywhere? You know how to call for the nurse?' Her mum looked at the time on her phone. 'I really should try and see the doctor.'

'I'm hurting everywhere but they're busy, Mum. Maeve and Mackenzie are much worse than me. Why don't you come back tomorrow and then the doctor will have been and they might be able to tell you when I can go home?'

Was she ever going to go? Ella checked the time again, wondering how long Tiernan would be. At least she could text him now.

But first she needed to get her head around this whole court thing. What if they asked her about the fight? When she'd been questioned after the party, they'd asked her over and over again who had hit who. She hadn't even known Tiernan's name then, but she did now. Could he get prosecuted for assault or something if she gave his name? He was going to go *mad* if she had to testify, she just knew it. She'd have to swear an oath – could she say she genuinely didn't know who was involved because she didn't at the time? Was that the truth and the whole truth, or half the truth?

Ella closed her eyes; she was going to have to tell Tiernan. But perhaps she could wait. One problem at a time, as her mum was always saying. He was so wonderful, but she was always so worried that she might say something to upset him. Some days he didn't text at all, and then others he sent her hearts and checked in on her every five minutes. She just prayed it wasn't because he was seeing someone else. She ticked herself off for even thinking it, but deep inside she could feel something wasn't quite right.

But she couldn't think about that now.

Tiernan had to be on his way in and even after this long, she *really* wasn't ready for her mum to meet him yet.

BULLET JOURNAL
Behind Every Successful Woman is Herself

This place is crazy busy during
visiting time. Which suits me. Means
I can blend in. I'm looking for my
chance.

I'm sitting waiting by the main doors
near the smoking area so I thought I'd
update my journal. I'm too hyped to sit
here doing nothing.

I know where everyone is now.

I've been to the different wards and
worked out which bed everyone is in
— it's amazing what the nurses will tell
you with a bit of chat.

Sorcha was the only one with her
curtains pulled back. And Frankie's only
just got a bed.

Apparently Ella's got more pain meds
coming pretty soon so I think she'll
sleep well. At least the nurse I spoke
to thought she would. Useful.

I had a wander around the Emergency Department, and I found out where Becky is too. Her mum was with her. I almost died when she came out to go for a smoke. Handy I had my lighter with me — she'd lost her matches. She hates vaping as much as I do. And it turns out she doesn't really know any of Becky's friends. She seemed a bit surprised that we were so close.

Apparently, Becky's in some sort of frozen state and on a drip. They want to move her to a specialist unit, so I might not have much time.

The Wi-Fi signal is pretty bad out here but it's strong enough for me to check a few things.

I'm going to have to move fast.

ST JOAN'S WARD
ST ANTHONY'S HOSPITAL
7 p.m.
16 hours 25 minutes remaining
Sorcha

WHAT WE KNOW: Explosion in Chemistry Lab,
Raven's Hill School

Six girls in St Anthony's Hospital: Frankie in
St Thomas's Ward, Sorcha in St Joan's Ward,
Ella in St Valentine's Ward, Mackenzie in ICU,
Maeve in St Raphael's Surgical Recovery
Ward, Becky in Emergency Department side
ward.

~~Gas explosion~~
~~Accident? How?~~
Deliberate: if so, **who** was the target?
Theory #1: Mackenzie/international girls –
racist attack?
Theory #2: Revenge against Mr Murray.

Wriggling against her pillows, Sorcha could feel the bars at the back of her bed pressing into her back – hospital beds really weren't designed for sitting up in. She scanned the Google doc again, as if more answers might magically appear, and looked over at Jess.

'The nurse must have misheard whoever it was who said they were my sister. I mean, who'd do that? But I'll text Beth and see if she can find anything out from her friend in the *Irish Times* newsroom – I know she's still in touch with them. Can you ask your dad if there's been any sort of claim from a far-right group that the press isn't allowed to report yet?' Sorcha sighed. 'I don't know what the significance of the two bangs is, but if they don't believe me about that, there could be other bits they don't take into account. I might be sixteen, but I'm not an idiot.'

Jess lifted her eyebrows in agreement. 'You're so right. And Frankie's right about focusing on who the target might be. If we can work that out, we might be able to figure out who did this.'

'When the Guard was here, he kept saying about the school itself being the target – I'd guess they don't think any of the students could be.' Sorcha pulled her bobbed hair off her face as she spoke. 'But if it was Mr Murray, how would this Hailey girl have got into the lab?'

Jess leaned on the edge of the bed. 'I can't see how she could have just wandered in. The lab's usually locked, unless the lab assistant's in there. Maybe there was no class in the lab this morning and she got in before break?' Jess screwed up her nose, thinking. 'It's possible Mr Murray left the lab unlocked, I suppose – he can be a bit ditsy when he's between classes. He always seems to have his head full of the latest scientific papers. We'd have to get a look at his timetable, or ask him, to know if the room was empty earlier.'

'There was a class, definitely, because there was a spillage.' *At least Ms Rowan had agreed with Sorcha's memory of that.* 'Mr Murray said something about the lab assistant cleaning it up when Becky asked about a smell. That's why Mackenzie was coughing. The lab assistant used bleach and it was really strong.'

Jess ran her silver dolphin pendant slowly along its chain. 'So that narrows the window of opportunity to plant a bomb. The Guards must be looking at the CCTV, though; it covers all the outside areas.'

'You can get to the Science Block from the main building, though, without going outside. Nobody's going to just walk in with a bomb, are they?' Sorcha chewed the end of her pen. 'If it was one of those political groups, and they were targeting the school, surely it would have had to have been planned. Someone could have joined the cleaning staff and have been walking around for weeks working out the best place to plant it. And if you're going for impact, a lab several floors up with windows on two sides is ideal – it's visible from the road and all that glass breaking …' Sorcha winced.

Jess wrinkled her nose. 'A far-right activist group feels more possible than this Hailey girl being involved, honestly. Though people *are* saying she's a bit out of control, and there was that fire at her old school.' Jess put her head on one side. 'But maybe that *was* just a coincidence? Let's see if there was anything on the news about her school catching fire. That must have been right at the start of term. Maybe there was some sort of explosion before the fire took hold?'

Sorcha shifted against her pillows again; her bum was going a bit numb sitting in one position, but she couldn't get too far from the socket, or the charging cable plugged into her phone wouldn't reach. She found the YouTube app she'd downloaded, punching in a search. The Wi-Fi wasn't amazing in the hospital but a second later there was a full page of results, topped by RTÉ News. She twisted the screen around to show Jess a clip of what looked like a Tudor manor house going up in flames. It was like something out of a movie.

'Whoa, that's major.' Jess glanced up from the screen. 'I heard them say there were loads of fire engines but that's *really* big.'

Sorcha looked at Jess. *Maybe this theory was a real possibility.* 'Can you tell Frankie about this Mr Murray idea when you get to her, see what she thinks?' Sorcha leaned back into her pillows. 'Who else was there in the room who could have been a target?'

'You?' said Jess.

Sorcha pulled a face. 'I think there are easier ways of getting someone off the swim team. What about Ella or Maeve? Or how about Becky? She was right next to where it went off.'

'But she'd swapped places with Maeve. I don't really know her well, but Becky is so shy, who could she have upset so badly they'd want to try to kill her?' Jess's mind flashed back to Jasper. Exactly the same thought had occurred to her earlier about him.

'You're right. I've chatted to her about school stuff, but I don't know much else about her. She's very private, she doesn't talk about home really. I don't think she's even on the year group chat. I've never seen her post or comment.' Sorcha screwed up her face. 'She's really not the type to be embroiled in scandal, though, is she?'

'Is there a type? Georgia says she lives in Kilmurray Point. But I think it's just her mum at home; she runs some sort of wellness business or is a counsellor or something.' Jess narrowed her eyes, trying to remember. 'I have a feeling Georgia might have gone to see her about something, then realised she was Becky's mum, and felt it was a bit too close. She said she was a bit odd, too, I think.'

Sorcha pulled the pillow up behind her where it had slipped. 'Could her mum have a disturbed client? Maybe she's got a stalker or something?'

Jess looked quizzically at Sorcha, and raised an eyebrow. 'Now you're getting carried away. I'd hope not. Becky seems so vulnerable, but perhaps that's just because she's a bit younger than everyone else.'

'I just wish I could remember more clearly what happened before everything blew up. I'm sure I would have noticed if someone had left a suspicious package behind, the lab is so tidy. There was some stuff on the counter under the window, but it was just a box or something.'

'No wires coming out of it?'

Sorcha gave Jess a withering look. 'I definitely heard two bangs, though. They were really close together, but I'm sure of it. And there was this fizzing noise and I'm sure there was a flash when the first one went off.'

'It could have been one of the other girls who went into the Physics lab who was the target. We're going to have to look at the whole Chemistry class, aren't we, not just the five of you who were in there at the time?'

Sorcha pursed her lips for a moment. 'True. But you know, the Chemistry room has loads of windows. If it was some sort of radio-controlled device and someone was watching from outside, they'd have seen half the class leave. So maybe it *is* just us five we need to think about.'

Sorcha thought back to the photo in the paper that had been taken from across the road. She'd assumed it was from a journalist, but what if it had been sent in by someone who had been watching the school? From that height you must be able to see into the lab easily with binoculars.

Jess sighed. 'That feels like a lot of maybes, but I wish someone had been watching when Jasper got attacked. Whoever it was gave him a real kicking.'

'I'm sorry, I didn't even ask how he was.' Sorcha winced, embarrassed.

'You're fine, you've got other things to worry about. God, it's mad, isn't it? It's only Monday and first Jasper and then those photos and now this.'

'Those photos are awful. That would have been the big story if this hadn't happened.' Sorcha cleared her throat. 'I didn't see anything recent on Rave-fess. Is there any news?'

Jess shook her head. 'It's stopped updating. But listen, I was talking to Tara before we left school, God, I totally forgot with everything else and this Mr Murray stuff.' Jess took a breath. 'Tara said the last text she got from Maeve was right before Chemistry started, and it was about those photos.'

Sorcha's eyebrows shot up. 'What did it say?'

'Maeve thought she knew who it might be. It's something to do with an Instagram account. She wanted to talk to Tara because she didn't know what to do.'

Sorcha looked sceptical. 'If she thinks it's someone who has an Insta account, that's the whole school.'

Jess leaned forwards in the chair, keeping her voice down. 'But I think she must have recognised the account; I mean the person whose pictures they are.'

'And then she got blown up.' Sorcha's eyes met Jess's. 'She couldn't have been the target, could she? If she knew who was in the pictures, maybe she knew who shared them? Maybe she'd already messaged them and said she was going to go to the Guards.' Sorcha's eyes opened wider as the full possibility hit her.

Jess rubbed her face, considering it. 'But how could someone have had time to set a bomb?'

'I don't know, I really don't. But you know something, Maeve's usually on that back bench, the one near the window. Becky went down there so she could finish her homework without Mr Murray noticing. So maybe you're right, maybe *Maeve* was the target.'

Theory #3: Maeve knows who is in the photos.

WHAT WE KNOW: Explosion in Chemistry Lab,
Raven's Hill School, Kilmurray Point

Six girls in St Anthony's Hospital: Frankie
in St Thomas's Ward, Sorcha in St Joan's
Ward, Ella in St Valentine's Ward, Mackenzie
in ICU, Maeve in St Raphael's Surgical
Recovery Ward, Becky in Emergency
Department side ward

~~Gas explosion~~

~~Accident? How?~~

Deliberate: if so, **who** was the target?

Theory #1: Mackenzie/international girls –
racist attack?

Theory #2: Revenge against Mr Murray.

Theory #3: Maeve knows who is in the photos.

Maeve knew who was in the photos? Frankie pushed her dark hair out of her face as she scanned Sorcha's update, feeling her stomach flip. This was getting bigger with every idea they had.

Frankie hoped Jess would get here fast so she could explain Sorcha's thinking to her. Now that she was in a proper bed on a proper ward, at least she could have visitors. She couldn't wait to see Danny, but she really needed Jess to fill her in.

Before Frankie could think about the rest of Sorcha's theories, Katie appeared through the ward doors in a burst of colour. She'd tied her blonde hair up in a pony-tail and was wearing silver hi-tops with jeans and a bubblegum-pink cropped sweater that made Frankie immediately think of the ColourMeHappy Instagram account. As if to complete the look, she was carrying a bouquet of lilac, pale pink and cream silk flowers wrapped in pink tissue paper.

'Oh my God, Franks, I can't believe you're in here. I'm so sorry I didn't see your texts, I'm such a terrible friend.' Plonking herself down on the edge of Frankie's bed, Katie put the flowers down beside her and leaned in for a hug.

Pulling back to look at Frankie, Katie continued, 'I turned my phone off after breakfast and went and hid in my room. I only heard this evening. What on earth happened?' She sighed loudly. 'I can't believe today – it's one thing after another. First the trial news and then this.' She picked up the flowers and handed them to Frankie. 'You're not allowed flowers in hospitals any more, apparently, so I got you some silk ones to match your room.'

Frankie grinned. 'They're gorgeous. Thank you, that's so thoughtful. They're much better than flowers that will die.' She paused. 'I know what you mean about today – Ms Cooke grabbed me on the way in this morning and pulled me into her office to tell me. I was already so late, and then this ...'

It felt like a cascade of events, dominoes in a row knocking into each other. If Ms Cooke hadn't held her up at breaktime, she might have been able to give Becky the iPad earlier and she'd never have been outside the Chemistry lab when it blew up.

Cookie's face had been so serious when she'd asked her to sit down in the leather chair opposite her desk. For a minute Frankie's life had rushed before her eyes as she'd tried to work out what on earth she'd done wrong. And then she'd said that the court date had been set.

Frankie must have gone pale because Cookie had made her have a glass of water. Frankie closed her eyes at the memory. It had been her first shock of the day.

She dreaded the thought of having to go back over everything again – the fight and calling her brothers and then … Frankie pushed the images away. It had been like a horror film.

Frankie wished Danny would hurry up and come in. She needed a Danny-hug – she really wasn't able for everything today. He'd been working at the Berwick Castle Hotel for ages before they even started dating, and she felt like she'd known him forever. He was like an oasis of calm, somehow managing to make everything feel all right.

Frankie took hold of Katie's hand, giving it a squeeze. 'At least the press will be more interested in this bomb thing than your party, for a bit at least. That's something.'

Katie's face betrayed her feelings. 'Have they said it was definitely a bomb?'

As she spoke, a commotion at the other end of the ward drew their attention. A nurse in pale blue scrubs was trying to stop someone coming in, and as she moved out of the way, Frankie could see why. It was Danny, juggling a pile of pizza boxes, three big bottles of Coke jammed under his arms and a huge white teddy sitting on top of the boxes. He could barely see over the teddy's ears but a moment later he was heading towards them, having obviously managed to charm his way past the nurse.

Frankie felt herself tearing up. Even from this distance she could see the bear was huge and super soft and had the cutest face.

'God, this place is like a prison. You'd think I was smuggling in a file.'

Katie grinned. 'Why did she stop you?'

'She's worried about the pizza. Mainly the smell. She does have a point, but I think she's more concerned that there'll be a stampede when the patients see some decent food in the hospital.' Danny slid the pizza boxes onto the bed and let the Coke bottles fall on top of them. Katie reached out to catch them and block them from rolling off the bed. He presented the bear to Frankie. 'How are you feeling, babes?' The last word came with a teasing smirk.

Frankie took the bear from him, gave it a hug and then play-pushed him. 'Do not call me babes, Danny Holmes, you know how much I hate it. I'm not a pig.' He only did it to tease her because she'd been in floods of tears when they'd watched *Babe* on TV with Max and then they'd heard a boy saying it in Starbucks and she hadn't been able to stop laughing. 'Better now you're here, though.' Frankie smiled, feeling the glow that always came with Danny. He leaned over to kiss her.

'So, do we know what happened? What have you heard?' Then he added quickly, 'And how is everyone?'

Frankie sighed. 'Nobody's telling us anything, but it must have been something big. Sorcha was inside the Chemistry lab, she helped Maeve, she's been in surgery all afternoon.' Katie's brows furrowed as Frankie continued, 'I mean Maeve, not Sorcha.' Frankie could feel herself getting muddled. As soon as she'd been settled on the ward, her mum and Ollie had left, telling her to sleep. Being in the corridor all day had been draining.

That and getting knocked out by a ceiling falling on top of her.

She hadn't let herself dwell on it, but for a split second Frankie had thought she might be about to die. She pushed the thought away as Danny gave her another kiss. It only took her a few moments to update him on everyone else's whereabouts.

'I need to get a pizza over to Sorcha and catch up with her so I can come back and chat. You two tuck in and save me some.'

As he spoke, Jess arrived in behind him. She grinned at the pizza boxes as she got to Frankie's bed. 'They say not all superheroes wear capes. Sorcha will be very pleased to see you, Danny.'

'How is she?' Frankie said, as Jess reached over to give her a hug. 'She's in case-solving mode and every time I ask her how she's feeling she asks another question.' Before Jess could answer, Frankie caught Danny's expression, eager curiosity replacing concern. He was a born newshound. 'Have you been texting her, Danny? She's supposed to be resting.'

'How can you look at me so suspiciously?' He pretended to look affronted. 'I've been worrying about you. I haven't even got her number – yet.'

Frankie gave him a side eye. 'Have you got enough pizza for Ella?'

'I certainly have. I didn't get any for Beth, though, but I guess she can go to the restaurant.'

Frankie patted the bed beside her, indicating Jess should sit down. 'Sorcha's sister, Beth? She's not here yet. Her plane got delayed.'

Danny looked confused. 'Oh, I thought she was. I met Becky's mum outside the front door having a cigarette when I came in, and she commented on all the pizza.'

Frankie wrinkled up her nose and looked at him. 'How does that connect to Beth?'

'She made a joke about the boxes, and I said it was for you lot, and then she said her daughter was still in the ED. She said something about you guys all being very caring and how even Sorcha's sister had come down to check on Becky.' He frowned. 'Sorcha's only got one sister, hasn't she?'

Frankie nodded. 'Yeah, and she's still in Edinburgh Airport, unless she's changed airlines.'

Settling herself, Jess cut in, 'She is, we were just talking about her.'

Danny shrugged. 'Maybe Becky's mum got mixed up. She looked pretty stressed. And a lot of you girls do look the same.' He pulled a face and ducked as if he was expecting one of them to swipe him.

'We do not, Danny Holmes, stop messing. Ella, Georgia and Amber just have the same colour hair …' Frankie looked at the time on her phone. 'Visiting time only lasts till 8.30 – can you drop these off and come back quickly?' She looked at him sternly. 'And don't quiz Ella on what happened yet. Wait a bit.'

'Me?' His face was a pantomime of innocence, but seeing her serious expression, he relaxed. 'I won't, I promise. Am I allowed to see if she's up for a chat tomorrow, though?'

Frankie threw him a warning look. Grinning, he raised both hands to calm her. 'Got the message. Maybe you can see when she's ready for a star interview?' He ran his hand through the blond curls on the top of his head. 'Let me get these pizzas delivered before they get cold.'

'Sorcha's on St Joan's Ward, and–'

'And Ella's on St Valentine's, can't forget that.' Danny grinned. 'Gimme five. Clark Kent never moved so fast.'

This is taking too long

Chill, it'll all be fine

You keep saying that???

This needs to be done properly.
Trust me. It'll all be sorted soon

But what if the guards get involved?

TRUST ME

📷 Ⓐ   iMessage   ➤ 🎤

Ella tried to settle the blankets around herself. Her other hand was wrapped around her chest, cradling her ribs. When she'd first come around, she'd never felt pain like it. It didn't hurt so much now but she wasn't very comfortable either. Trying to look amazing when you were in a hospital bed, exhausted and sore all over, was a whole new challenge.

The nurse had pulled the curtains around her bed to give her some privacy during visiting time. She'd looked horrific before her mum had come and hadn't wanted to see anyone, and she definitely didn't want people looking at her. At least her mum had brought in her make-up and helped her put it on. It wasn't anywhere near her full face, but she looked less like a ghost.

Ella heard the curtain rattle and turned, smiling, expecting to see Tiernan. But it wasn't Tiernan, it was

Frankie's boyfriend, Danny, holding a pizza box, a huge grin on his face.

'Hiya, emergency delivery. Franks said the food was disgusting so I brought supplies.'

Ella was about to laugh but stopped herself, wincing at the pain. 'Oh Jaysus, that hurts.'

He slipped the box onto the bed beside her. 'Don't move. Here, I've got napkins.' Rooting in the leg pocket of his combats, Danny pulled out a wad of serviettes. 'Are you okay to eat? What was the damage?'

'Okay to eat, just don't make me laugh. I've got two broken ribs. I was lucky, though, I think. I got blown onto the edge of the lab bench. I mean, Maeve ... did you hear?'

Danny stuck his hands in his pockets. 'I did.' He paused. 'And about the trial, did you know they set the date?' He grimaced. 'It's a while yet, though, and we'll get lots of warning from the Guards, I think.'

As he spoke, Tiernan appeared behind him. 'What's this about the Guards?' Ella's heart sank; she wasn't ready to tell him yet. How much had he heard? Before she could respond, Tiernan continued, 'Who's this?' Tiernan looked from Ella to Danny, his face expectant.

'I'm Danny, Frankie O'Sullivan's boyfriend. I'm doing a pizza run.' Nodding towards the box, Danny stopped speaking, as if he was waiting for Tiernan to introduce himself. He didn't, and the silence suddenly became awkward. Tiernan seemed to be waiting for him to say more. Ella glanced between them, suddenly anxious at the shift in atmosphere. She wasn't up to this right now.

Tiernan looked at the pizza box. 'I'm not sure she wants pizza, do you, Els? So many calories.' Tiernan managed to sound amused and confused at the same time, like it was the last thing Ella could possibly want.

Danny's eyebrows shot up. 'Why don't I just leave it here in case she changes her mind?' He grinned at Ella as if there was nothing wrong. 'I'll tell Frankie you said hello. Enjoy.'

Turning, he waited for Tiernan to move so he could slip out between the curtains of the cubicle.

As Danny vanished, Tiernan grinned at Ella. 'How are you feeling, sweet pea? What was he saying?'

Ella reached out for his hand. 'Just about the explosion; he says the Guards still don't know anything. Come and sit, thank you for coming over.'

'Course, babes, what did you expect? God, it's hot in here.' Tiernan unzipped his fleece, and slipped it off, laying it across her knees. Moving the pizza box to the end, he sat down beside her on the bed, leaning over to kiss her. 'I was so worried when I heard. Some of the guys from Raven's Park were over doing the scenery for *Macbeth*, they'd just left when it happened, said you could hear the explosion down the street.'

Ella sighed. 'There was a big bang, alright. I don't remember much. I thought you were coming over this morning with them?'

He smiled and chucked her under the chin. 'Did you want me to? I had some stuff to sort out. Do you know Mackenzie Smyth? She's in your school, isn't she?'

Why on earth was he asking about Mackenzie? 'Yes, she's pretty sick, though, she's up in the ICU. She's lovely; her brother's in your school.'

He rolled his phone through his fingertips, concentrating on it as he did so. 'Yeah, cool guy. Do you want a Coke, babes? I saw a machine on the landing.'

Ella was about to shake her head, but he'd already turned around, patting the back pocket of his jeans to check he had his wallet.

She just wanted him to stay and talk to her. She needed to talk about what had happened. But he obviously had something on his mind.

'That would be lovely, thanks.'

'Back in a sec.' He kissed her again and vanished out through the curtains, his wallet in one hand, his iPhone in the other.

Ella closed her eyes. She felt like the energy had drained out of her. Why hadn't he texted her to say he wasn't coming into school this morning? She'd been so excited about seeing him at lunchtime, had been thinking that they could sneak off to Starbucks. There were times when he wanted to know her every move, and times when it was like he forgot she was there. She had been amazed when they'd started chatting that he was single, guys like him were just never single, but as time went on, she was starting to get really worried that he had something else going on. With someone else.

And she could hardly ask him, could she, because what if it was true? And if it wasn't, he'd go nuts.

He got really mad when she asked him something simple like what he was doing at the weekend, if he wasn't meeting her. She was just trying to make conversation and get to know him, but he said that she was prying, or being too possessive. He needed his space, he said; she needed to trust him.

A buzzing interrupted her thoughts. Ella opened her eyes, confused. Something on the bed was vibrating. It felt like it was Tiernan's fleece. But he'd taken his phone with him. She moved and his jacket started to slip. Reaching out, she felt a stabbing pain in her chest, but she caught the jacket and pulled it towards her. Something was still buzzing inside the zipped pocket.

It definitely felt like a phone.

Did he have another one?

Why would he have two phones?

ST THOMAS'S WARD
ST ANTHONY'S HOSPITAL
7.14 p.m.
16 hours 11 minutes remaining
Frankie

WHAT WE KNOW: Explosion in Chemistry Lab, Raven's Hill School.

TWO BANGS

Six girls in St Anthony's Hospital: Frankie in St Thomas's Ward, Sorcha in St Joan's Ward, Ella in St Valentine's Ward, Mackenzie in ICU, Maeve in St Raphael's Surgical Recovery Ward, Becky in Emergency Department side ward

~~Gas explosion~~

~~Accident? How?~~

Deliberate: if so, **who** was the target?

Theory #1: Mackenzie/international girls – racist attack?

Theory #2: Revenge against Mr Murray.

Theory #3: Maeve knows who is in the photos.

'Revenge against Mr Murray? And Maeve knew who the photos were of? Wow, how on earth did she guess?' Frankie looked up at Jess, who had got comfortable beside her on the bed. 'And what's the new note on two bangs about?'

Jess's face was serious as she answered. 'Sorcha's absolutely sure she heard a sort of fizzing, cracking sound and then two bangs really close together, but Ms Rowan and the Guards don't believe her.'

Frankie gave Jess a side eye. They both knew Sorcha didn't make things up, and *really* didn't like it when people didn't take her seriously.

'Look what the nurse gave me. This should be big enough, shouldn't it?' Katie's voice cut through Frankie's thoughts as she put a plastic vase down on the bedside locker. 'The best bit is these flowers don't need any water and they won't wilt in this heat.'

Katie peeled off the paper wrapped around the silk lilies and roses, arranging them as she glanced over at Frankie.

'What are you two looking so serious about?'

Frankie handed Katie her phone. The Google doc was open with Sorcha's notes at the top. Looking at it hard, Katie pushed a stray blonde curl behind her ear and sat down heavily on the end of the bed.

'Maeve knew?'

Jess nodded. 'Her cousin Conan sent her the photos. The thing is, Tara told me that when Maeve realised who they were of she texted him as well – about the photos being illegal.'

Katie looked at her, puzzled. 'I'm not seeing how knowing who was in the photos or who shared them, even if she *did* mention telling the Guards, could be related to the explosion or who set it?'

Jess ran her hand through her hair, the purple tones bright under the overhead lights. 'That's the thing, Maeve told Conan that she'd realised who was in the photos. Conan's in the Raven's Park group who shared the pictures. He could have easily messaged the group to warn whoever originally shared them.'

Katie wrinkled up her nose. 'But assuming this Raven's Park group all knew, and they wanted to stop Maeve from saying anything – why the science lab? Wouldn't it be easier to catch her on the way home from school and give her a fright? Look at what happened to that friend of yours, Jess – Jasper, is it? I saw it on Ravefess.' She passed the phone back to Frankie.

Frankie sighed, pulling at her woollen blanket. 'And who could have set the bomb? Like, how did they even get into the lab in the first place?'

As she spoke, a lady wearing blue overalls walked in, laughing. Behind her came Danny, pushing her tea trolley for her. Delivering it into the middle of the ward, he bowed, as if presenting it to her. She slapped him on the shoulder playfully. Smiling, he came over to Frankie's bed.

'Wow, you've got a full house. Sorcha wants to know what you think of the doc she's working on. And who's that dude visiting Ella? He's a bit in your face, isn't he?'

Jess rolled her eyes. 'I bet *that's* the mysterious Tiernan.'

Are you there?

Any update?

You said it would all be fine, you better be right

????

Will you answer???

We need to make sure the photos and video are secured

Did you say 24 hrs?
Only 16 left!!

iMessage

S orcha pushed back the blankets and swung her legs out of bed, reaching for the new dressing gown that Frankie's mum had brought her. It was a lovely soft fleece and wrapped around her like a hug. Which was exactly what she needed right now.

Jess had just been to see her, and Ollie. Frankie's mum had been amazing, and her sister Beth was on her way, but right now Sorcha wanted to go home.

Really wanted to go home.

She was fed up with being in here, on a ward with none of her friends, where she was the youngest by about fifty years, and she *hated* not knowing what had happened this morning.

Frankie always said she was a control freak, but when you had to train to the level she did and study, and you had goals, a bit of control was vital to make things happen. Which meant that something this out of control was just a little bit terrifying. Sorcha knew her *WHAT WE KNOW* doc was as much about trying to find order in the chaos as it was about finding solutions. Frankie was always trying to fix things – in a good way, but it drew her into all sorts of situations anyone else would just walk away from.

Sorcha pushed her hair behind her ear and did up the tie on the dressing gown. She was starting to feel cross; no, more than cross – angry – absolutely livid, in fact, that this could have happened.

She stood up and looked for her slippers, steadying herself against the bed as the room began to swing, each theory in her document appearing in her head like a soldier ready for inspection.

Theory #1: Mackenzie/international girls – racist attack?

Theory #2: Revenge against Mr Murray.

Theory #3: Maeve knows who is in the photos.

Theory #1 was nagging at her. Could their school have been targeted by someone making a huge political statement about foreign nationals in Ireland? The councillor who had spoken out in the press was definitely vociferous in his views, and had led the debate at some really toxic rallies.

At this stage anything was possible.

Sorcha walked carefully to the end of the bed and held on to the metal frame for a minute as the room spin began to slow down. The ward was full, the curtains drawn around most of the beds, the noise of visitors and patients talking a gentle hubbub over the swoosh of the doors and the general clattering of the ward.

Sorcha closed her eyes, letting the room steady. Whatever had happened, she needed the loo, and she couldn't wait any longer.

Getting to the loo had been a lot easier than getting back was proving to be. Sorcha was moving very slowly, limping on her bad ankle, but as she'd pulled the door open to go out into the corridor, everything had started spinning again. Perhaps that had as much to do with the fright she'd got when she'd looked in the mirror over the sink as anything else. Her normally sleek dark bob was mussed up and she was as white as a sheet, which she'd always thought was a ridiculous expression, but right now, it was pretty accurate, her dark eyes like coals in a very, very pale face.

She really needed to get back into bed.

As she slipped out of the toilet, using the wall to support her, an orderly with a patient in a wheelchair whizzed past her and Sorcha had to stop for a minute to recentre. This was ridiculous – how long would this last? She was super fit and rarely even got a cold; this was as maddening as it was scary.

Now she just had to navigate the drinks machine and then she'd be almost at the door to St Joan's Ward. She probably should have called a nurse to help her, but that just seemed ridiculous. There were actual sick people who really needed help; she was just feeling a bit dizzy, although now she was pretty exhausted as well.

Pausing for a moment to let her head catch up with the rest of her, Sorcha leaned on the side of the drinks machine. It seemed to be at a junction – she could see a sign for the stairs hanging in the middle of the corridor, pointing to a door that must be on the other side of the machine. *How ridiculous was it having a fizzy drinks dispenser in a hospital?* There was a tax on sugar precisely because it was bad for your health.

Sorcha was about to move again when she heard the clatter of what sounded like the door to the stairs and a voice that stopped her in her tracks.

'I thought I'd find you here. Visiting your "friend", are you?' The voice was filled with intensity and malice.

Curious, Sorcha peeked around the machine and then pulled quickly back. She could only see the back of the head of the speaker, in side profile, but he was tall and wearing a Raven's Park rugby shirt, the white collar turned up. Who was he talking to like that?

'You better not do anything with those photos, or you'll regret it. It won't just be two of us next time. Tomorrow morning your time's up.'

Sorcha didn't hear a reply, just a door again, slamming closed.

What the actual … ?

lla glanced back towards the curtain as the phone in Tiernan's jacket buzzed again. Someone wanted to talk to him badly. Could he really be seeing someone else? Was that what this was about? Ella felt her mouth go dry.

It would explain the two phones.

When they'd started seeing each other he'd been so gorgeous. He'd texted constantly, sending her love hearts and wanting to know her every move. He'd met her at the school gates and walked her home, and met her in town when she was going shopping, helping her choose outfits. It was like he was totally, wonderfully obsessed with her. He'd even texted her in the middle of the night to say he was thinking about her.

She'd thought it was a bit weird that he wouldn't let her put up pictures of him on her public Instagram or even mention his name; she had to keep all that for her private account. And he'd never put up pictures of her. He said they were exclusive but didn't need to be public as well.

Then he'd wanted to know her phone password so he could look at her messages – she'd adored the attention, had thought he was totally in love with her, but now she thought about it, he didn't give her any space – and he rarely told her what he was doing. If he was late to meet her, she was just expected to accept it.

Like tonight – why had he come in so late? And why hadn't he texted her today? She'd scrolled through all the notifications on her phone but there had been nothing from him. The explosion had to have been on the national news, everyone would have been talking about it – *what had him so busy that he couldn't text to see if she was okay?*

And seriously, two phones? Only drug dealers had two phones, everyone knew that.

Her eyes on the curtain, Ella reached into the pocket of the jacket, pulling it out. It was another iPhone, top of the range like his usual one. It even had the same guerrilla case that he was always talking about, but this one was khaki and the other one was black.

Moving her knees up under the blankets to block the view of anyone coming into her cubicle, Ella pulled the jacket over so if he suddenly appeared, it would look like the phone had fallen out.

It hurt to move, but Ella needed to find out what this was about. The screen was flashing with notifications.

The last two made her freeze.

> We need to make sure the
> photos and video are secured

> Did you say 24 hrs? Only 16 left!!

What photos?

The only photos anyone was talking about were the nude photos.

But what did Tiernan know about them?

Ella glanced anxiously at the curtain. He was taking ages. She didn't remember seeing a drinks machine on her way in, but then she hadn't been fully concentrating. Maybe he'd met someone and was talking?

Could she unlock the phone and look at the messages? *Did she have time?* Ella knew his password from his other iPhone; she'd seen him open it often enough. Would it be the same?

She had to look. She needed to find out what the hell was going on.

Her thumbs flew over the keyboard.

He'd used the same password. *Idiot.* She was in.

Her eyes flicking to the curtain, Ella grabbed her own phone and sent him a message:

I'd love some chocolate if you
can find any xoxoxxxxxoooxxxx

Would that buy her a bit more time?

She opened WhatsApp, looking for the account that the message about the photo had come in from.

Tiernan had named the caller Barbarian in his contacts. *Was that something to do with rugby?* There was a team called the Barbarians, wasn't there? *But who could it be?* There were lots of messages, going back ages. They obviously knew each other well.

She closed the thread and scrolled down the other messages looking at the usernames, checking to see which had hearts or thumbs-up emojis. All Hail the Queen had sent him a photo of her lips – at least Ella assumed they were her own lips. Her tongue was just visible, poking suggestively between them, and she was wearing heavy red lipstick, a diamond stud – like a beauty spot – caught in the photo. *Who on earth was she?*

Ella scrolled back through their messages, shock setting in as she saw rows of love hearts. She didn't have time to read them all, but she didn't need to. They were just like the messages Tiernan had sent to her.

Holding her breath, conscious that Tiernan could be back at any moment, Ella scrolled on. There were a couple of groups too. One for the rugby team, and one called AllFansHere.

What the?

She opened it and scrolled down, immediately wishing she hadn't.

Photos.

The nude photos everyone had been talking about, the Raven's Hill sweater bright in the corner of one of them.

Her mouth dry, her heart beating so loud in her ears she couldn't hear the noise of the ward around her, Ella closed the thread quickly. She shut her eyes, trying to slow her racing thoughts down and calm the wave of panic that was making her feel even sicker.

How long did she have? If he came back now, what would she do?

Quickly, she opened the group messages and photographed them with her own phone. Closing the group, Ella scrolled down further, spotting another message.

> How could you share those photos? HOW? You said you loved me. You said I could trust you.

It had been sent this morning. From someone called Rainbow Princess.

Ella held her breath as she opened up the thread.

They'd been sent to Tiernan.

The photos had been sent to Tiernan.

Whoever Rainbow Princess was, she'd been sending Tiernan nude photos. That he'd messaged her to ask for.

And then he'd shared them with his friends.

Ella felt sick. Really sick.

As Mackenzie began to surface, she realised that she could finally breathe more easily. There was an oxygen mask clamped to her face and she could hear the beeps and whirrs of the machinery beside her, feel the pull of a drip in her arm. The first time she'd had an asthma attack she'd been absolutely terrified when she'd woken up, clinging to her mom's hand, trying to fight off the mask, sure she was dying.

It didn't get any easier when it happened, but at least this time, she knew she was in the right place.

Mackenzie shifted slightly in the bed. She was sore all over and her back hurt. Memories began to appear in her head, fragmented like pieces of a jigsaw puzzle. She'd been in school. But she'd heard Greg's voice. That couldn't have been in school.

She'd been talking to Becky, probably for the first time ever, properly, she was so shy. But she'd skipped a year or something and was only 15, so Mackenzie could see why. She'd never lived anywhere but Kilmurray, and she was an only child, her mom was English, and she worked a lot. Parts of the conversation began to lock together.

What had Greg said? He'd been asking her what to do. What about? Somewhere deep inside, a memory she couldn't quite grasp nagged at her. He'd sounded desperate, like the world was about to end. Worry unfurled inside her like like the petals of a rose. What had he been so worried about? Had he done something?

Mackenzie heard a door suck open and someone humming as they came closer to her. Then a clatter as her chart was picked up, the tapping of a pen on the page. The door sucked open again.

'How's she doing?'

'Good, a lot better than I expected.'

'Her brother's been here all day – he thinks we haven't seen him lurking in the stairwell.'

The humming nurse laughed sympathetically. 'Poor lad, he must be worried sick. She gave us all a turn. How's her friend?'

There was a pause, Mackenzie wasn't ready to open her eyes yet, but she could almost hear the shake of the other nurse's head. 'Bad. The mother keeps saying she's very shy but not anxious, she can't understand it.'

'Must be something. The explosion must have been terrifying but for her to close in on herself like that, to totally shut down ... I don't know. I saw it once when I was training in London. Poor girl, social media puts them under so much pressure these days, who knows what's actually going on in their heads?'

'It's often the quiet ones. They focus on coping but it's an act: they're like swans gliding past but it's all under the surface, frantic paddling to keep themselves afloat.'

The nurse beside Mackenzie sighed. 'They're talking about moving her to the mental health unit, but the mother won't have it. She's supposed to be a psychotherapist – makes you wonder how her daughter got into this state.'

Who were they talking about?

And what had happened?

Mackenzie remembered coughing in the lab, the smell of bleach irritating her throat and lungs. She'd been drawing, doodling in her notebook, thinking about ... thinking about Jess's friend, the one who'd got beaten up. And her chest had started to tighten ... She'd been concentrating on breathing, had been about to reach for her inhaler, and then ... had Becky pushed her? It was all so muddled, but she was sure Becky had pushed her off her stool.

Mackenzie rolled it back through her head. She'd been concentrating on her doodling, and then there had been a flash or something and Becky pushed her sideways. *What on earth had that been about?*

Jess punched the lift button again, but it was taking ages. *Perhaps she should have gone back to the lift and stairs near Sorcha's ward – the lift there might be quicker.*

There was under an hour left of visiting time and she wanted to go up and see how Mackenzie and Maeve were doing, and to see Ella, and get back to Frankie if she could. She wasn't sure they'd let her into the ICU, but Frankie had given her three white silk roses from the flowers Katie had brought in, to give to Maeve, Mackenzie and Ella. It was a lovely idea. Frankie was always trying to make everyone and everything better – it was one of the things they all loved about her.

Jess looked at the lift indicator. It was still on the seventh floor. When she'd left Sorcha, she'd popped to the loo, which had seemed like it was miles away – Jess reckoned she must have missed the one nearest Sorcha's ward. There was no way they could expect patients to walk so far to find one. The hospital was huge, and now she was at totally the other end from where she wanted to be. When she finally got up to Ella's floor, she'd probably have to walk the full length of the building back again to find her.

Beside Jess, the door to the stairs opened and a nurse appeared. He'd obviously given up on the lift.

Jess glanced at the time on her phone. The longer she stood here, the less time she had to see the others. She had no idea if Maeve was awake, but Danny had said Ella was, and Katie was going to check on Becky, taking the iPad with her. If she wasn't awake, Katie was under instructions to bring it back to Frankie.

Jess glanced at the lift again. It still hadn't moved. Out of the corner of her eye she saw movement beyond the glass doors as someone else crossed the landing to the stairs. *Obviously nobody was waiting for this lift tonight.*

Making her decision, Jess pulled open the door to the stairs and, following whoever had gone up ahead of her, sprinted up. This part of the hospital was new and modern, the corridors and stairwells bright white and well lit. Jess swung around the landing and up the next flight, very glad that she'd gone home and changed into her jeans and hi-tops after school. The stairs were definitely the best option; it was mad waiting for the lift when Ella was only two floors away. Danny had said her ward was right at the end of the corridor. Jess just hoped she could find it.

Speed-walking, her trainers squeaking again on the polished floor, eventually Jess spotted a sign for Ella's ward. Pushing open the dark grey doors, Jess could see everyone had visitors, but the curtains were drawn around one of the beds. For a minute Jess hesitated. Beds with curtains drawn around them made her feel queasy. Her mum had always had her curtains drawn; she'd hated how the ravages of cancer had changed her.

But Danny had said Ella was second from the end on the right, so that bed had to be hers.

Pushing through the curtains surrounding Ella's bed, Jess had expected Ella to be miserable, but she hadn't expected her to be in floods of tears, the pizza box Danny had brought abandoned on the end of the bed.

'My God, what's happened?' Jess went straight to her, sitting on the side of her bed and putting her arms around her, careful not to jar her.

Ella drew in a sniffly breath and buried her head in Jess's neck.

'What's wrong? Are you hurting? Will I get the nurse?'

Ella pulled back and wiped her face with her hand, mascara running down her cheeks. She sniffed again, seemingly unable to speak. She took a sobby breath, wincing in pain.

'I need to get you a nurse–'

'It's not that.' Ella winced again. 'It hurts when I breathe, but it's not that. I don't know what to do.' The words came out in bursts, Jess could barely understand her. 'I …' She drew in another breath as Jess leaned in instinctively to hug her again but held back, afraid she might hurt Ella even more. *Perhaps some sort of delayed shock from the explosion was hitting her.*

'You're fine, you're safe here and you'll probably be able to go home in a day or so. Frankie wanted me to bring you a rose – will I put it over here?' Jess pulled one of the silk roses from the tissue paper that Frankie had wrapped the stems in and popped it on Ella's bedside table. Her phone was lying face up on a pile of magazines. Jess started to reach for it. 'Sorcha's got a new phone, and she wants to give you her number. Will I put it in?'

For a moment a look of panic flitted across Ella's face. Jess froze, trying to work out what she'd done wrong. She put the phone back down on the top of the locker.

Ella sniffed again, her eyes filling up. 'I have to tell you; I have to tell someone.' Ella glanced anxiously over Jess's shoulder. 'Those photos –'

Jess interrupted her, her voice low. 'We think Maeve knows who they are of. She texted Tara before the explosion.'

Ellas's face froze. 'Seriously? Who?'

Jess rubbed her face with her hand. 'That's the bit we're missing. Maeve's still out of it as far as I know, but hopefully she'll be able to remember who she thinks it is when she comes around.' Ella stared at her wide-eyed as Jess continued. 'Sorcha's made a list of everything we know about the explosion. She's trying to work out what might have happened, if someone was maybe a target.'

Ella's eyes filled with fear. 'Like who? Who could be a target?' It came out as a whisper.

BULLET JOURNAL
Behind Every Successful Woman is Herself

Damn, damn, the one with the purple hair almost saw me. I think her name's Jess. I saw her in reception earlier and then she almost ran into me on the landing. She came through the door to the stairs, just as I was starting up the next flight. I had to fly to get ahead of her. She must have given up on the lift too. There are three lots of lifts and stairs in this place and I was deliberately using the one furthest away from the wards where the Raven's Hill lot are.

I'll have to wait here now, until I'm sure she's gone. This waiting area is beside the nurses' station, but there's no one here at the moment. It's perfect, and I can see the ward doors clearly. I'm keeping my head down so it looks like I'm scrolling, and no one can see my face. The mask helps, and I've seen a few people with them on, so it doesn't look odd.

I really hope Jess leaves quickly. I only need five minutes, maybe less. Visiting time is almost over so my chances of being able to sort this out tonight are getting smaller with every tick of the clock.

Which is very annoying.

Coming back early in the morning wasn't part of the original idea but it's looking like the best option. And it does mean that I can do more research overnight and work out a proper plan that will be quicker to execute.

I think I'll need to do the other one first. She should be easy, but I haven't been able to get near her today with everyone coming and going.

Bomber to assassin, it's amazing what you can do when you have to.

OMG, what?!?

I do NOT believe it, what the hell is he doing here? He's just come up the other stairs right by the drinks

machine. He's even looked this way
and hasn't seen me.

What, am I invisible?

He couldn't be visiting her?
SERIOUSLY?

This just got real.
That. Is. It.

Jess took a breath, suddenly realising what she'd said. Ella had been in the lab too. She'd gone even paler now, her mascara in black streaks down her face.

Jess cleared her throat. 'We were wondering if it could have been something to do with the international students – there's a far-right local councillor who made a whole load of nasty comments right after it happened.' She paused. 'But I overheard Mr Murray saying he'd turned down a girl from Ardmore Wood School who'd been expelled –'

Ella interrupted her. 'Hailey de Búrca?'

Jess nodded. 'Do you know her? Her school burned down the same day she was chucked out. Anyway, we thought she might be hating on Mr Murray, but then I remembered that Tara said Maeve had texted her cousin about the photos. She sent him a link about them being illegal and said she'd go to the Guards.'

'Could that be the reason? For the explosion, I mean. Does Sorcha think someone set a bomb to blow up Maeve, to stop her telling the Guards?'

Jess shrugged. 'We're speculating but maybe they didn't intend for it to be this big – perhaps it was just supposed to scare her. The thing is, if the girl in the photos is underage, it's *really* serious. It's really serious anyway, but whoever got her to take the pictures and then shared them could be facing a prison sentence.'

As Jess had been speaking, Ella had got paler and paler. Then she let out a breath: 'Who's Maeve's cousin?'

'Guy called Conan. He's in the Raven's Park rugby squad; he sent the photos to Maeve asking who the girl was. All laughing emojis.' Jess hesitated. 'It's one possibility, but I don't see how they could have got a bomb into the lab.'

Ella took a shaky breath. 'They could have done it at breaktime.'

Jess did a double-take. 'What do you mean?'

'A bunch of Sixth Years from Raven's Park came over to Raven's Hill this morning to help with the *Macbeth* scenery. I thought Tiernan was with them, and he'd come and say hello, but he didn't text. I think most of them were rugby team and they were in the school at breaktime. Tiernan said they were leaving when the explosion happened. They could have gone up to the science labs; there's never anyone up there at first break.'

Jess looked at Ella, processing what she'd just said. *There had been boys from Raven's Park in the school this morning?*

That put everything into a *whole* new light.

A bomb sounded a bit extreme, but a prank gone wrong? Or a prank that was designed to scare someone, that wasn't a prank at all? That sounded a lot more possible.

Jess shook her head in disbelief. 'Oh my God, maybe that *is* it. Maybe someone *was* trying to scare Maeve, to stop her going to the police?'

'What's her cousin's name again?' Ella's voice was so low it was hard to hear over the chatter of visiting time.

'Conan, I think.'

'Like Conan the Barbarian.'

Jess shrugged. 'Maeve calls him that sometimes. He's pretty awful, she says.'

The tears began to slide down Ella's face again. Jess opened her mouth to speak but she jumped as she heard Tiernan's voice behind her.

'Hey, babes, sorry I was so long. What's wrong?'

Turning towards him, Jess was about to say hello when she realised Ella was gripping her arm, digging her fingers right in. Jess glanced at her in surprise. There was something wrong here. Something between Ella and Tiernan.

Jess rubbed Ella's free arm protectively to show her she'd got her message as she answered. 'It must be shock,

I think. It can be delayed. The whole explosion was such a big thing.'

Tiernan looked concerned and, leaning forwards, put a can of Coke down beside Ella's phone on the bedside table. Jess felt Ella freeze. *What on earth was the problem?*

'Here's the Coke. I was looking for chocolate for you, couldn't find any.'

Ella's eyes flicked to the bedside table.

Was she looking at her phone? What had made Ella so sensitive about her phone all of a sudden? Jess reached forwards and picked it up, tucking it in beside Ella as if she was putting it within easy reach.

Then Jess realised what he'd said. There was a chocolate machine near the lift on every floor, along a bit from the drinks machine, you couldn't miss it. Jess had noticed it as she'd shuttled between wards. She'd been trying to decide if she should get some for Frankie. It would be easy to find chocolate. *He had to be lying. But why?*

Tiernan reached for a fleece jacket lying across the bed behind Jess. 'Look, I'm sorry, babes, but I've got to get to training. I'll come back in tomorrow. Text me?'

Ella smiled weakly as he leaned in to give her a quick kiss and then raised his hand. 'Laters.'

As he vanished out of the curtains, Ella burst into tears again.

Becky felt like she was trapped under a heavy blanket of worry. She could just hear what was going on around her, but it was muffled by the thoughts in her head that felt louder than everything outside. She didn't know what was wrong, but she couldn't move, and she couldn't open her eyes. It was like she was frozen. Perhaps she was dead. Perhaps this was what being dead was like …

Her mum was back, giving out again to the nurse. At least Becky guessed it was a nurse. Her thoughts felt like they'd slowed down, like the worries around her were a fog that was trapping her. The nurse sounded calm. A lot calmer than her mum, that was for sure. Her voice was too loud and angry. It made Becky want to sink into the fog and hide.

'You must be able to do *something*. This is ridiculous. There must be something you can give her? And why is she still here and not on a ward?'

'We are treating her; we're giving her benzo-diazepines via her drip. And we're monitoring her closely. This is a very unpredictable condition that's unique to each sufferer. A catatonic state is part of the body's flight, freeze or fight mechanism. Freezing is a reaction to extreme shock or anxiety. That's essentially what we think has happened to Rebecca.' There was a rattle, like a clipboard was being slotted into the end of the bed. 'And she's still here because we need to work out the best place for her to go. We're hoping if she responds to treatment she can stay here, but if she doesn't there are other units that might be more suitable.'

'But why would she freeze? Everyone else is fine. Well, not fine, but they're not locked in like this.' Her mum again. Becky wished her dad was here, or her granny. Her granny had died when Becky was little, but for some reason she was suddenly missing her.

'The explosion was very sudden and from what the police have told us, it was close to Rebecca. It's possible that she could have been so frightened that she thought she was going to die. And in response to that, her body shut down. We most commonly see it in people who are already being treated for anxiety, or who have been depressed.'

'She's not depressed. And everyone's anxious at this age.'

Her mum said it so fiercely that Becky automatically reached out for the ColourMeHappy theme song in her head.

No matter how bad she was feeling, the music always caused colour bursts in her mind, yellow and pink. Even if they only lasted a few minutes. Becky tried to picture Maeve standing in the common room, scrolling through the ColourMeHappy Insta posts, her face alight. It made people happy, made everyone happy.

Becky loved the account so much; it was like stepping into another world, one ruled by order, where everything was themed and organised and everything meant something, had an impact. Everything was always perfect: the music, the videos and still photos. It was like a safe corner of the internet, and it wasn't just Becky and Maeve who loved it – the follower numbers had snowballed since it started.

The nurse took a moment to answer. 'Catatonia usually occurs when the patient experiences a very intense emotional state. It's a built-in defence mechanism triggered by fear or trauma and interferes with their ability to communicate. We're doing all we can. Perhaps you'd like to get a cup of tea and come back a bit later. We'll call you if anything changes.'

That was a good idea. The further away her mum was right now, the better. She always had more time for her clients than she did for Becky and now wasn't the time to suddenly get interested.

Becky couldn't really remember how she'd got here but she knew her mum wasn't helping things. Whatever had happened had been bad, though, something really *really* awful that was making her feel sad and lost. Something really terrible.

The Guards are still in the Chemistry lab. There's a Northern Irish registered van parked outside now. I heard it's the bomb squad from Belfast.

> Don't the bomb squad defuse bombs?
> Bit late for that.

> I think they're forensics. CSI from Belfast. The Guards must think it's a bomb to call them down 😦

> Who would put a bomb in a school?

> Don't people put bombs where they can get the most press coverage and create the most chaos? It's been all over the news. They've got pictures

of everyone. There's a terrible one of
Mr Murray – who knew he was in a
tribute band?!!!

A class full of schoolgirls getting blown
up is pretty big news. So lucky that it was
only half the class. Go Faraday.

Who's Faraday?

Dude who invented the box that stops
phone signals. My mum's threatening
to buy one. That's what the demo was
of in Physics.

Heard they were interviewing everyone. That lab assistant with the glasses
was there for ages.

The one that came in with odd shoes
on at the start of term?

Seriously, someone who can't tell
what colour their shoes are is left
in charge of dangerous chemicals?
Recipe for disaster.

She's really sweet, she helped me with the Lego competition, our robot kept flipping over and she fixed it. They have to talk to everyone, doesn't mean anything.

Any update on the photos? Whoever shared them should be in jail.

Rumour is that she wouldn't sleep with him, so he shared.

I heard he was going to *share more* if she didn't sleep with him.

That doesn't make sense, why would she ever speak to him again if he did that?

That's blackmail. If she did, it would be rape.

J ess didn't want to leave Ella, she was so upset, but she knew she was running out of time to check in on the others. Even if she could only drop Frankie's silk roses into the ICU, she wanted to see how Maeve and Mackenzie were.

But what on earth was the story with Tiernan? When he'd walked in behind Jess it was almost as if Ella was frightened of him. It was so unlike her – Ella was the most confident of all of them, she never worried what other people thought. Georgia had told Jess that Ella wanted to go to London to university – she looked like she was all about having a good time, but actually she was really focused on studying.

And recently she'd been a lot less mean, according to Frankie and Georgia. Her friend Ruth leaving Raven's Hill had been good for the whole class. Jess knew from the other schools she'd been to that some people were just toxic and affected everyone around them. They might come across as joking and funny, but the little digs added up like pinpricks, and after a while their obsession with themselves became really boring.

Jess had given Ella another gentle hug before she'd left and told her to text if she needed anything. Now she was running up the stairs again. With luck she could get to the fourth floor in the ten minutes left of visiting time.

Upstairs, the ICU floor had a different atmosphere to the lower wards. It was hushed, more intense. Jess spotted the nurses' station and went straight to it. The nurse behind it looked up as she arrived.

'Hi, I'm from Raven's Hill. My friends Maeve and Mackenzie are up here, I think.'

The nurse smiled back. 'They're popular today. Would you like me to give them a message?'

'Can I see them? How are they?' Catching her breath, Jess leaned on the counter.

'I'm afraid it's family only, but they're getting the best care up here.'

Jess could tell she was avoiding answering. Frustrating but understandable. She'd have to text Tara to get an update on Maeve, and if she could get Greg's number, find out about Mackenzie. Someone would have it.

'Could you give them these?' Jess held up the two remaining roses. 'They're from Frankie O'Sullivan – she's on St Thomas's Ward.'

'Of course, they're lovely. I'm sure they'll both be delighted.'

'Thanks.' Jess wanted to ask her more but at that moment a Tannoy announcement asked visitors to leave. That had to be the fastest two hours on record.

As Jess trotted back down the stairs to the main entrance, her mind kept going back to Ella. Jess had really felt like Ella wanted to tell her something more, but there hadn't been time. Maybe she'd text, or Jess could text her when she got home and see how she was.

Jess still couldn't believe what Ella had said about the boys from Raven's Park being in the school this morning. What did they always say in detective stuff on TV – you had to prove means, motive and opportunity?

Reaching the bottom of the stairs, Jess headed for the main doors. Her dad would be waiting to pick her up, but he'd probably be parked somewhere in the huge car park. And before she texted him, she needed to text an update to Frankie and Sorcha.

Jess looked around and, seeing a bit of vacant wall beside the car park payment machine, went to lean on it. She quickly opened WhatsApp and started typing:

> Just spoke to Ella. Rav Park
> rugby boys were in Rav Hill this
> morning to do Macbeth scenery.
> Could have got into Chem lab at
> first break.

She waited for the blue ticks to appear. Sorcha was first. It was like she was reading Jess's mind.

> Means?

Frankie's text came a second later:

> Motive?

Jess would have laughed it if wasn't so serious. Her thumbs flew over the keyboard:

> Frighten Maeve into NOT going
> to the Guards?

The more Jess thought about it, the more plausible it seemed. Maeve had texted Conan about what could happen with the photos – if he wanted to scare her, coming up with a harebrained scheme to set a bomb off in the Chemistry lab was exactly the level of genius – not – you'd expect from a bunch of lads who were sharing nude photos. Although that said, if it was them, Jess was pretty sure they hadn't meant the explosion to be so big. But getting whatever the ingredients were wrong, or in the wrong quantities, sort of went with the territory.

Anyone who thought a bomb in a chemistry lab could possibly be a good idea needed their head examining.

Jess felt anxiety flutter inside her, stretching its wings. She bit her lip. She needed to text her dad to come get her and when they got home, talk it through with him, see if he'd heard anything from his contacts in the Guards about the explosion.

As Jess hit send, she pushed herself off the wall and paused for a moment, biting her lip. *Was this it, was this the reason for the explosion?* Turning to head towards the huge sliding front doors, Jess suddenly realised that Mackenzie's brother Greg was sitting on a chair on the other side of the atrium, his head in his hands. He looked utterly dejected, his shoulders slumped. She couldn't leave without checking he was alright.

'Hi again.' Greg looked up sharply as Jess spoke. His lashes were wet. He sniffed and tried to smile. She kept talking, giving him a minute to compose himself. 'How's Mackenzie? I was just up at ICU, but they couldn't tell me anything.'

Greg cleared his throat. 'She's doing good. Well, not good, but better. A bit. Conscious, anyway. I just saw her.' Greg's face didn't seem to reflect her improvement; he looked worried, almost frightened.

'That's brilliant news. The others are desperate to hear.'

Greg opened his mouth, about to speak, and then closed it again. It was like whatever he wanted to say wasn't coming out. Jess didn't know what was wrong, but something was definitely up with him.

'I'm just waiting for my dad; he'll be here soon. Are you heading back to school?'

He looked awkwardly towards the main doors to the hospital. 'I'm not sure, I … Christ, this is such a mess.' He shook his head, avoiding her eyes.

He looked trapped, that's what it was. What on earth had happened? 'Why don't you come home with me for a bit? We're only ordering pizza but it's just me and my dad. You'd be really welcome.' Jess hesitated, her voice soft as she continued, 'Maybe we can help with what's bothering you?'

Greg looked shocked for a moment, fear in his eyes, then his face softened. 'Is it that obvious?'

Jess smiled warmly. 'Whatever it is, I'm sure we can help. A lot happened before I came here. I know how it feels to be a blow-in and not have anyone to talk to.'

BULLET JOURNAL
Behind Every Successful Woman is Herself

Visiting time's over. I'm either going to have to come back during the night, or first thing in the morning. But I know where everyone is. And I've had another idea, so I know what I have to do.
I can be in and out in minutes.
Then everything will be sorted, and we can get over this blip and get on with our lives. Be properly together.
You know, I'm starting to think this will make an amazing podcast. I can interview everyone who was involved and get their take on the situation, find out exactly how the explosion impacted them.
I'll enjoy that.

S orcha turned over in bed, trying to read on her
Kindle app on the phone Ollie had brought in
for her. At least she had something to distract
herself from the monotony of the ward. It felt weird
being here. And it wasn't even like she was that sick.
Well, not really.

After her trip to the loo, she'd come back to bed
exhausted, turning over what she'd heard in her mind.
She wasn't totally sure, but she thought the boy she'd
overheard by the drinks machine might be Ella's boyfriend, and he'd been talking about photos.

*It didn't take a genius to work out what that could
be about.*

Tiernan was in the rugby team too – and they seemed
to be at the heart of the whole nude photos issue.

And then Jess had texted about the Raven's Park boys
having access to the lab.

Minimising her book, Sorcha opened Google Docs and looked at her list.

Theory #1: Mackenzie/international girls – racist attack?

Theory #2: Revenge against Mr Murray.

Theory #3: Maeve knows who is in the photos.

They needed to look properly at every idea and work out which ones were the strongest.

The news clippings she'd found about that local politician had been really worrying. There was a whole right-wing political swing in the world at the moment and immigrants were getting the blame for the failings of governments all over the place. It felt scary. But could they really have targeted a *school?*

Had the bomb been set by anti-immigration activists who wanted to make an example of them? There was definitely a huge mix of nationalities at Raven's Hill. Its international feel was part of its appeal to lots of parents sending their children there.

It was a bit terrifying to think that someone could have targeted Raven's Hill. Sorcha glanced at her document again and suddenly started to feel overwhelmed. She needed to give her head a break from all of this speculation; there seemed to be so many possibilities and any one of them felt like they could be the reason for the explosion.

It was nuts. Yesterday she'd been worrying about her 400m breaststroke time and getting her Maths homework done, and today she was in hospital. *What if one of them had died?*

She couldn't deal with that now.

Opening Instagram, Sorcha clicked through to her private messages, looking to distract her wandering thoughts. Beth had sent her a load of funny animal videos from the airport to try and cheer her up.

Beth hated airports – well, not so much the airport, but the waiting. None of them liked sitting about doing nothing, and airports were the worst. It was definitely some sort of genetic trait; her dad was always in trouble for trying to cut down the waiting time, arriving as close to take-off as possible. But getting delayed was a whole different level of pain. They all tried to avoid evening flights as they always seemed to run late, and here it was happening again.

But Beth had to be in the air by now. Sorcha hoped so; she really wanted to chat this all through with her big sister.

She flicked to look at Beth's Reels. When Beth had finished the coding assignment she'd been working on, it looked like she'd started roaming through every single shop in Edinburgh Airport. Sorcha smiled to herself.

She must have been really bored. She'd even gone to the designer store and had tried a load of tops on, the lights in the cubicle making her dark hair gleam. Beth's Reel moved on from a white T-shirt to a pretty purple silk blouse with star-shaped buttons. Purple really suited Beth.

Sorcha looked at the Reel again. The purple reminded her of something. It was like an echo, something she couldn't quite remember, just out of reach. But whatever it was, she knew it was important. She put down her phone and closed her eyes.

Where had she seen purple?

Then she had it.

Back in the Chemistry lab, as she'd bent to pick up her pen, she'd glanced down the room, and Becky had been doing something with her phone.

And there had been a pinky-purple flash. And the fizzing sound had happened at exactly the same time. The flash had made her look up and the first bang had happened right then, with the next one going off what felt like less than a second later.

Had the purple flash been connected to the bang?

JESS'S APARTMENT
LAMBAY HOUSE, MAIN STREET,
KILMURRAY POINT
9.02 p.m.
14 hours 23 minutes remaining
Jess

As Jess's dad pulled up outside the main doors of St Anthony's Hospital, she pulled open the passenger door of the Mini and stuck her head in.

'Dad, Mackenzie's brother Greg's here. His parents are flying over from the US, but he's on his own right now. Can he come home with us for pizza?' She leaned in, her voice almost a whisper. 'He's really worried about something, and I think he needs someone to talk to.'

Her dad's eyebrows rose marginally. 'Jump in – we'll order pizza on the way back.'

Jess smiled at him gratefully. She didn't know what was up with Greg, but she knew fear when she saw it. Maybe she could get him to talk to her. And failing that, her dad was used to talking to people: he had to build trust with anyone he needed to interview. If Greg couldn't talk to Jess, maybe her dad could find out what was worrying him so much.

Jess gestured to Greg, who was hovering just inside the automatic doors of the hospital. He crossed the pavement quickly as Jess got into the back seat, leaving the front passenger door open.

As Greg buckled up, her dad grinned across at him. 'Cormac McKenna – you're Greg?'

'Yes. Thanks, Mr McKenna. Greg Smyth, my sister is in Jess's class.'

Jess's dad checked his mirror and pulled away. 'You guys decide what you want and order. Have you eaten today, Greg?'

As if in shock, Greg took a moment to respond. 'No, sir, not yet.'

✕ ✕ ✕

The hospital was only a ten-minute drive from Jess's apartment, which was on the fourth floor of a new building overlooking the pier and the bay. The thing she loved most about it was the view – even on a freezing winter night like tonight, it was amazing. The lights on the piers and on the tankers out in the bay shone like beacons of hope. There were days when she couldn't believe she lived here – it was so totally different to London and the Middle East.

Showing Greg into their comfortable living room, the side lights glowing warmly in the corners of the room, she moved her iPad and the remote controls off the soft sofa so that Greg could sit down.

'We can eat in here. Can I get you a Coke, or a cup of tea?'

Nodding nervously, Greg sat down on the edge of the sofa and played his phone through his hands. He was over six foot, made their big squishy chairs look small. Behind Jess, her dad appeared with sheets of paper towel to use as napkins and three cans of Coke.

'I'm ahead of you.' As he spoke the main door buzzed. 'You sort that out, Jess.' He gave her a meaningful glance that said 'take your time'. She knew her dad had picked up on Greg's mood as soon as he'd got into the car.

Jess smiled warmly at Greg and headed for the intercom by the front door, pulling the living room door closed behind her.

She glanced at the screen as she reached it and, checking the video image, buzzed the delivery man up.

What was up with Greg? Did he know something about the explosion that he was too frightened to talk about?

Jess's head was whirring. Her phone had pinged with a message from Sorcha as she'd got in the car, but between ordering the pizza and trying to keep the conversation going so Greg would relax she hadn't had a chance to look at it yet. And she couldn't focus on it now. As she waited for the delivery man, Jess paced the hall, going over everything she, Frankie and Sorcha had heard today. There was a lot, but something was nagging at her.

The pizza delivery man must have run up the stairs from the ground floor, and Jess jumped when he knocked on the apartment door. The boxes were warm as he handed them to her.

Smiling her thanks, Jess closed the front door and the thing that had been bothering her slowly clicked into place. There had been so much going on today, and with running around the hospital, this was the first time her brain had had a chance to calm down. She looked at the box in her hand – it was the pizza that was joining all the bits together.

Her dad must have heard the door shut. His voice carried through from the living room.

'Bring them through, Jess.'

'Won't be a second ...' Hurriedly, Jess went into the kitchen and put the boxes down on the table, reaching for her phone. She opened the WhatsApp group.

> Guys, listen up, I heard TWICE today that Sorcha's sister was asking questions about who was in which ward/what was wrong with them.

Sorcha was obviously still awake:

It wasn't Beth, she's only on her way now.

Jess replied quickly, her fingers flying over the keys:

EXACTLY, that's my point, so someone was pretending to be Beth, someone who wanted to know where the Raven's Hill girls were in the hospital.

WHO and WHY?

Frankie joined the conversation:

Do we know when?

Jess glanced at the kitchen door, conscious her dad was waiting. But their video doorbell had given her an idea.

Danny, do you know what time it was when you spoke to Becky's mum?

She'd seen his thumbs-up on her original message – now he came right back:

> Yep 7 p.m. on the dot. And she
> sounded like she'd only just
> spoken to 'Beth'.

Jess fired a message to the group. She knew this was
going to sound a bit dramatic, but it was the best way she
could think of to get the information they needed and
quickly. They could take it to the Guards, but they hadn't
even believed Sorcha about the explosion, so were they
going to waste time on what they'd probably think was
mistaken identity – didn't all teenage girls look alike?

The more Jess thought about it, the more she was
convinced that the Beth impersonator had to have something to do with what had happened today. Otherwise,
why would she be in the hospital at all?

> Sorcha, can you get into the
> hospital CCTV and get a look at
> who was talking to Becky's mum?
> Becky's in the ED, so it has to be
> there, in the corridor or outside.
> We need to find out why someone
> is impersonating Beth and, more
> importantly, WHO they are.

Hacking the hospital CCTV sounded a bit extreme.
Jess knew from her dad that huge money had been put

into strengthening the data systems after a big ransomware attack on the HSE a few years ago, but in the midst of the chaos had they thought to strengthen the internal CCTV systems?

She doubted it.

There was a good chance there were vulnerabilities there too – CCTV ran on Wi-Fi and wasn't hard to hack. Random cameras from all over the world were streamed to the dark web every day. And Sorcha knew more about computer systems than anyone else Jess had ever met – apart from her sister Beth, who was in Edinburgh doing a degree in Cybersecurity.

If Sorcha couldn't manage to get into the system herself, Beth could tell her how to.

And Sorcha couldn't resist a challenge.

Jess smiled as she read Sorcha's reply:

> Leave it with me. I have my laptop. Beth's landed, she's on her way home.

> Do you think whoever this is, is behind the bomb?

Jess bit her lip as she answered; maybe she was wrong, but something very weird was going on.

Impersonating your sister
seems very extra. And what's
that thing about criminals
wanting to watch the impact of
their crimes, going to funerals
and stuff? Worth a look.

Three thumbs-up emojis appeared after Jess's message.

Quickly she put her phone on the top of the stack and picked up the pizza boxes. Manoeuvring the living room door open, her arms full, Jess could see Greg was sitting forwards on the sofa, his head bowed, elbows on his knees, his phone held loosely in his hands. Trying to focus on the situation here and not on her somersaulting stomach, she slipped the boxes onto the coffee table and sat down on the sofa closest to the armchair where her dad was sitting.

Would Sorcha be able to hack the cameras and how long would it take her?

Her dad leaned forward to open the boxes and grab a slice of pizza.

'That took a while.' He glanced at Jess enquiringly and she felt her colour rise. She couldn't tell him now, but she was sure she was on to something.

Her dad turned his attention back to the pizza. 'Tuck in, Greg, or I'll have to eat the rest for breakfast, which won't do my waistline any good.' Her dad glanced over at Greg. He seemed to be in a world of his own.

Jess's dad caught her eye. 'We'll cut to the chase. Greg's worried about going to the police with some information he has.' He paused. 'But he's got some photographs – and video – that they need to see.'

Jess leaned forwards, grabbing a slice and trying to look like she hadn't just had all the wind knocked out of her. She glanced at her dad, then looked back at Greg. *Photos.* Did he know something about the nude photos, and who they were of?

As soon as Jess had left, Ella had closed her eyes and pulled the blankets up as far as she could. She was in so much pain. She just wanted to hide, to burrow into a deep dark hole where she could think about everything that had happened. Her heart was broken. And not just broken, but smashed into tiny pieces. It hurt even more than her broken ribs.

It was the betrayal that was worst. And it made her feel like she was nothing, like she didn't matter, like she wasn't good enough to care about.

She'd thought Tiernan loved her.

He'd showered her with texts and flowers and little video messages. He'd told her she was beautiful and that she didn't need anyone else, that he'd always look after her. He'd said she was too mature for her friend group, that she should hang out more with him. He always wanted to know who she was talking to; he'd made her change the password on her phone so he could 'share' her messages.

She'd thought it was cute, that he really wanted to be with her. Ella could feel the tears starting again as she thought about the times when he'd ghosted her, when he hadn't answered her texts.

Was he with her then, this Rainbow Princess? And who was All Hail the Queen? Another girl he had on the go? Had he told them he wanted to keep their friendship private, to keep it special like he had said to Ella? Had he love-bombed them both as well, convincing them that they were wonderful, making them feel like they were the centre of his world and that they didn't need anyone else except him?

Whatever about All Hail the Queen, he must have had something going with Rainbow Princess for her to send him intimate photos. He must have *really* convinced her that she was the centre of his universe, to make her trust him.

And then he'd betrayed her.

Ella thought back to the Barbarian texts. It sounded like he wanted more photos – and in the next 24 hours. What on earth was he going to do with them then?

It didn't make sense to Ella, but Rainbow Princess must be absolutely terrified.

But who on earth was she? If she went to Raven's Park, she had to be in Fifth or Sixth Year, which *must* mean she knew Ella and Tiernan had been inseparable for the last two months. It was the longest Ella had dated anyone. She hadn't mentioned his name online, but she'd talked all about him in the common room.

Maybe she hadn't connected Ella's Tiernan with the one she was seeing? Or perhaps he'd told Rainbow Princess that he loved her more and they needed to keep their relationship a secret while he worked out how to break up with Ella. That was exactly the sort of thing a two-timing cheat would do.

And Ella bet he'd got the photos from her so he could pressure her into doing something she wasn't ready for.

The more Ella thought about it, the angrier she got. A bit with this girl, but even more with Tiernan. Who did he think he was? Just because his dad was loaded and they lived in Ballsbridge and he had his own car, it didn't mean he could treat girls like shit.

Whatever he'd done by cheating on Ella, sharing Rainbow Princess's pictures with his rugby mates was way worse.

And that made Ella *really* mad.

Rainbow Princess probably thought he was crazy about her too. Ella bet he'd bought her presents and sent her love heart emojis as well. He'd obviously sent them to All Hail the Queen, whoever the heck she was.

Ella could see now exactly why he had two phones. He must have done this before. If someone saw him with the wrong phone, then he'd just pretend he'd changed the case. But it meant he could keep things separate, the girls separate. How many others were there? She hadn't had time to go through everything, but maybe she and Rainbow Princess and All Hail the Queen weren't the only ones. She hadn't read the message that was under that selfie of All Hail the Queen's lips, the nude pictures were a much bigger issue, but she'd taken a photo of it for when she challenged him later.

Because there was no way she was letting all this rest.

Ella looked at her own phone. She needed to call this girl, to talk to Rainbow Princess and find out what had been said, to see if she could help her. Ella closed her eyes. She'd taken a photo of the girl's contact details with her own phone as well, and of the nude photos, and of Tiernan's messages to Rainbow Princess. There was no way he was getting out of this.

She just needed Rainbow Princess to answer her call.

Ella bit her lip. This could be the most difficult conversation she ever had in her life. For God's sake, she was lying in a hospital bed with broken ribs and Tiernan hadn't even turned up until halfway through visiting time and he'd stayed about five minutes.

He'd obviously had other things on his mind.

Ella pulled her phone out from under her blankets. The last thing she'd wanted earlier was for Jess to open her phone, or for Tiernan to pick it up. Thank goodness Jess had realised what she meant when she'd squeezed her arm.

Ella looked at the screen and opened the photo she'd taken of Rainbow Princess's contact page. *What sort of name was that anyway?* Tiernan seemed to give stupid names to everyone in his phone. Ella was Sparkles because her surname was Diamond. She'd thought it was adorable at the time. Now she could see that it was a way to conceal people's identities. Like Barbarian. But Ella had a very good idea who he was.

Tapping Rainbow Princess's number into her phone, Ella's finger hovered over the dial button. The number hadn't come up in her contacts, so it wasn't someone she knew.

Ella felt her mouth dry. *She had to do this. She needed to know. And Rainbow Princess needed help.*

She hit dial and waited. She could hear the phone ringing out somewhere. Then the answer message came on.

'Hi, I can't answer the phone right now but leave a message and I'll get back to you as soon as I can.' Ella waited for the beep. What should she say? Her heart was pounding but she kept her voice light.

'Hi, this is Ella Diamond, call me back when you can.'

Suddenly breathless, her head whirring, her mouth dry, Ella hung up.

The message hadn't given her a name, but the voice sounded weirdly familiar.

Maybe she did know her. Ella just had to work out who it was.

JESS'S APARTMENT
LAMBAY HOUSE, MAIN STREET,
KILMURRAY POINT
9.16 p.m.
14 hours 9 minutes remaining
Jess

Jess took a bite of the slice of pizza in her hand, almost choking on it in her effort to keep calm. It was like she was chewing wood. *Greg knew something about the photos.* He really didn't seem the type to be involved in this sort of thing. She stopped herself – *was* there a type? She didn't know. But what had her dad found out?

She looked from her dad to Greg, waiting for one of them to elaborate. Greg cleared his throat.

'He said he'd kill me if I didn't send them to him and delete them. And then there was the explosion and Mackenzie … I couldn't live with myself if something I've done has put her in danger. He's already half killed Jasper.' Greg's lip curled. 'If I hadn't been there on the field to call the ambulance, Jasper could be dead right now.'

Jasper? What had he got to do with the nude photos?

Jess leaned forwards; she hadn't been expecting this. 'Who? Who beat him up? Did you see?'

Greg sighed. 'I was trying to catch him up, Jasper, I mean, but he was way over the other side of the field when I heard them.' Greg shook his head. 'I should have stopped it but there were two of them, and ...' He took a ragged breath. 'He would have twisted things to make it look like I did it. I couldn't ... Christ, I'm going to regret that for the rest of my life. All I could do was yell and at least that stopped them, but it meant he knew I'd seen him. I got a text like ten minutes later. He recognised my voice, obviously. Nobody else in the school has my accent.' Greg glanced at Jess.

Stunned, she stared at him, the slice of pizza still halfway to her mouth. 'So, what's with the photos?'

'There was just enough light where they attacked him, from the streetlamps on the other side of the hedge. I videoed them and took stills. They were a bit away but it's just about clear enough to see who it was.'

Jess opened her eyes wide, willing him to continue. 'So, who was it?'

'Tiernan Reece, and this guy Conan who's on the rugby team with him. I don't know his surname.'

Jess did. He was Maeve's cousin. Stunned, she shook her head slowly. 'But why? Jasper doesn't play rugby – why on earth did they beat him up?'

Greg shrugged. 'Tiernan kept saying something about

staying in his lane and keeping away from what was his, apparently. I think he said something about Jasper keeping away from "her".' He shook his head. 'That bit *really* doesn't make sense. Jasper isn't interested in girls.'

Jess looked at him, and everything began to triangulate. 'Oh God, I think he means Ella.'

Greg looked at her, confused. 'Like Ella in Mackenzie's class ... in your class?'

Jess nodded. 'Her laptop kept crashing. She texted me to ask if I knew where to get it fixed – Georgia told her the same thing had happened to mine. And I was with Jasper. He said he could take a look.' Jess looked at her dad. 'He builds PCs for people, like as a hobby.'

Her dad had stayed quiet up to now, listening as he ate his pizza. 'So presumably Tiernan thought Jasper was moving in on Ella, and his solution was to beat him up.' He raised his eyebrows. 'Nice lad.'

Trying to hide her racing thoughts, Jess took a bite of her pizza. She'd been sure the photos they were talking about had been the nude ones, but these were a whole other pile of trouble.

'How does he know you've got these pictures?' Jess could see the fear and exhaustion in Greg's face. He didn't look like he'd slept since Friday.

'He texted me – he said I'd be next if I said anything, and there wouldn't just be two of them.' Greg closed his eyes. 'So, I sent him one of the pictures, to, I don't know, frighten him back, I suppose.' Greg shook his head. 'Bad move.'

Jess's mind circled back to the explosion – could this be the reason for it? 'Did you tell Mackenzie? Would he have known if you did?'

Greg sighed. 'Well, she's my twin so we tell each other everything.' He shrugged. 'I met her in Starbucks on Saturday morning. Someone could have seen us.' He shook his head again. 'It's like Tiernan has this control over everyone. I reckon he's got stuff on the whole year, stuff that needs to be kept secret, so they spy for him. I bet they all know he beat up Jasper. It's so alpha male, especially if you're right and it was something to do with Ella. Everyone's shit scared they could be next.'

'This Tiernan guy sounds like a bundle of fun. So now we need to work out the best course of action. We don't know he was involved in the explosion – yet – but we do know he beat up Jasper, so one thing at a time.' Jess's dad took a bite of his pizza, chewing thoughtfully. 'Eat, Greg, you need to keep your strength up.' He looked at Greg pointedly until he reached into the box.

'I've no idea what to do …' Greg raised his free hand helplessly.

Jess looked from Greg to her dad.

'Dad, could you talk to your editor about doing a story on the bullying in Raven's Park? Get them to focus on what happened to Jasper?'

Greg's eyes brightened as he realised what Jess was saying. 'Tiernan's like the king of the castle there because his dad paid for the new sports building or something. The teachers all turn a blind eye. He gets away with everything.' He chewed thoughtfully. 'Maybe you could do something about privilege. It's sickening to see the way they fawn over him, and other people get suspended for having their hair cut too short.'

Jess's dad pursed his lips, thinking. 'It's not my normal gig but I certainly could. You know you really need to take this to the Guards?'

A shadow of fear passed across Greg's face at the mention of the police. Jess cut in. 'The Guards here aren't like cops in America, but could you give them the video and photos, Dad? You're allowed to protect your sources, so nobody needs to know they came from Greg. If you write a story, it'll blow everything open and Tiernan won't be able to go after Greg, 'cos everyone will be watching him.'

Jess's dad pursed his lips as he thought for a minute. 'Okay, here's the plan. I'll get the phone footage to one of my contacts in the Guards, they bring this Tiernan in. It's public knowledge that Jasper was attacked. I can talk to the headmaster and get some quotes. I can't identify Tiernan or it could prejudice the case, but if the paper agrees to print the photos, it'll spook him. They will need to be enhanced by the Guards for a proper identification, but he'll know it's him, and I'd guess a few other people will too. You're going to have to testify in court though, Greg, if Tiernan's arrested, you know that?'

Greg rubbed his hand over his head. 'Yeah, I get that, I just don't want him twisting things. The cops could be in his father's pocket too. If this Conan guy says he saw me there, they'll make it about me. The 911 call, I mean 999, came from my phone. And Jasper and I are good friends. I was hoping we'd be able to get a bit closer, before all this happened. I was supposed to be meeting him to walk across the field. It's because I was late that this happened.'

Jess's dad's face was serious. 'It'll be fine, Greg, you did the right thing: you stopped the fight and you've got video and photographic evidence. It'll be very hard to get out of that.'

Greg's face was still clouded. 'There's one more problem. He said I had twenty-four hours, so I've only got until tomorrow morning to send him the photographs. I've no idea what he's going to do if I don't send them, but I don't really want to find out.'

'He can't beat you up if you're safe here.' Jess looked at Greg. She could see in his face that his imagination had played out what might happen.

Greg looked from Jess to her dad. 'I just don't know if that explosion was supposed to be some sort of warning. There was a bunch of Raven's Park rugby dudes at

Raven's Hill this morning. I'll never forgive myself if I've put Mackenzie in danger too.' Greg put down the pizza slice he'd only taken a single bite out of.

Jess's dad shook his head, his face angry. 'The police are investigating the explosion, but this is about control, Greg, about power. Nothing's going to change in twenty-four hours. If he wanted these photos that badly he would have asked for them immediately, but he's deliberately given you a deadline to intimidate and frighten you even more.' Jess's dad paused. 'And sending them to him, saying you've deleted them, doesn't mean you have – he knows that. It's nonsense. But that ticking clock plays right into our hands. What time did this start?'

'I got the message at 11.25 this morning.'

Jess's dad looked at his watch. 'It's 9.30, that's almost fourteen hours until this supposed deadline. For you, this ends *right now*, but let's make these fourteen hours Tiernan won't forget, will we? Where's my phone?'

ST JOAN'S WARD
ST ANTHONY'S HOSPITAL
9.34 p.m.
Sorcha

WHAT WE KNOW: Explosion in Chemistry Lab,
Raven's Hill School, Kilmurray Point.

A purple flash AND TWO BANGS

Six girls in St Anthony's Hospital: Frankie
in St Thomas's Ward, Sorcha in St Joan's
Ward, Ella in St Valentine's Ward, Mackenzie
in ICU, Maeve in St Raphael's Surgical
Recovery Ward, Becky in Emergency
Department side ward

~~Gas explosion~~

~~Accident? How?~~

Deliberate: if so, **who** was the target?

Theory #1: Mackenzie/international girls – racist attack?

Theory #2: Revenge against Mr Murray.

Theory #3: Maeve knows who is in the photos.

The ward was almost dark, but Sorcha had put on the reading light above her bed so she could see her keyboard. Her fingers had been flying since Jess had texted. She stopped for a moment now to let the data she was accessing scroll up the screen. Beside her, her phone was open, Beth's instructions clear. If she got stuck, Beth could access her computer remotely and take over, but Sorcha was through the first layer of encryption already. *This really should be a* lot *more difficult.*

Everything was swirling in her head now. As the screen changed, Sorcha tried desperately to remember back to the Chemistry lab and what she'd seen before the world had come tumbling onto her head. What had Becky been doing with her phone? Sorcha could definitely remember seeing her holding it, Becky's head bent forward against the light from the window behind her.

Mackenzie had been coughing. Sorcha could remember that clearly too.

And then boom.

But the purple. There had definitely been a pinky-purple flash. And it had been right in front of Becky.

There had to have been more, she *must* have seen more. But there was so much happening now, and she needed to focus on this.

Who on earth was pretending to be Beth, and why? It didn't make any sense at all, but it *did* feel like the urgency of this situation had suddenly gone up a level. If the explosion was deliberate, did the Beth impersonator have something to do with it?

The screen stopped scrolling, and Sorcha checked it, her concentration back on the problem at hand. If she could get into the CCTV recording system, she should be able to see the feeds from all the security cameras. Then, with luck, they could see who had spoken to Becky's mum.

More data began to scroll. Sorcha was pretty sure she was almost there. Waiting for her laptop to finish this next stage, Sorcha thought back. The purple was nagging at her.

The flash hadn't totally registered in the moment that she'd looked down the lab. The part of her brain that had seen it had thought it was on Becky's phone screen or something. She'd been thinking about her lost pen, and the nude photos, and her swim session that morning and the competition against Kilmurray Point that weekend. Her head had been full.

But the experiment they were about to do was with potassium, which, Sorcha knew, burst into a pinky-purple flame. That was the point of Mr Murray demonstrating the sodium first – it was a bit of a downer, but lithium got people interested and potassium was the wow factor.

But they didn't have the chemicals to do the experiment themselves. Mr Murray was doing them – because they were dangerous.

Had the lab assistant left the experiment samples in that box at the back of the classroom, intending to put them away later, and Becky had seen them when she sat down?

Had Becky done the experiment herself, and that's what had caused the first noise, the fizzing and the cracking Sorcha had heard?

Her laptop screen stopped scrolling and Sorcha focused back on it to input more instructions. This might take a while, but if Jess was right, then whoever was impersonating Beth was doing it for a reason, and Sorcha didn't imagine it was a good one.

There was a cough on the other side of the ward, and more lines of data appeared on the screen. Sorcha needed to let her system do its thing. At least it was quieter here now; visiting time was well over and the lights were dimmed. It helped her think.

Waiting for the laptop, Sorcha strained to remember exactly what had happened that morning.

Could Becky have used too much potassium and her experiment set off a chain reaction with something the boys from Raven's Park had left in the lab? Had the extra power from the potassium explosion made their explosion even bigger than they'd intended?

That still didn't account for the two bangs Sorcha had heard, but it made some sort of sense.

Sorcha pulled out her phone to text Frankie, just as a message came through from her.

> Sorry, fell asleep after visiting.

> Update: Katie says Becky still bad, she's sort of conscious unconscious.

> Katie couldn't see her so brought back iPad.

> Feel so bad that I still have it.

> How is hacking going?

Sorcha rolled her eyes. Frankie always broke things into separate messages instead of one long one. She always knew when it was Frankie because a bunch of notifications came in together.

> Getting there, shouldn't be much longer. Looking good so far.

Frankie replied:

> Excellent.

> Aoife says the doctors want us to go and talk to Becky when we can.

> We should record messages so she can hear our voices.

Sorcha smiled; that was a lovely idea. They said people in a coma could hear ... Sorcha's mind clicked forward like the hands on a clock.

Recording.

Had that been what Becky was doing with her phone in the lab? Had she been recording a video of the potassium experiment? Could she have caught more of what happened on her video?

Before she could respond to Frankie, another message arrived from her:

> Never going to be able to sleep here now. Head wired.

Sorcha texted Frankie back.

Mine too.

It really was. Images of the lab before the explosion merged with images afterwards. The dust. Maeve's blood.

If Becky had been recording on her phone, they needed to see what she'd captured. But the phone would probably have been smashed to pieces. There had to be a backup, like the recordings Sorcha was accessing here. Sorcha checked the progress on the screen again as a thought struck her. She sent Frankie another message:

Have you got log in password for Becky's iPad?

Frankie replied immediately:

Obvs. Had it for project. Why?

Sorcha picked up her phone:

Can you look on iCloud for last phone camera upload?

Why? Gimme a minute.

Sorcha looked back at her laptop screen. She was through another layer of security. This felt like it was taking ages, but she was confident she'd get there. She turned back to her phone, messaging Frankie again:

> Think she was filming in Chem.
> Look for a purple flash.

Sorcha bit her lip as she waited for Frankie to respond. Sorcha didn't have an iPhone, or a Mac, but she'd used the Google cloud to retrieve photos and video from her Android. It often saved the stuff she'd deleted from her phone, the really cringey pictures, which she found when she needed to get something off the cloud.

On the other side of the ward someone coughed again. Sorcha pulled up her pillows, trying to get more comfortable.

Then Frankie texted back.

> Found it

> Fizzing and big flash, centre is purple.

> She *was* filming experiment.

> Phone fell but facing up.

> Can see ceiling and hear a bang and then a much bigger one. TWO BANGS. Stuff whooshing everywhere. You were right about two bangs. Looks like her phone was blown off bench.

> Second bang massive.

Sorcha could feel her heart beating hard. Had Becky's experiment set off the chain of explosions?

Sorcha's phone pinged again:

> Weird, there's only three videos on the cloud and no photos.

> The other ones are of bees in a big lavender bush and then pile of books with purple covers.

Before Sorcha could reply another text came through. This time into their private WhatsApp group. It was from Jess.

News on Squirrel. Can't share
yet, will explain but evidence on
who beat him up. Dad working on
it. Wondering if bomb could be
threat to someone in class who
knew what happened. Join the
dots with previous messages.
Means/opportunity.

Stunned, Sorcha looked at her phone. They hadn't
even considered that Jess's friend Jasper could be part
of this, but … maybe the timing wasn't a coincidence?

He'd been beaten up on Friday night. The explosion had happened Monday morning. Had something
happened over the weekend? Sorcha read Jess's text
again.

Their previous messages had been about the rugby
boys from Raven's Park being in the school. *Means and
opportunity.* But what was Jess not telling them – someone in the class knew something about the assault? Who
could that be?

Another text came in from Frankie.

Becky has a password-protected
file called videos? Who
password-protects their files?

Sorcha texted back:

> **Anyone with a nosy mother!**
> **Could be video diary?**

Sorcha's head was whirling. Could this really be to do with Jasper Parks? She opened their Google doc *WHAT WE KNOW*.

Theory #4: Threat ref Jasper assault?

Just as she typed the question mark, her laptop screen sprang into life, segmenting into multiple rectangles, each one a camera feed from a different part of the hospital. She was in.

Sorcha tapped out a message to Jess, Beth and the others.

> **In the security system,**
> **accessing recorded data now.**

ST THOMAS'S WARD
ST ANTHONY'S HOSPITAL
10.49 p.m.
Frankie

rankie had no idea how she was going to get to sleep. Her head was spinning. Around her she could hear the night noises of the ward: gentle snores, the sound of the nurses' shoes squeaking on the floor as they came in to check on the other patients. The curtains were drawn around the bed and Frankie reached up to switch on the reading light above her head, a bright pool suddenly spilling over her pillow in the semi-darkness. Frankie reached for her phone to see if Sorcha had sent her an update. She was itching to hear what Sorcha had found, if the cameras had caught Becky's mum talking to anyone who could be impersonating Beth.

It sounded mad.

How much could happen in 24 hours? This time last night she'd been finishing the voiceover on their group video *The Truth About Gatsby* and the internet cutting out had been the end of the world. Now they were trying to find out the truth about a brutal assault, who in Raven's Park had shared nude photos, and why there had been an explosion that had almost killed five of her friends.

With the trauma of the morning, the drama of the photos had been subsumed, but Frankie knew it didn't lessen their impact. *Those photos* … If they'd been of her, Frankie knew she'd want to die, or go and hide in a cave and come out in ten years when *maybe* everyone had forgotten. And when whoever had shared them had been murdered in a painful and grisly way by her brothers. It was just such a hideously awful thing to do.

It sounded terrible, but the girl had to be secretly breathing a sigh of relief with the drama of the explosion keeping the gossips busy for a while at least. Frankie knew she had to be praying everyone would forget about the photos with everything else that was happening. Frankie hadn't even told Danny about them, but it didn't feel like it was her business to be spreading gossip.

Frankie turned onto her side. The cast was so hard to sleep with; it made her arm heavy. Not that she was likely to get any sleep.

Frankie closed her eyes.

Was the explosion something to do with the Raven's Park rugby team as well? They'd shared the photos but could they *really* have thought it was a good idea to set off something to explode in the lab? That was next level nuts. *And why?*

When Danny had come back from seeing Sorcha earlier, he'd been full of the *WHAT WE KNOW* doc. His voice was still in her head.

'*You have to give that to the Guards.* Seriously, and that's me saying it. It's ready-made for my *Breaking News* feed or, even better, a true crime podcast.' She could see a lightbulb had gone on in his head, as if the idea had hit him while he was speaking and he needed a moment to catch up. Then he was back with her. 'Seriously, you've got a take on this that could take the Guards ages to get to. And they'll be able to check out your first theory about far-right political activists pretty fast, they keep tabs on groups like that. If they *are* going to find out who did this, they need as much info as you can give them – as soon as possible.'

She'd looked at him, his brown eyes sincere. He was right. Frankie had kept her voice low as she'd answered. 'I bet they don't even know those lads from Raven's Park were in our school this morning. I'll get Ollie to find out who we need to talk to. There's bound to be someone from the station in the bar tonight – they all drink there. Do you think they'll take us seriously?'

He'd kissed her on the top of the head. 'I think you guys have a bit of a reputation for problem-solving in Kilmurray Point.' His faced twitched into a smile. 'You've got form.' She'd play-thumped him. They hadn't been dating then, but he'd been involved in everything that had happened after Katie's party.

Katie had arrived then, looking worried, Becky's iPad in her hand. 'Becky's still downstairs. I saw her mum, and she says she's not responding as well as they hoped to the drugs, but they're going to keep her in that little ward beside the Emergency Department and see how she is in the morning. Her mum's really cross.'

Frankie had raised her eyebrows. 'Why's she cross?'

Katie had shrugged and rolled her eyes. 'I don't know really – they're doing their best. I think she's making this about her, she said something about her branch of psychotherapy – I wasn't really listening, to be honest; I know it sounds mean, but I haven't got room in my head for her problems. Becky's more important.' Katie sighed. 'I saw Aoife on the way – she said to say that she'd pop up to you before she goes home. She's due to finish at 8.30 but she's covering for someone for a couple of hours after that, and she said to text her if you need anything.'

As Katie had finished speaking a voice had come over the Tannoy to say visiting time was over.

'Come on, Danny, I'll drop you home, it's freezing out tonight. I'll be back tomorrow, Frankie. I'm not going to school – I'll bring you lunch if they haven't turfed you out.'

'I hope they have. Drive safe.' Frankie gave her a hug.

Now, in the darkness, Frankie reached for her phone with her good hand, hoping there was a message from Sorcha that she'd missed. Nothing yet. She scrolled through Rave-fess. It had been quiet for a while, and since the explosion seemed to be only updating in bursts. But that was understandable. Frankie looked at the time. Aoife still hadn't come up to see her and it was almost eleven, but perhaps she'd got caught up.

As if she'd heard her thinking about her, Frankie heard the ward doors suck open and a moment later Aoife popped her head around the curtains of her cubicle. She had her coat over her arm and her bag on her shoulder. She looked exhausted, her strawberry blonde curls escaping from her ponytail as if they'd had enough of the day too.

'How are you doing?'

Frankie smiled, her spirits lifting to see a friendly face. 'Can't wait to go home. How are the others?'

As Aoife put her bag down on the visitors' chair, Frankie's phone pinged with a message from Sorcha.

I'M IN, STAND BY.

Sorcha had accessed the CCTV – what on earth would she find? Frankie turned the screen over. Some things Aoife didn't need to know.

'I'm just on my way to check on Sorcha but everyone else is fine.' Aoife sounded exhausted. 'Ella wants to go down to see Becky in the morning. She's still really sore, but she needs to move around and we want Becky to know her friends are nearby. We'll have a better idea of Becky's condition tomorrow, and then we can decide where she needs to go.'

'Like to a ward, do you mean?'

'Maybe, or perhaps to another hospital that's more set up to treat her. But listen, I've got news.'

Ella's phone pinged with a message and her eyes fluttered open. She was barely asleep, her mind churning over everything. She'd hidden the photos she'd taken of Tiernan's phone screen in a folder on her own phone now, but not before she'd looked at them a second time and her stomach had turned over.

Ella had felt the shock reverberating through the girl's texts to Tiernan – how could he have shared them? Asking for them in the first place was bad enough, but to then share them, like Rainbow Princess was some sort of object …

That was the bit that had made Ella really mad.

Tiernan was a two-timing cheat, but he was also some sort of lower form of pond life that thought he could manipulate the girl he was cheating with by sharing her intimate pictures. That was even worse than being a two-timing cheat in the first place.

Ella had tried calling Rainbow Princess again. She hadn't answered, but this time Ella had recorded her voice message so she could play it back. There was something about her voice that Ella couldn't quite pin down, but she was sure she'd heard it before. Right now, though, Ella felt so dopey it was hard to tell if she was imagining it. She could be mixing it up with something she'd heard in a podcast or on YouTube. The message was so short that it was hard to tell, but there was something about her accent.

The one thing she did know was that the girl went to Raven's Hill, which narrowed it down a bit. But Ella knew there were loads of different accents in Fifth Year alone, and there were others in Sixth Year, and even Fourth Year. But Tiernan couldn't have been dating a *Fourth Year*, could he?

The thought made Ella feel sick. Tiernan was in Sixth Year. She could see how easy it could be for him to manipulate a Fourth Year into sending him photos. He could be very charming and very persuasive when he wanted something. Look how he'd charmed Ella into thinking he loved her. They'd been dating for two months and she hadn't realised.

Ella had decided to text her then, just in case Rainbow Princess was someone who never picked up her voice messages. Or, more likely, was deliberately not answering her phone. Unless she happened to have Ella's number, which was unlikely if Ella didn't have hers from one of the groups, she'd have no idea who was calling, and Ella didn't want to frighten her more.

Ella knew if they were her photos that had been circulated, she'd be hiding at home working out ways to change school and leave the country. Part of her curled up inside at the thought. She couldn't imagine how bad Rainbow Princess must be feeling, and reading the Ravefess posts, knowing everyone was talking about it, just made it a million times worse.

Getting a call from an unknown number could freak her out.

Ella's phone pinged again, and she picked it up. She'd slipped it under the covers beside her, so she didn't have to keep reaching for it. Even with the painkillers it hurt to breathe and the nurse had said to hold a pillow over her chest if she needed to cough. Thankfully she hadn't yet.

The phone screen was alight with a pile of incoming messages. It looked like a load had arrived before the one she'd just heard. Perhaps she had been asleep after all.

Confused, Ella looked at the screen.

They were all from Tiernan.

Maybe he was saying good night.

Or maybe not.

Another message came through:

Need you to answer babes

xxxxxxxxxx

What? Lots of kisses when it suited him.

Why did he need her to answer? And why now?

It was late, she was in hospital, she'd been blown up and had two broken ribs and a dose of painkillers. What could be so important at his end that he needed to wake her up and maybe disturb other people on the ward? Other sick people.

She scrolled back. The message before said:

> **Are you there, sweet pea??**
> xxoxoxxoxxxooxoxoxooooxox

She felt like texting back:

> **Not here. Never will be here.**
> **Go feck yourself.**

But before she got a chance another message came in.

> **Just message me babes.**
> **You know how much I love you**
> xoxooxx

Ella snorted and a pain shot through her chest, making her wince. *Loved* her? That was the funniest thing she'd heard all night. But he obviously wanted her for something. What on earth was this about?

She scrolled back to the first message. It had come in ten minutes ago.

> Cops here. Can't talk. Need to tell them that we were together on Friday night, you remember – okay?

The cops? *She remembered?* Ella felt her mouth drop open. They hadn't been together on Friday, and that was the weirdest way to phrase the text. It sounded like he thought someone else would be reading his messages.

Had Rainbow Princess reported him? The pieces began to fall into place in her head. If the cops were there to talk to him, there was a very good chance that they'd be looking through his phone. A smile began to curl across her face. Those pictures were going to take a lot of explaining if they found them.

But what had Friday night got to do with anything? Was that when the photos had been shared?

Ella wasn't sure. But one thing she *was* sure of was that Tiernan was asking her for an alibi.

And she knew where he could stick that one.

ST THOMAS'S WARD
ST ANTHONY'S HOSPITAL
11.05 p.m.
Frankie

Frankie patted the side of the bed. 'Tell me. And sit down, you look fit to drop. What did you hear?'

Aoife sighed. 'Thanks. Long day.' She added her coat to the visitor's chair and sat down heavily on the side of Frankie's bed. 'I was talking to one of the Guards downstairs – he's just brought in a D&D.'

Frankie cocked her eyebrow, confused. *What did Dungeons and Dragons have to do with Accident and Emergency?* As if Aoife realised, she continued, 'Drunk and disorderly. I was checking him in, and we got talking about what happened at Raven's Hill. You won't believe this.'

She paused and Frankie grabbed Aoife's arm, her voice a loud whisper. 'What? Tell me.'

Aoife grinned at her impatience. 'He's not detective unit, but he heard that they questioned the technician who looks after the Chemistry lab this afternoon, and they think they've found out what might have caused the explosion. Obviously, this isn't official yet but ...' Aoife pushed a curl back behind her ear. 'And this is totally confidential until the official version is released, so you can't breathe a word.'

Frankie pulled a *who, me?* face as Aoife continued. 'I'm sure it'll be public soon; your principal will want to stop all the wild rumours in the press.'

Frankie had looked at the headlines, but she'd seen the inaccuracies and clickbait reporting straight away, and she hadn't taken any of their reasoning seriously. Aoife was right that some of it was wild. Sorcha's master list of theories seemed way more sensible, and more importantly each one was a real possibility.

Aoife glanced over her shoulder at the curtains pulled around Frankie's bed, as if she was checking for eavesdroppers. But the ward was quiet, the gentle snores of the other patients rhythmic in the darkness.

Turning back to her, Aoife kept her voice low. 'Apparently, the lab assistant was clearing out some cupboards and she found a pot of something called 2, 4-Dinitrophenylhydrazine. I think I've got that right. She wasn't sure what it was, so she put it down next to a box of the equipment she was using to set up the experiment Mr Murray was going to demonstrate.' Aoife leaned closer to Frankie. 'The forensics guys found part of the container; that's what put them on to it. Basically, it's incredibly unstable and when it comes into contact with air, it can explode. Like *really* explode.'

Stunned, Frankie drew in a breath. 'Air?' She couldn't keep the shock out of her voice. 'What on earth was it doing in the lab?'

'It used to be used in an experiment on the old Leaving Cert syllabus, but most schools got rid of it when the syllabus changed. I googled it and a whole load of schools over the years have found it and had to call the bomb squad to get it professionally removed. It's stored in oil to keep it stable but if it dries out, it can be really dangerous.'

Frankie felt her mouth drop open. 'The army bomb disposal squad were called to Raven's Hill over the summer – there were photos of the soldiers all over Rave-fess for days. We couldn't believe it happened in the holidays and we missed all the uniforms. They blew something up in the middle of the field and it made this huge crater in the grass. Perhaps some got left behind?'

Aoife nodded. 'That's what it sounds like. The lab assistant said it was a really small pot – she took a photo of it next to her keys to show Mr Murray and ask him about it. The thing is, there was some sort of emergency, a spillage that she had to clear up – sometimes chemicals from a spill can linger in the air and she was really worried about someone breathing them in or them catching fire or something. That put her under pressure to get Mr Murray's experiment set up in time, and the class started before she could ask about it or move the box at the back.'

'That was why Mackenzie was coughing so much, because of the bleach. Sorcha said it was the main thing she remembered, but she's sure that there were two bangs. One really soon after the other, but definitely two.'

'I don't know about that, but Mackenzie had a big asthma attack. I can't imagine her breathing was helped by all the dust in the air, but the coughing would suggest something was affecting her before the explosion. They should really use a fume hood; if the fumes are flammable, even a phone could set them off.'

Frankie suddenly felt very pleased that she didn't do Chemistry. There was enough danger crossing the road to school these days without the risk of toxic fumes.

Aoife continued, 'Mackenzie's attack could definitely have been brought on by the lab assistant cleaning the surfaces with bleach before your lesson – that would be a reasonable trigger when you've a history of asthma.' She shifted on the bed. 'Anyway, this 2,4-DNPH as they call it looks like the culprit for the explosion. They just aren't sure what caused it to fall off the shelf and the container to break, but I'm sure it could have been knocked.'

Frankie grimaced. 'We think Becky started the potassium experiment; she filmed it – we reckon she wanted to get a video of the purple flash. If she found it at the back of the lab, with the flasks and stuff, she could have used too much. There was definitely a flash before the big bang. That doesn't explain Sorcha hearing two bangs, but if the potassium–water reaction created enough of a blast wave to knock this stuff off a shelf, and the pot smashed, it would be exposed to air.'

'And *boom*. Literally.' Aoife sighed. 'That sounds like a distinct possibility to me. Becky was at the back of the room, wasn't she?'

Frankie nodded, trying to process the information. It all made sense, but it *still* didn't explain the first sound Sorcha had heard.

How could something that dangerous have been missed? If it had fallen off the shelf in the supply cupboard it could have set off a chain reaction with all the other chemicals in there and blown up half the school. It sounded like the lab assistant was a bit vacant – Frankie wouldn't be surprised if she'd left the potassium right next to this 2,4-DNPH stuff. They were lucky that Becky hadn't picked that up and had it blow up in her face.

Frankie sighed. 'Wow, we were so sure that the explosion had been deliberate – there has been a whole load of mad stuff this week.'

Aoife reached over to give her a hug. 'Conspiracy theories tend to develop legs of their own. But no, thank God, it looks like it was an accident.'

'Did you say you're going to see Sorcha? We've both been too worried to sleep.'

'She's my next stop. Hopefully both of you can go home tomorrow. Ollie said her mum and dad and sister will be here in the morning, so she'll have someone to look after her. Now, sleep. I'm back in at 7.30 – I'll smuggle you in a croissant.'

Aoife was the best. Frankie hoped she and Ollie lasted. She was fabulous, and with her four brothers and her dad there *really* weren't enough women in her house – Aoife helped even up the numbers. And Max loved her.

Aoife reached for her bag and coat as Frankie picked up her phone. Aoife looked at her reproachfully. 'Franks, sleep really would be a good plan.'

'I'll sleep, I promise. I just need to update something.'

As she heard Aoife walk away, Frankie quickly texted to warn Sorcha that she was coming her way. She was brilliant, but Frankie was sure Aoife wouldn't be too impressed with them hacking the hospital security CCTV, even if it was for a very good reason.

Frankie let out a sigh of relief as a thumbs-up emoji appeared on her message. Turning onto her back, Frankie opened the Google doc Sorcha had created.

WHAT WE KNOW: Explosion in Chemistry Lab, Raven's Hill School: <u>A purple flash AND TWO BANGS</u>

Six girls in St Anthony's Hospital: Frankie in
St Thomas's Ward, Sorcha in St Joan's Ward,
Ella in St Valentine's Ward, Mackenzie in ICU,
Maeve in St Raphael's Surgical Recovery Ward,
Becky in Emergency Department side ward

~~Gas explosion~~

Accident? How? Abandoned chemical

~~Deliberate: if so,~~ **who** ~~was the target?~~

~~Theory #1: Mackenzie/international girls —
racist attack?~~

~~Theory #2: Revenge against Mr Murray.~~

~~Theory #3: Maeve knows who is in the photos.~~

~~Theory #4: Threat ref Jasper assault?~~

Theory #5: Accident?

Googling the name of the chemical, Frankie found
the news reports that Aoife had mentioned about the
bomb disposal squad being called to the other schools.
Frankie added a line to their doc.

Theory #5: Accident – potassium/
water reaction caused
2,4-Dinitrophenylhydrazine to explode.

BUT *what* was the first bang if this was the
second one? What set it off?

She added a question mark after 'accident'.

There was still stuff going on at Raven's Hill that they
needed to get to the bottom of.

Jasper's assault wasn't an accident.

And the naked photos weren't an accident.

*And someone was pretending to be Sorcha's sister Beth
and asking lots of questions.*

Would the morning bring any answers?

TUESDAY

TUESDAY

'**G**ood morning. How are you feeling?'

Maeve opened one eye to see who was speaking. Then she registered the uniform and hair pulled back in a ponytail and realised that the voice belonged to a nurse. The information took a minute for Maeve to process as she looked around her. She could see polystyrene ceiling tiles and blue curtains, a tubular white metal frame at the end of the bed. Why was she in a hospital?

But the how and why wasn't her first problem. 'Terrible. Can I have a glass of water? I'm so thirsty.'

The nurse smiled. She was pretty. Her green scrubs were a sort of turquoise colour that made her eyes look super blue. 'Of course, here you go.'

Picking up a glass from beside the bed and leaning over, the nurse tilted Maeve's head so she could take a sip. The water was warm, but she really needed it. She could feel her lips were dry, her throat sore.

'Oh God, thanks, that's much better.'

The nurse put the glass down as Maeve looked at her searchingly. 'What happened?'

'My name's Aoife. I'm usually in the Emergency Department, I was there when you were brought in yesterday, but I know Frankie, so I've been keeping an eye on you all.'

'Frankie? Frankie O'Sullivan? She's here too?' Surprised, Maeve interrupted her. What did she mean *all*?

'Yes, she's broken her wrist but she should be going home today. There are a few of you here. There was a bit of an accident at your school. An explosion in the Chemistry lab. Can you remember any of it?'

Maeve tried to think. Chemistry. Mr Murray had gone out with the other half of the class, and she'd been trying to find a lab coat that fitted. Ella had been there, and Sorcha. And then there had been a flash at the back. Had it been pink, or maybe purple?

'A bit. There was this huge bang. Is everyone else okay?'

Aoife nodded. 'That's right. And everyone's fine. You're all a bit battered but nothing for you to worry about.'

'But how?'

'We can tell you later; it's important you rest now. You had to have surgery, but you should be on the mend.' Aoife's eyes were warm.

'*That's* why I feel like I got hit by a truck.'

Aoife smiled sympathetically. 'We'll keep on top of your pain medication. There's a button by your head – if you need anything buzz immediately. I have to go back downstairs but the nurses on this floor will be in to check you. Don't wait to buzz if you're worried about anything.'

Maeve let out a shaky sigh. 'Is my phone here?'

Maeve could see Aoife's mouth twitch. 'Your mum said she'd be in as soon as you woke up, and Tara was here all day yesterday. They left their numbers, so I'll let them both know you're back with us. I'm afraid your phone might not have survived so well. There's quite a lot of rubble but the Guards will get it back to you if they find it.'

'The Guards?' This was all getting very confusing. And Maeve felt so tired, like she just wanted to sleep.

'The Guards had to investigate, in case the explosion wasn't an accident.'

Okay, that made sense. Sort of. *In case it wasn't an accident?* What on earth had happened?

Maeve knew Tara would tell her everything when she got there. Maeve took a breath. There was something she needed to tell Tara. Something really … It was to do with her phone, she was sure.

It took her a few moments to work out what it was.

'Can you give Tara a message? It's *really* important.'

'Of course, I'll call her in a sec, and I'll let your friends know you're okay – they've been asking for you.'

'Can you just tell Tara that the photos are ColourMeHappy? She'll know which photos – it's an Instagram account I follow. I don't know who she is, but I'm sure they were taken in the same place she does her filming.'

RAVE-FESS
ONLINE
8.30 a.m.

Explosion update: Fellow armchair detectives
stand down. Hot press! Some of the stuff the
bomb disposal squad removed during the
summer got missed! Guards think it blew up in
the lab.

That's mad, how did it get missed?
How did no one realise? What was it
anyway?

I heard Jennifer the lab technician
found it but didn't know what it was.

Could you imagine if the army
hadn't come, it could have blown up
half the school!!!

Isn't she supposed to know what chemicals are? Does she not use Google?

Maybe it wasn't clear on label. Thank goodness everyone's okay.

Heard everyone okay except Becky Hartigan, still in a coma.

Just heard Tiernan Reece from Sixth Year in Raven's Park got arrested last night!!! Will update when know more.

Isn't he the one with the amazing car?

I heard he was dating Ella Diamond??? What did he do?

Allegedly he beat up Jasper Parks from Raven's Park Model UN team on Friday night.

How do you know all this? Who's dating a Guard and hasn't said?!

Probably someone's brother.

OR SISTER, eh hello.

The minute Sorcha opened her eyes, she reached for her phone, cursing herself that she hadn't set an alarm. Last night she'd managed to access the hospital security camera recordings, and cross referencing with a professional photo of Becky's mum she'd found online, had made the first breakthrough discovery at about 1 a.m.: a girl with long, dark brown hair wearing a black hoodie and leggings had stopped to talk to her in the Emergency Department corridor.

But she'd been wearing a surgical facemask as if she was worried about airborne germs, and her face was turned away from the camera.

Was she the girl who had claimed to be Beth? The timing seemed right.

Sorcha had switched to different cameras, following their progress outside to the smoking area where Becky's mum had had a cigarette. The girl went back inside just as Danny appeared with the pile of pizza boxes.

Was she trying to avoid him?

Sorcha had pushed herself as far as she could, but the events of the previous day had begun to catch up with her in a pounding headache that made her vision blur. She might be super fit and have a dogged determination that had taken her to the top of the county swim league, but in the end she'd had to admit defeat and pass what she had to Beth, who had been working alongside her as soon as she'd got home last night and caught up on Sorcha's texts.

Now, despite the noise and clatter and comings and goings on the ward, Sorcha had only just woken up.

But her WhatsApp had been busy. Sorcha couldn't believe it as she looked at the additional stills and video that Beth had sent through in the early hours of the morning.

Looking at the time on the last message, 6 a.m., Beth had been working at it all night. In the movies detectives whizzed through CCTV footage, but in reality, it was incredibly tedious to watch, and the cameras in the hospital weren't amazing quality, which made concentrating on the slightly blurred footage even harder. At least the video was in colour.

But Beth had come up trumps.

Sorcha flicked between the different images that Beth had grabbed from the CCTV cameras, each one telling a different part of the story. The first image they had was of the girl talking to Becky's mum at 7 p.m., but Beth had gone back further, checking cameras all over the hospital from the time of the explosion. The same girl had waited in the main reception area before speaking to the nurses behind the desk at just after 3 p.m. She'd been across the atrium when Jess had arrived just after 6 p.m., Jess's purple hair unmistakable.

Then she'd been at the nurses' station on the second floor right outside Sorcha's ward and then had walked repeatedly up and down outside Ella's ward.

Beth had found more footage of her coming out of the stairwell later in the evening. Jess had appeared right behind her and gone along the corridor to Ella's ward, followed by a boy Sorcha was sure was Tiernan. He'd only stayed a few minutes, had appeared at the ward door and pulled the collar of his rugby shirt up, shouldering on a team fleece before he headed for the lifts. He looked a lot like the boy she'd heard talking on the other side of the drinks machine. She'd only seen him from the back, but who wore their rugby shirt collar pulled up anymore?

Even on the grainy recording, this girl was everywhere. And even with her mask on, Sorcha had a strong idea who she was. She just needed to find a photo from Ardmore Park to be absolutely sure, but it was her trainers that gave her away – Louboutin suede sneakers with spikes. The camera had caught them multiple times as she'd passed Ella's ward, the red soles flashing against the grey-blue lino floor.

But why would Hailey de Búrca be here, in St Anthony's Hospital, and why was she pretending to be Beth?

BULLET JOURNAL
Behind Every Successful
Woman is Herself

I'm all set. I've got a gym bag with
me with night things in it so I
can say I'm checking in if anyone
challenges me, look confused, pretend
I've got the wrong place. People
always seem to have bags with them
in hospitals, it'll help me blend in.

I found a letter online about an
appointment for something horrible-
sounding at another hospital. I've
used it as a template, so I'll be able
to wave around some paperwork if I
need to.

It pays to be prepared.

And I've got my fake ID, and the
name matches the letter. Today, fans,
I'm Sorcha's sister, Elizabeth Bennett.

Even if the spelling isn't quite
right, *Pride and Prejudice* is my
favourite, it couldn't be better.

More importantly, I know exactly what I've got to do. I can fix Becky no problem. I read about air bubbles in drips being fatal — that should only take seconds.

Ella's a bit trickier, but it turns out there's a cocktail of drugs in my mum's bathroom, and now they are all crushed up in a little bottle of sparkling French wine with zero alcohol. It's not exactly Bolly but it's like rocket fuel — on the way back from the hospital I ran into the fancy deli on the Main Street and got a really cute mini peach juice bottle to go with it. I've no idea of how much it will take to knock her out properly, so just in case I have to add more later, I've brought the powder with me.

Ella's always posting about how much she loves Bellinis. Today she's going to have the strongest one of her life. Mixed with her pain medication it should give her a nice long sleep. And once she's asleep, if she were to get her face caught in her pillow, she'll stay asleep. She might need some help there, so I'll go back up after I've sorted things with Becky.

And then everything will be perfect. It'll be just me and T. Like it should always have been. He worked hard to catch my eye but he's mine now. And I don't share.

He should know that. He will do now.

All Hail the Queen.

He's not answering his phone again, but I'm not worried. We'll catch up later and celebrate with a proper bottle of Bolly. It's time to go public.

Now I just need to pick my moment. I need to look like I'm meant to be here.

Everyone's so busy, it should be easy.

ST THOMAS'S WARD
ST ANTHONY'S HOSPITAL
9.05 a.m.
Frankie

Frankie yawned and leaned back on her pillows looking at her phone, trying to work out where she should start with her messages. She'd been very pleased to see Aoife with a bag of croissants, and toast and marmalade had never tasted so good earlier this morning, but in the five minutes it had taken her to eat her breakfast, her phone had literally started hopping. It was going to take her ages to go through everything and reply, and even more messages were coming in now.

Frankie rolled the metal breakfast tray stand towards herself and rested her cast on it so she could hold the phone and scroll at the same time. It wasn't ideal, but scrolling with the heavy cast didn't work either. She was fed up with this whole broken wrist situation already, and apparently she had another four to six weeks to go.

The year group WhatsApp was flying like the updates on Sky News and their group chat had a whole side conversation unfurling, on top of individual messages to Frankie. And that was before she even got to Rave-fess.

She decided to start with their private group messages; she could save Rave-fess for later.

Frankie smiled to herself. Danny had sent her another sunshine emoji, asking if she'd slept okay. A warm feeling flooded through her.

As she was about to read the next message, a new one popped in from Sorcha.

> Found out who was impersonating Beth – I think it's Hailey de Búrca – she was here all day yesterday??? Why and why?

Frankie looked at her phone screen, shocked. *Wow, had Hailey got something to do with all of this after all?*

But now they knew the 2,4-DNPH had been the reason for the explosion. The big explosion, at least.

Sorcha's insistence that there had been two bangs came back to Frankie. Even after Aoife had left last night it had been in the back of Frankie's mind. She looked at her phone, frowning, then sent Sorcha a reply.

> Look at *WHAT WE KNOW* for latest update.

Frankie's phone pinged again, but it wasn't Sorcha responding, it was a text from Jess. Frankie scanned it, wondering why she hadn't used the group WhatsApp.

> How are you feeling? Message from Tara. Maeve awake, doing good. She thinks naked photos are of ColourMeHappy???

Frankie narrowed her eyes and read it again.

How could a massive Instagram influencer be at their school, and they didn't know it? That seemed a bit unlikely. Surely Maeve was mistaken? Maybe that's why Jess had messaged her privately. Another message came through.

> Can't see how M can be right.

Frankie messaged back:

> Perhaps she's misremembered. What made her think that?

Jess's next message was longer:

> Tara said Maeve realised the girl
> in them had the same book in one
> of her photos as ColourMeHappy,
> and the same medication. She
> takes same brand.

Frankie screwed up her nose, thinking, then sent a message back.

> But loads of people take the
> same brand of meds, and we've
> all got similar books. So there's
> no actual proof?

> How could we have someone
> that huge in our school and not
> know?

> We all follow that account; unless
> she's super clever, there would
> have been something else in her
> photos to give us a clue.

Jess came straight back:

> Agree. Not going to say anything
> just in case.

Jess was right. Maeve was obsessed with the ColourMeHappy account; perhaps everything had got mixed up in her head. She'd had a pretty traumatic few days.

The next message was from Sorcha and made her sit up.

Have you checked Rave-fess???

Part of Frankie's stomach fell. What had happened *now*? She couldn't really deal with any more bad news. Frankie opened the site on her phone.

Around Frankie the ward was getting busy – other patients being moved, everyone's blood pressure being taken, or at least that's what it looked like to Frankie. But she could barely concentrate, as she read the latest Rave-fess post again. It was as if the shock waves were coming off her phone. This was huge news.

Tiernan had been arrested for beating up Jasper.

This must have been what Jess meant last night but couldn't say anything about. She'd said it was big.

Had Ella seen this? Frankie felt her heart flood with worry. Ella would be devastated. She was mad about him.

Even if Tiernan *was* actually a total scumbag.

He had to be absolutely horrible to pick on Jasper. Frankie had only met him once when she'd gone to support Jess at a Model UN debate, but his nickname

– Squirrel – suited him. He was gentle and curious and passionate about debating ... And Tiernan had half killed him ...

Danny had felt Ella's amazing boyfriend had been very spiky when he'd met him yesterday. He could be like that all the time, but equally, visiting your girlfriend in the same hospital where the guy you'd just beaten to a pulp had been admitted must have been a bit fraught.

Frankie had a feeling there was more to this story that they were yet to learn. *What on earth could have prompted an attack like that?*

'Good morning, Frankie, how are you feeling?'

A nurse in dark blue scrubs appeared at the end of her bed, and picked up her clipboard, making her jump.

'This all looks great; I gather you're feeling better.'

'Much, thanks. I was wondering ...'

The nurse interrupted her. 'If you can go home?' She smiled at Frankie's nod. 'That's what I'm here for. Do you need to call anyone to pick you up?'

Oh, thank God. Maybe she could go down and see Ella and Becky on the way out.

What the hell's going on?

Why haven't you replied??

Have you got the photos???

Hello, photos and video are all in very safe hands. We need to have a chat about them.

????? Someone said you'd been arrested??? WTF is going on???

This is Kilmurray Point Garda Station, a detective will be with you in a few moments to explain. We look forward to talking to you.

iMessage ➤ 🎤

When Frankie got to Ella's ward, she could see from the doorway that Ella's curtains were closed. She hovered for a minute. It wasn't visiting time but the nurse who had discharged her had said she'd be fine to slip in to see Ella, once she didn't stay long.

Did Ella know about Tiernan? Oh God, Frankie suddenly realised that she was going to have to tell her if she didn't.

Frankie pushed the ward door open with her shoulder and headed down to Ella's bed, slipping inside the curtains.

Ella looked like she hadn't been awake long – her hair was mussed up, but she was still managing to look very together in a gorgeous pair of pink satin pyjamas. And her smile was real.

'I am *so* glad to see you. Are they letting you go home?'

Frankie dumped her backpack on the floor, pulling the chair around with her good hand, and sat down. 'Yep, I just have to come back in for this.' She waved the cast. 'But otherwise I'm all good. Sorcha is too. Her mum and dad landed early this morning and her sister arrived last night; I'm meeting them at reception shortly. Mum's taking us all out for hot chocolate. Well, not exactly out – we're going to the hotel bar.'

Sitting down and looking at Ella properly, Frankie realised her eyes were red-rimmed under her make-up. It looked like she hadn't slept well.

Frankie could relate to that.

'That sounds heavenly. I'd love a hot chocolate. But look, someone's left me the makings of a non-alcoholic Bellini, isn't that sweet? I bet it was Amber, she knows I love them, and she'd know I couldn't drink with all these pain meds.'

Frankie laughed. '*Everyone* knows you love them. They're all over your Insta. Will I make it for you?'

Ella smiled warmly. 'Please. Look, she even left a fancy cocktail glass. No note, but that's Amber all over, she can be such an airhead.'

Frankie smothered a grin; she didn't know Amber that well, but she'd helped her through a bout of 'food poisoning' at Katie's party that had been an interesting experience.

Frankie leaned forward and started to peel the gold foil off the top of the bottle, twisting the wire to release the cork. It really was the cutest thing. She paused. She really needed two thumbs to pop the cork, but maybe she could pull it with her good hand.

It took her a few moments but then it came free, with a very disappointing dull sound, as if the gas had somehow already been released.

'Oh, sorry, that wasn't very sparkling sounding, was it?' Frankie looked at the cork critically. 'I hope it's not gone off. You don't want an upset stomach on top of everything else.'

Ella peered at the bottle. 'There does look like there's some sediment. Maybe it's a bit old or something. I'll see if it tastes okay.'

Frankie poured the sparkling wine into the glass and picked up the peach juice. It looked like the lid had already been untwisted. Amber must have done it so Ella didn't have to strain and hurt her ribs more – she was so thoughtful. But both bottles felt cold; she must have just missed her.

Frankie looked at the glass closely – the mixture did look a bit cloudy. 'You're right, maybe just sip a tiny bit. Ollie's been teaching me to make cocktails – he says you always have to use the best ingredients.'

Ella's eyebrows rose in question.

'He says it'll be useful if my photography career doesn't take off. He's helpful like that.' Frankie handed her the glass.

'Brothers are all heart, aren't they? Mine's only doing the Junior Cert.'

Ella's brother. Frankie stopped for a moment as a thought began to formulate about Beth's impersonator. It had been on her mind all night. But right now she needed to concentrate on Ella. 'Ollie says it's useful to have skills you can use anywhere in the world, in case you decide to travel.'

Ella took a sip of the Bellini. 'That doesn't taste amazing, but maybe it's just having non-alcoholic wine that makes it taste different.' Ella handed it back to Frankie. 'I'll have a bit more in a minute. It seems a shame to waste it after Amber's gone to so much trouble.' Ella winced as she shifted position in the bed. 'So, what's the news? I forgot to plug my phone in last night and actually it's quite nice not having it constantly updating. Amber probably left me a message about breakfast cocktails – she loves any excuse to celebrate.'

If she hadn't looked at her phone, Ella didn't know about Tiernan yet. Yikes. Frankie kept her face neutral as the thought shot through her head.

Gathering herself, Frankie leaned forwards, her voice low. 'Did you hear about the reason for the explosion?'

Ella's eyes opened wide. 'No, do they know what happened?'

It only took Frankie a moment to update her. 'Sorcha is still sure she heard two bangs, but Becky was definitely filming the reaction. It's possible that she used a bit too much potassium and the energy it created knocked this other stuff off the shelf.'

Ella screwed up her face. 'Why on earth was she doing that?'

Frankie shrugged. 'I think it might have been something to do with the colour. She had some photos of purple things on her iPad. Pretty book covers and flowers. Sorcha thought she might be creating a colour folder, you know, like that account.'

'ColourMeHappy.' They said it almost together.

Frankie smiled. 'So many people follow that girl.'

'Yep, me too.' Ella said, like it all made perfect sense. 'I've got a whole folder of pink. ColourMeHappy said making folders can really help your mood. Perhaps Becky was doing that.'

'Maybe. Maeve's always talking about yellow too. She's probably got a bunch of photos saved. But listen, Maeve told Tara she thinks ColourMeHappy goes to our school.'

Ella started to laugh, but stopped quickly, her hand around her chest. 'Oh my God, that hurts too much. Seriously? How did she work that out?'

'Well, apparently she saw those nude photos and there was something in one of them that is the same as something she saw in a ColourMeHappy post.'

Ella shook her head slowly. 'That's mad. She's

obsessed. There's no way that's right. But poor Becky, why did she try the experiment? We were about to watch Mr Murray do it in class.'

'Maybe she wanted to film it – you know what Mr Murray's like with phones. I've really no idea.' Frankie paused. 'Sorcha and Jess and I had this list of theories for the whole explosion thing. We thought someone in the class could have been a target.'

'I was wondering about that too; it was just so random. Too random to be random, if you know what I mean.' Ella's face clouded. 'Things really aren't always what they seem.'

'That's for sure.' Frankie hesitated for a moment, wincing inside. *This was so awkward.* 'So, if your phone was dead, you haven't seen Rave-fess yet this morning?'

Ella shook her head. 'Should I have?'

Frankie curled up inside. 'It's just there was a post about Tiernan.' Ella's eyebrows shot up as she continued, 'He was arrested last night. For attacking Jasper Parks, Jess's friend, on Friday night.'

'Really?' Ella looked stunned, but not in the way Frankie had expected. 'Jasper? On Friday? Wow.' It took her a moment to absorb the news. Then she must have read the concern on Frankie's face. 'You are lovely, but don't look so worried – we broke up. Properly.'

Frankie looked at her, her mouth falling open.

'Yes, I was pretty surprised too. He's a total cheat.'

Ella reached for her phone, still on charge, opening it to show Frankie a screenshot of a girl's lips, bright with red lipstick, a diamond piercing like a beauty spot beside her mouth. 'I found this on his phone.'

The image had been sent from All Hail the Queen. Below it, the message was short:

> Soon you'll be all mine.

Ella shook her head. 'I wish I could stomach more of that cocktail – we should be celebrating. I never want to see him again. I hope he rots.'

EMERGENCY DEPARTMENT SIDE WARD
ST ANTHONY'S HOSPITAL
10 a.m.
Frankie

When Frankie got out of the lift on the ground floor, she knew exactly where to go. After seeing Ella, she really wanted to look in on Becky before she left the hospital.

Frankie had always liked Becky; she was shy but once you got to know her she was so creative. She'd had brilliant ideas for their Gatsby video. The thought of her lying in hospital in some sort of frozen state made Frankie's heart break. Perhaps hearing her friends' voices really would help her come back to them. It was worth a try. Frankie had read somewhere about music helping people in comas. Perhaps if they played happy music, that would help too.

To her left, the corridor behind the emergency department had trolleys lined up along one side and a scattering of exhausted-looking visitors hovering beside them. There was an air of desperation that surrounded them like a cloud. Further down the corridor were the dark grey double doors that she'd spent much too long looking at the previous day. Right now, they were firmly closed.

Frankie hitched her backpack onto her good shoulder. Telling Ella about Tiernan hadn't been as bad as she'd expected, thank goodness.

Just before Frankie left, Ella had opened WhatsApp to find a pile of messages. She hadn't even checked to see if they were from him – instead she'd gone straight to read the new post on Rave-fess. And had actually smirked.

Frankie felt her jaw tighten as she thought about Tiernan Reece, her head filling with expletives. According to Ella he was a two-timing cheat, and being arrested for beating up Jasper was just one of his problems. She hadn't wanted to say more, but it had made Frankie wonder about the nude photographs. Ella obviously knew something she wasn't going to share, and Tiernan was in the Raven's Park rugby team.

Maybe Frankie was joining the dots all wrong, but there seemed to be an awful lot of dots pointing in Tiernan's direction.

'Hi, Frankie, how are you feeling? I heard you'd been discharged.'

Frankie swung around to see Aoife walking towards her, a clipboard in her hand.

'I'm good, I'm going to meet Mum soon, but I was wondering if I could see Becky?'

Aoife smiled. 'That's lovely of you. I think she could do with hearing all the friendly voices she can. She's that way.' Aoife pointed in the direction of the ED ward beside the one that Frankie had been brought into originally. 'You guys have had a tough time; I still can't believe that lab assistant of yours left out such dangerous chemicals.'

Frankie rolled her eyes. 'It must have been a mistake. But you know Sorcha's convinced there were two bangs, that something else set it off. I hope the Guards don't stop looking now they think they've got the answer.'

'I'm sure they won't. How's Sorcha this morning? She'll be glad to see her family.'

'She's being discharged too; her mum and sister are meeting us at reception.'

'It's funny that her sister doesn't look anything like her, isn't it? Sorcha's so tiny, I sort of expected her sister to be too. You and Ollie and the twins and Max all look really alike. Sorcha looks more like you guys than she does Beth.'

Frankie looked at her, confused. Aoife knew Sorcha fairly well, they'd met in the family kitchen of the Berwick Castle Hotel often enough, but Beth had been travelling for most of the summer. Frankie didn't think they'd ever met. 'Beth's a bit taller than Sorcha but not much. They look pretty similar; Beth has that same pixie vibe.'

It was Aoife's turn to look confused. She pulled a face. 'She's really slim, same dark hair, but long?'

Frankie shook her head slowly as Aoife continued, 'But she said hello. She knew who I was. She said she'd just been with Sorcha.' Aoife's brow creased. 'I asked her about Edinburgh – she said it rained a lot … She was wearing a mask, she was worried about bringing airport germs into the hospital …'

Frankie's mind flew into overdrive. Aoife was wearing a badge with her name on it: it wouldn't be hard to pretend you knew her, and she must see a million people a day. 'Did she mention the airport *after* you asked about Edinburgh?' Then, more urgently, 'When did you see her?'

'About two minutes ago – she's just gone in to see Becky.'

Frankie felt Aoife's words hit her in the chest like the original blast wave that had sent her flying.

'I don't think that was Beth.'

INTENSIVE CARE UNIT
ST ANTHONY'S HOSPITAL
10 a.m.
Mackenzie

'How you feeling?' Mackenzie heard Greg's voice and opened her eyes. Lying back on the bed, one arm tethered to her drip as if it was an anchor, she was still feeling a bit disorientated. And totally exhausted.

She knew the scientific explanation about what happened when she had an asthma attack, about the build-up of carbon dioxide in her system, how toxic and life-threatening it could be. But it felt like being a fish out of water when it happened, the panic growing as she fought to take a proper breath. The inhalers and medication helped day to day, the oxygen and nebulisers when she got to hospital, but every time it was more frightening.

Mackenzie patted the blankets, reaching for Greg's hand as she looked up at him. He grinned. 'They said you were awake. Mom's just landed, and she's on her way.'

Mackenzie felt a surge of relief. It always took her a while to get over a big attack – the hospital could help her breathe again but the shock didn't leave as easily. She needed her mom now.

'What happened? I can remember this loud noise and then Becky was pushing me off the stool …'

'There was an explosion. A really big one. Your friends Jess and Frankie and Sorcha have been trying to work out what happened.'

Mackenzie's eyebrows shot up. 'A what? How the …?'

Greg squeezed her hand. 'Some explosive chemical was left on the worktop – turns out it was like a ticking bomb. They don't know what set it off yet but some of your friends think Becky might have found some potassium and tried to do the experiment.' He shrugged. 'The cops are working it out.'

Mackenzie frowned, trying to figure out the pieces. They were like bits of a jigsaw that had been tossed on the floor, but as Greg spoke, the picture was slowly starting to form. Becky had opened the window beside them to get rid of the smell of bleach. The blind had rattled with a gust of wind that had made Mackenzie shiver, but at least the air had been fresher.

Becky had seemed a bit subdued, more than just worried about her homework. Mackenzie had been about to ask her if she was okay.

'Becky was talking about that Instagram account, the colour one everyone's following – about how she was collecting videos and photos to make mood boards.' Mackenzie paused. 'I remember her saying dark purple represented sadness and frustration, but lighter shades are creativity and magic. And something about amethyst stones giving you wisdom and inspiration. She had one in her pencil case.' Mackenzie bit her lip. 'I wasn't looking at her, but I remember seeing a flash out of the corner of my eye and then she sort of shoved me under the bench.'

'It sounds like Becky got between you and the blast; she must have pushed you out of the way.'

Mackenzie nodded slowly. 'It all happened so fast. I'd been coughing, and then it got really hard to breathe. I don't remember anything after that.' Panic suddenly flared inside her.

There was one thing she *could* remember very clearly.

'What day is it? What's happening with the photos?'

'It's Tuesday, and in …' Greg looked at his phone, 'about an hour and a half the twenty-four hours will be up.'

Mackenzie felt a jolt of fear shoot through her, but Greg looked almost happy. He was sort of smirking.

'But … what's happening?' The fear that was coursing through her made her voice wobble. Greg squeezed her hand.

'Don't worry, the clock stopped ticking at about 9.30 last night.' He grinned, 'Squirrel's fine – well, not exactly fine, but he's going to be okay. And Jess's dad has been amazing.'

Mackenzie felt her eyebrows shoot up – *what had Jess's dad got to do with all of this?*

Greg smiled, pausing before he continued, as if he was enjoying every word. 'Tiernan Reece has been arrested for attacking Jasper, and Jess's dad has run a story about bullying in Raven's Park. I haven't been in this morning but loads of people have texted to say it's hitting the fan big time. Some bishop has arrived to talk to the principal, apparently. Which seems to be a huge deal. I guess the bishop is his boss.'

It took a moment for the news to sink in. 'So, it's all okay?'

Greg smiled. 'It really is. There's no way Tiernan can deny it's him in the photos, and the Guards have some sort of forensics, something they found on the field that ties him to it as well. I think it was a button, but it had Jasper's blood on it.' Greg looked at her seriously. 'Without knowing it was Tiernan's they didn't have anything to check for a match, it's not like he's on a criminal database or anything, but now they have a suspect, they can tie it all together with my photos.'

'Oh, thank God.' Mackenzie felt as if a weight had literally been lifted off her.

Greg rubbed her arm. 'We'll find out more soon. Right now, you need to get better. Mom's staying at your friend Frankie's hotel. Jess's dad sorted it all out.'

'How did Jess's dad get involved?' Mackenzie looked at him, confused.

'I bumped into Jess last night. I remembered you

telling me he was a journalist.' Greg rubbed his face. 'The short version is that Jess persuaded me to talk to him. I showed him the video and he took it to the Guards. I'll have to give a witness statement, but I think it's going to be fine.' He grinned again, the relief clear on his face. 'Tiernan won't dare come near me now, and his friends are being brought in too.'

ownstairs in the Emergency Department, Frankie barrelled through the doors of the ward that Becky was in and looked around frantically for her bed. The curtains were drawn around one in the far corner. Running towards it, Frankie ripped the curtains apart, cursing her sling and her broken wrist.

Becky was lying inside the curtained cubicle, her red curls spread across the pillow, surrounding her like a halo. She didn't look good at all. Her eyes were open, but she was sort of staring at the ceiling, like she was frozen or something. Frankie faltered at the sight of her. *No wonder Becky's mum had been upset.*

Behind her, Frankie heard the ward doors thumping, swinging with the force that she'd run through them, and Aoife's voice: 'What on earth are you doing, Frankie? You can't just ...'

Frankie stood stock still, every muscle tense. Where was 'Beth'? Had she run out the far doors when she'd heard Frankie coming? Had Frankie been quick enough to catch her?

Then Frankie spotted a movement. Someone was crouching on the other side of the bed, half under it, a manicured hand in a dark sleeve snaking up Becky's drip stand.

The girl who was impersonating Beth.

It had taken Frankie a while to figure it out, but she'd realised, as she left Ella, that Ella had mentioned her little brother. She didn't have any sisters. Frankie had four brothers, Jess was an only child, Maeve had a brother too. Sorcha was the only one of them here who had a sister, and a sister who was quite close in age to them all. Beth was in her second year at Edinburgh University.

Whoever this was had done their homework. Which creeped Frankie out even more than the security stills that Sorcha had shared earlier – someone had been checking up on them all. She obviously had a strong motive for hiding her identity.

In the split second that the girl's hand moved towards the infusion line taped into Becky's frozen arm, Frankie yelled at her.

'Leave her alone. Don't touch that!'

'What's going on?' Aoife arrived behind her as Franke sprinted around the bed, reaching for the girl's arm and grabbing her wrist as tightly as she could with her good hand. The girl immediately reacted, trying to pull away and crawl under the bed. But Frankie was ready for her and she wasn't loosening her grip. She put all her weight into pulling her back out from under the metal-framed bed.

'Let go of me. How dare you grab me?' The girl had long, dark hair and was wearing a black hoodie. As she snarled at Frankie and tried to fight herself free, slapping Frankie's good hand hard, the surgical face mask that was hiding half her face came unhooked, and Frankie could see that she had a diamond piercing, like a beauty spot, close to her lip.

Was this the girl Tiernan had been cheating on Ella with, the girl who had sent him suggestive photos of her lips?

Still trying to pull away from Frankie, the girl twisted and changed direction. Instead of trying to get further under the bed, she scrambled out and tried to push Frankie backwards. Staggering, one hand trapped in her sling, Frankie didn't let go, but with the movement, she caught sight of the girl's trainers. Louboutin black suede hi-tops with silver metal spikes on the toes and heels.

This had to be Hailey de Búrca. *All Hail the Queen.*

Struggling to stand, using Frankie's weight to lever herself up, Hailey tried to lash out. But she was built like a straw. For once in her life Frankie was very glad that she was bigger than Sorcha, and clearly significantly heavier than Hailey.

Hailey tried to thump Frankie, aiming for her cast. Still holding Hailey's wrist in a vice-like grip, Frankie dodged, protecting her broken wrist. Hailey lifted her foot to kick out at Frankie, the spikes on the toes of her trainers gleaming in the fluorescent lights. Frankie was wearing her jeans, but she wasn't about to risk being gored.

Now she'd really had enough.

Watching her twin brothers Cian and Kai training at home, she often joined in their Taekwondo sparring sessions. And they practised self-defence with her whenever they could, teaching her simple but effective moves.

Frankie had been in this situation – in her kitchen – many times before. But she hadn't been nearly this mad before.

Holding onto Hailey's wrist, Frankie yanked it and twisted it up behind her back, at the same time hooking her foot in front of Hailey's leg to destabilise her. It worked, and Frankie pushed Hailey hard onto the end of the bed, away from Becky's drip stand. Trapped, Hailey kicked out behind her, at the same time looking up and trying to appeal to Aoife.

'This girl's crazy. I was feeling a bit faint, and she just *grabbed* me.'

'Why is Frankie always the last to arrive?' Frankie's mum looked impatiently at her watch. She was wearing a navy trouser suit and heels, and had her blonde hair clipped up. Leaning back against the wall in the hospital reception area, Jess exchanged an amused glance with Sorcha, who was sitting opposite her sister Beth on one of the easy chairs, her backpack on her knee. Sorcha opened her mouth to say something, but Liz, Sorcha's mum, shot Sorcha a warning look.

'I'm sure she's on her way, Sinéad. I can bring these guys back to the hotel if you need to go.' Liz leaned forward on the plastic-covered sofa they'd gathered around. She looked exhausted; her flight had been delayed as well last night. 'I can get a cab; you head off for your meeting.'

Frankie's mum shook her head impatiently. 'It's ridiculous getting a cab when I've the hotel minibus outside – that was the whole point of everyone meeting here, I thought?'

Jess could feel the tension brewing again. Apparently, it had been Liz's idea to collect Sorcha and Frankie and meet everyone here this morning, but she hadn't checked with Frankie's mum, who had a meeting with her contact in the Health and Safety office scheduled for 11. And Max had been so excited to see his aunt and uncle that he'd been up all night, and for some reason had let Ollie's dogs into the family kitchen at midnight, which had resulted in a lot of shouting and barking and the twins going nuts because they had a test this morning.

Sorcha's mum and dad had arrived into the middle of everything to discover that Beth had gone straight to their house in the city, instead of coming out to the hotel, as they'd expected.

One of the things that Jess loved about Frankie's family was the chaos that regularly bubbled to the surface – there were so many of them, and they were all so super busy, all the time, so coordinating anything was a military operation. One that didn't always go to plan.

For Jess, getting her dad to the opening night of *Macbeth* was going to be a challenge, but nothing on the scale of coordinating the O'Sullivans.

When Sorcha had texted her to come down and meet them too, Jess had been relieved. She hadn't been able to face the thought of school. Her dad had dropped her over to the hospital on his way in to meet the head of Raven's Park College, who, after seeing the papers that morning, had been straight on the phone to give an interview.

Tiernan's arrest had sent shock waves around all the group chats, and with her dad's name on the headline about bullying, Jess didn't want to be the centre of everyone's questions.

'Will I go and find her? Maybe they needed to check her wrist again before they let her go?' Jess pushed herself off the wall she was leaning on with her foot.

Frankie's mum looked undecided for a moment. 'We'd better give her another few minutes in case she's in the lift. This place is so big you could pass each other.'

Beth yawned suddenly, clamping her hand over her mouth. 'Oh God, sorry. Couldn't sleep when I got in last night.'

Sorcha raised her eyebrows innocently and avoided looking at Beth. Jess knew that between them, they'd been up all night.

'That's because the house was freezing. I told you there was no heating on, *that's* why you were supposed to go to the hotel.' Liz sounded tired. 'Have you girls heard anything new about what happened?'

Jess shook her head. 'I think we'll hear as soon as they announce anything.' She was working hard to try and look like she wasn't itching to go. *Where was Frankie?*

The minute that they got away from the mothers this morning, Danny was going to join them for a summit meeting. They needed to work out how to give the information they had about Hailey de Búrca to the Guards, *without* revealing how they'd got it.

The important thing, as Danny had said in their group chat early this morning, was to keep the explanation simple, and as close to the truth as possible, but make sure that the Guards realised that Hailey de Búrca hanging around the hospital and asking questions could be strongly connected to the explosion.

Jess hadn't had a chance to say it yet, but she was sure it would be simpler to get her dad to pass on the information – his sources were protected, and his Garda contacts took what he said seriously. It would be safer for everyone.

Frankie's mum looked up from her phone. 'We'll give Frankie another five minutes, but then I think you might have to go and look for her, Jess.'

As she spoke two Guards came jogging in through the huge glass main doors beside them, and went straight up to the reception desk. They were both wearing heavy bomber jackets, the female Guard the same height as her male colleague, her dark hair pulled back in a pony-tail under her hat. Something urgent was obviously unfolding if their body language was anything to go by. A moment later they headed towards the corridor that connected the main reception area with the Emergency Department.

Frankie's mum looked after them, exasperated. 'Now what on earth?'

'You can't keep me here. This is ridiculous – it's false imprisonment.' Pouting, Hailey de Búrca was slumped into a hard chair beside one of the round lunch tables in the nurses' kitchen, her arms tightly folded. The toe of her trainer with its embedded spikes was tapping faster than Frankie's heart was pounding.

Frankie really did need to get fit; the struggle had left her breathless, and her heart was still rattling inside her chest, although perhaps that was adrenaline rather than exertion. Everything the twins had taught her had come straight back. Taekwondo was about technique over strength and Cian and Kai were blackbelts for a reason.

Leaning back on the wall, Frankie watched Hailey carefully. There were so many questions jumping into Frankie's head. *What had Hailey been trying to do to Becky's drip – what was she doing here at all? And how long had she been involved with Tiernan?*

And more importantly, had she had anything to do with the explosion? *Means, motive, opportunity.* She'd had the opportunity – she'd been seen in the school yesterday morning. Was Tiernan the motive? They were still missing parts of the picture, especially the means, but there was something crazy going on here. Or maybe it was Hailey de Búrca who was crazy. She definitely seemed to have some significant issues.

It all seemed a bit extreme, even to Frankie, whose imagination was prone to running away with her – but *something* had happened to set off an explosion in the Chemistry lab. It wasn't like Frankie was making that up.

And Hailey had already punched a girl in the middle of her school canteen. Had she had something to do with Ardmore Wood school burning down as well?

As Frankie watched her, Hailey threw her an evil glare.

'We're waiting for the Guards, young lady, that's what you're doing here. Maybe you can explain to them what the story is here?' Aoife was pacing like a protective lioness. Frankie had never seen her this angry. Security had responded to Aoife's panic alarm in seconds, then she'd checked Becky's drip and immediately called the Guards.

As Aoife moved between them, Frankie slipped her phone into her sling, switching it on to record.

'I told you I felt faint. I was using the drip stand to pull myself up off the floor.' Hailey shook her head as if they were all making a fuss about nothing.

'You tampered with Rebecca's drip. It was turned off. I know it was working properly when I was in the room five minutes before.' Aoife glared at her. 'And you pretended to be Sorcha's sister Beth, so I let you in to see her.'

Hailey shrugged. 'You misheard me – I never said my name was Beth.'

Still leaning on the door, Frankie cut in, 'You were all over this hospital yesterday pretending to be Beth. It's on the hospital CCTV. You told Becky's mum that's who you were.' Frankie kept her voice level, but inside she was fuming too.

'She must have been muddled – it's stressful having a child in hospital, and she's old. She's probably menopausal.' Hailey threw Frankie a searing look. 'I've as much right to be in this hospital as anyone else.'

Frankie rather doubted that.

But why had she gone after Becky? What could she possibly have done to upset Hailey de Búrca? Frankie looked at her hard, trying to work it out. She could understand why Hailey might hate Ella if they were both dating Tiernan – who knew what he'd told her, what excuses he'd made – but Becky?

Frankie felt her phone vibrate with a text, but she didn't want to look at it. It was probably her mum or one of the others wondering where she was, but if there was a chance Hailey would say something incriminating, there was no way Frankie was going to miss it.

Beside Hailey was a black sports bag. Aoife bent down to pick it up.

'Put that down, that's my property.'

Aoife slipped it onto another table, well away from Hailey, and pulled a pair of latex gloves out the pocket of her trousers. Looking back at Hailey, Aoife snapped them on and opened the zip. Right on the top was a clear plastic bag. She lifted it up.

'Visitors don't usually come into hospitals with sports bags packed full of syringes. What else have you got in here?'

Frankie looked at Hailey pointedly as she replied, 'Those are for personal use. And nothing in there is illegal.' Hailey glared at Aoife like she knew it all.

Frankie just wished the Guards would hurry up; they'd been everywhere yesterday and now they were nowhere in sight.

Aoife shook her head in disbelief as she lifted out another clear plastic bag, this one containing what looked like, from where Frankie was standing, a pill canister with a red lid.

Taking out the contents of the sports bag and laying them on the table, Aoife glanced at Hailey as she removed each item.

A letter in an envelope, a spare T-shirt, a pink wash bag. It looked like she was planning to stay overnight.

Scowling, Aoife picked out a bag from the fancy delicatessen near Jess's apartment. She opened it and looked inside, pulling out a till receipt. 'You can explain yourself to the Guards, madam, and they'll be analysing everything in this bag, right down to this receipt for ...' she turned it over to read it, 'fruit juice.'

Fruit juice? Frankie frowned and did a double-take.

'Was that peach juice by any chance, Hailey?' Frankie moved away from the wall to stand beside Aoife so that she could see the receipt. Before Hailey could answer Frankie picked up the plastic bag and looked at the pill canister. But it didn't contain pills: it had some sort of powder in the bottom, like pills that had been crushed.

Frankie felt her stomach flip as she realised what must have happened.

She glanced at Hailey. 'Was this the fruit juice that appeared next to Ella's bed this morning, with a little bottle of sparkling wine?'

It had been flat when Frankie had opened it – had Hailey pierced the cork with the syringe? Had she poisoned the wine? And then put the powder into the peach juice to be sure that Ella drank one of them? Ella had said it tasted a bit odd ...

Frankie felt her stomach heave and her mouth go dry but she tried to keep her voice light. 'I think we need to check in with Ella, Aoife, and tell her not to drink any of that cocktail that's next to her bed. The Guards will want to test it and to fingerprint the glass too.'

Hailey shook her head disparagingly. 'You think my fingerprints are going to be on it?'

Shrugging, Frankie put her head on one side. 'Maybe not, but if there are traces of any of the drugs in this canister in that wine, it's going to take a bit of explaining, isn't it? You're a real criminal mastermind, aren't you?' Frankie's tone dripped sarcasm. 'Were you planning to put them in Becky's drip too?'

Aoife looked from one of them to the other and, putting the receipt down on the table, strode over to the internal phone on the wall beside the kitchen counter, punching in the numbers, Frankie presumed, for the nurses' station closest to Ella. Aoife's voice was urgent as she filled her colleague in.

She hung up the phone. 'Ella's fine – she wants to see Becky, so she's just asked for a wheelchair to bring her down. The girls upstairs will make sure no one touches the cocktail.'

Frankie exchanged glances with her, then looked at Hailey again. 'Was Tiernan the reason for all of this, Hailey? You've gone to a lot of trouble. I mean, really.'

All this. The planning. The sneaking around impersonating Beth – the research it must have taken to discover that only one of them had a sister, and then finding out her name.

Hailey *had* to have had something to do with the explosion that had landed them all in here.

'Tiernan?' Hailey looked confused, shaking her head. 'He's my boyfriend ...' She shrugged like she had no idea what Frankie was talking about.

Frankie could tell from her face that she thought she was in the clear here ... she was rich; Frankie bet she thought that an expensive lawyer could get her out of this. Would the Guards believe she was involved or swallow whatever lies and excuses she came up with?

Frankie didn't think she could cope with that, but she *could* try and use Hailey's arrogance against her. *If this girl had hurt her friends there was no way Frankie was going to let her get away with it.*

Frankie let out a theatrical sigh, shaking her head. 'It's a laugh really, all this planning, and if the lab assistant hadn't left a bunch of stuff on the shelf in the lab nothing would have happened. Whatever you left there would have only made a ... Tiny. Little. Pop.' Frankie put her head on one side and looked at Hailey pityingly as she drew the words out. She knew she was guessing here, goading Hailey, but she had the strongest feeling that Hailey had left something in the Chemistry lab that had set off the 2,4-DNPH. Becky's experiment was just an accident of timing.

Hailey scowled at her, her tone scathing. 'You can't prove anything.'

'I don't have to; the Guards are going to find the fragments of whatever you left and now they'll be able to match your fingerprints. Were you careful when you built it?'

'There won't be any bits big enough to find my fingerprints on. You're talking rubbish, Frankie O'Sullivan, like you think you're some big detective or something.' Hailey tossed her hair behind her. 'Do I have to stay here much longer?'

Frankie suppressed a smile. Hailey didn't seem to realise what she'd just said – she'd acknowledged there *might* be fragments but they wouldn't be big enough – so she HAD left some sort of device in the Chemistry lab. Frankie prayed her phone had recorded everything. Looking up, Frankie caught Aoife's eye across the room. She was trying not to smirk. Aoife had heard Hailey incriminate herself too.

No doubt Hailey would try to wriggle out of this as well, but perhaps the Guards would believe Sorcha now about the two bangs.

'**J**ust ten minutes, okay?' The nurse smiled at Ella as she wheeled the wheelchair in beside Becky's bed. Ella smiled her thanks and watched as she slipped back out through the curtains, waiting for the sound of the ward doors closing before she said anything to Becky.

Where would she even start?

Getting down here had taken much longer than she'd expected, but then the Guards suddenly arriving to take her cocktail and the glass beside her bed had been a bit of a surprise. By the time they'd taken her statement and everyone had calmed down, it seemed to take ages for someone to find her a wheelchair.

In the lift on the way down, the nurse had filled her in on what the Guards wouldn't explain, and told her that Hailey de Búrca had been detained for questioning for what sounded like an ever-growing list of offences. Starting with impersonating Beth Bennett to get access to Becky's drip, she was also under suspicion for con-structing a homemade bomb that had been instrumental in blowing up the Chemistry lab. The Garda Technical Bureau had confirmed that they had found parts of something that appeared to be a timer. And it *did* have a fingerprint on it.

They'd run it through their records but come up blank. Now they had prints to check it against.

Ella had tried to hide her racing thoughts. If Hailey thought she was dating Tiernan and she'd found out about the nude photos, she'd probably found Ella's texts too. Could she have been targeting Ella and Becky because she wanted to wipe out any competition?

Hailey was plainly as nuts as Tiernan. Worse, probably. Ella bet he'd been wowed by Hailey's family money and had moved in on her like he had on Ella. Tiernan's family were rich but Hailey's was super rich. And then he'd got a LOT more than he'd bargained for.

Since Frankie had left her this morning Ella had been going through the photos in her screenshots and what felt like thousands of ColourMeHappy posts, and she'd found what Maeve had spotted: a post with the book in the centre – the same book that was on the floor in the background of the photos Tiernan had on his phone. Behind the book was the same box of medication with the last three letters of a surname showing.

It had confirmed everything.

Ella took a deep breath. Now she was here with Becky, she didn't know what she was going to say, but she had to try. And she couldn't see that anything she said could possibly make Becky any worse.

She kept her voice low; she didn't want anyone else to hear her.

'Becky, can you hear me? It's Ella, from school. I'm going to guess you can hear okay.' She glanced back at the gap in the curtains where she'd come in. She didn't have much time.

'I don't know what you can remember. Did they tell you that there was an explosion in Chemistry? Everyone's okay now. Frankie was there too, she was bringing your iPad back when it went off, but she's fine. She has it for you, it's all safe.'

Ella took Becky's hand and rubbed it. 'I'm upstairs on another ward, I've broken a couple of ribs, but I'll be grand. Everyone's okay.' Ella paused; Becky really didn't need to know about Maeve's surgery.

'Mackenzie's fine too, she had an asthma attack, but Aoife, she's the nurse here, she's going out with Frankie's brother Ollie, so she's been looking after us all – she thought the asthma was caused by bleach. Do you remember the smell was making her cough?'

Ella glanced at Becky's face. Had anything changed? She was still staring at the ceiling. Ella cleared her throat. She was waffling here, trying to find the right words. She needed to get to the point.

'Listen, Becky, Frankie told me that you were filming

the potassium experiment and the reaction might have been a bit bigger than you thought. But it wasn't your fault. The explosion wasn't anything to do with you. The Guards think this crazy girl who set fire to Ardmore Wood school built some sort of bomb. She ... well, we don't know why exactly, but she's been seeing my boyfriend Tiernan on the side, and she wasn't very happy that Mr Murray wouldn't let her come to Raven's Hill.'

Ella had winced a bit when she said 'my boyfriend Tiernan.' *Did Becky think he was her boyfriend as well? Was this just going to make things worse?* But as Ella looked at Becky, she knew she had to keep trying.

'Anyhow, there was a really dangerous chemical left on the counter at the back of the lab. It's really explosive – it's what the bomb squad took away in the summer. *That's* what caused the worst part of the blast.' Ella rubbed Becky's hand. 'Greg told Jess that you probably saved Mackenzie's life by pushing her away from the experiment. Otherwise, you both would have caught the full force of the big explosion.'

Ella watched Becky to see if there was any response. After a second, Becky blinked. Was that an indication she was listening or some sort of automatic thing? Ella didn't know, she just prayed Becky could hear her.

She'd spent all night trying to work out how to say the next bit, and then Frankie had appeared this morning with the last piece of the puzzle.

'I think it might have been something to do with the colour. She had a load of photos of purple things on her iPad.'

Ella had nodded like she understood – didn't they all collect colours to improve their moods?

But there was a bit more to it than that.

And it was Becky's secret, not hers, to share.

'Becky, I don't know how to say this, but I know about the photos, the ones you sent to Tiernan. He's an absolute scumbag creep, Becky, and, God, I hope you can hear me – he's been arrested, Becky. He beat up Jess's friend Jasper. It was really bad, and I think it was because of me, so I know a bit about how you're feeling.'

Ella could feel tears pricking at the back of her eyes. 'I know he tricked you into sending those photos. He can be very persuasive. He makes you think that you're the centre of his universe but he's just using you. Both of us, Becky; he used me too. It's about control: he sees something he likes and he has to have it. He's used to getting his own way and it's going to be some shock now when he doesn't.'

She took a shaky breath before she continued.

'The thing is, you're only fifteen, and if you report him for sharing the photos, you'll be completely anonymous. Nobody needs to know your name. I know it's scary reporting him, but with the assault charge too, he'll be in a heap more trouble.'

It had taken Ella a while to work out why Becky had come to school on Monday, and she knew she was guessing, but perhaps Becky hadn't realised the photos had been shared until that post appeared on Rave-fess. And it was too late to disappear then: everyone would be wondering why. Whatever had happened, Ella could imagine Becky's shock when she'd realised they were her photos. She must have been sick to her stomach.

Maybe filming the experiment, and creating the purple flash, had been her way of coping, of distracting herself.

Frankie had said that Becky had really come out of herself when she'd been working on the ideas for their English video; it was like she was a different person, she'd been brilliant and creative and so sure of herself. It made complete sense to Ella that Becky had created a whole other world online, one where there were no difficult mothers, or school bullies, anxiety or worry, one where she was in control and could be herself, where she could make other people happy.

Ella took a shaky breath. 'If you do decide to go to the police, Tiernan might have deleted the photos, but I've got my own photos – I've got all the evidence that he asked for them and he shared them. He's probably done it to other girls. God knows, but I'll be here for you, Becky, and I swear I'll never tell anyone. He's conned me too.'

Tiernan really was a total narcissist. Ella couldn't believe that she'd been taken in by him. But she'd thought about it last night, about the constant heart texts and the gifts and making her feel awful if she didn't tell him what she was doing or who she was talking to. And then ignoring her when it suited him.

He'd been toxic since day one.

He'd even stalked her on Instagram after meeting her at Katie's party and she hadn't even realised. God, she felt so stupid. She wanted to major in psychology, and she hadn't even been able to see that she was in an abusive, controlling relationship. He was an expert manipulator.

He and Hailey de Búrca were actually made for each other.

Ella bit her lip; she hadn't been completely sure about the next bit until she'd spoken to Frankie about the purple video, but then everything Frankie had said had slotted into place and it had all made sense.

'Maeve thinks it's someone at Raven's Hill …'

'Becky, you are completely amazing. We need you to come back to us. I can't even believe it, but you're ColourMeHappy, aren't you? You've got Rainbow Princess on your phone ID, I know that could be anything, and Tiernan uses all sorts of nicknames in his contact list, that's why I didn't realise at first, but then Frankie said about the purple flash.

'Becky, if it *is* you, you've no idea how many people think you are incredible. You've pulled us all through really hard times – Katie and Maeve and all of us, and that's just Raven's Hill. There are people all over the world that you've helped with that account. I hope it's your happy place too. You are just amazing. I know that you know that it's got thousands of followers, but they aren't just numbers, they're real people with real problems and your account makes a real difference to their lives.'

ColourMeHappy was so simple but had had such a big impact. The more Ella had thought about it, the more she was sure it was Becky's creative outlet, a place where she could just be herself and not be held back by her age, or by not fitting in. Its success was down to the fact that it wasn't trying to be anything, or sell anything, it was just an honest place to discuss mood and things like anxiety and stress that impacted all of them. And colour. Everyone could relate.

Ella drew a breath. 'I swear I'm not going to tell anyone any of it. Really, you can trust me one million percent. But I wanted you to know that those photos weren't your fault, and nobody else knows it was you. Tiernan's in so much trouble there's no way he's ever going to tell, but if you decided to report him, he'd end up in prison for that as well, and it would be the best place for him.'

'And the explosion wasn't your fault either. Hailey de Búrca is utterly deranged and she's been dating Tiernan. I think she was after me as well, and Mr Murray. The stuff that was on the shelf was waiting to explode – it should have had a warning on it. And Mackenzie's asthma attack was because of the bleach. And we all think you're amazing. I'm totally in awe.'

As Ella finished, she felt Becky's hand tighten on hers.

'Becky, are you okay? Oh, please say you're okay.' Forgetting about her ribs, Ella stood up too quickly, a bolt of pain shooting through her. Stifling a yelp, she rubbed the back of Becky's hand with both of hers. This was the really difficult bit – she couldn't tell Becky that anyone had spotted a link between the photos and ColourMeHappy's posts.

'Becky, I can be ColourMeHappy while you're in here, I just need your login. Then *nobody* will ever guess it's you.' Ella prayed Becky could hear her. If she could get Becky's password to the Instagram account, she could take the photo down that Maeve had seen and remove all the evidence before Maeve was well enough to find it again.

Ella felt Becky squeeze her hand. Were Becky's eyes starting to focus? Oh God, she hoped so.

'Thank you.' It was barely a whisper. A tear slid down Becky's face.

Ella felt a surge of relief, her own eyes wet with tears. 'I'm here, Becky, and I'm your champion. I'll make sure nobody finds out any of it, and if they guess, I'll make sure that your secret is safe, whatever I have to do. Just know that you're amazing and that none of this was your fault.'

WHAT WE KNOW: UPDATED
BY SORCHA BENNETT

Double explosion in the Chemistry Lab,
Raven's Hill School: Six girls taken to hospital.

Explosion 1
Deliberate: Target – Ella and Becky.
Plus Mr Murray.

Explosion 2:
Accident: 2,4-Dinitrophenylhydrazine left in
lab, knocked off shelf by explosion 1.

Frankie O'Sullivan out of hospital with a
broken wrist, back at school.

Sorcha Bennett out of hospital, at home for the moment but moving back into the boarding house this week (yay!). Back at school.

Ella Diamond at home with two broken ribs, off school for a few more weeks.

Becky Hartigan fully conscious and at home, returning to school next week, we hope.

Mackenzie Smyth back at the boarding house, back to classes this week.

Maeve Andersson in post-surgical recovery at St Anthony's, home tomorrow.

Jasper Parks being discharged today.

Hailey de Búrca: arrested for setting a bomb in the Chemistry lab, trying to poison Ella and interfering with Becky's drip – in custody.

Tiernan Reece: arrested for attacking Jasper Parks and for sharing intimate photos of a minor. In custody.

Conan Johansson: arrested for attacking Jasper and for conspiracy to share intimate photos – on bail.

Danny Holmes making a true crime podcast about recent events.

Jennifer Ryan, lab technician: re-training in the Art department.

Mr Murray seen having dinner with Ms Rowan in new Italian restaurant on the sea front. We're all hoping something might be about to blow up there ☺

ACKNOWLEDGEMENTS

Every book is brought to you, the reader, by an army of people. I put the words on the page, but I'm hugely grateful to everyone who helps in that process, particularly the experts who helped me with getting the detail right in *Something's About to Blow Up*.

Rex Fox O'Loughlin is a massive YA reader and my go-to on anything social media related or techie. Huge thanks, Rex, for reading that early draft and all your plot input – you know that I couldn't do it without you!

Big thanks too, to Sam O'Loughlin for helping me with the proof read and double checking all the times and text messages.

Joy Rice, a real chemistry teacher and vice principal, was absolutely invaluable in assisting with all things chemistry related, and one of the first people I spoke to when I came up with the idea of an explosion. I had no idea what that explosion could have been caused by and it was Joy's knowledge that set me on the right track. Any classroom mistakes are definitely my own. Huge thanks, Joy, for all your help and for agreeing to meet me for coffee to discuss how to blow up a chemistry lab!

Margaret Williams-Muldoon read a very early draft and helped enormously with the hospital setting. Location is a character in many of my books, but I set myself a challenge with this one as it's set over 24 hours and essentially all in one place. Margaret is a nurse, and her input was absolutely vital on all things hospital related, blast injuries and what happened to the girls – many of her ideas became key to the plot. Margaret is a fabulous writer herself and I hope we'll be seeing a book of hers on the shelf very soon.

And thank you, Margaret Skea, for telling me exactly what broken ribs feel like – your awful experience was put to good use.

Huge thanks, too, to the team at Gill Books for all the work that you put into every book – from the editing to the cover to the PR, you make it all come together.

My agent Simon Trewin is the one who ensures that I can keep doing what I love most and call it my job – thank you for everything.

And a HUGE thank-you to all the book bloggers, reviewers, teachers, librarians and school librarians who have supported me and loved *Something Terrible*

Happened Last Night – I do hope you enjoy this one too. I really couldn't reach readers without you – you make it all possible!

If you are faced with any of the challenges that I've covered in this story, you'll find links that might help at my website www.samblakebooks.com. Please reach out: there are people ready to help you.

SBx

SOMETHING

TERRIBLE

IT'S THE DEADLIEST

HAPPENED

PARTY OF THE YEAR

LAST NIGHT

SAM BLAKE

NUMBER ONE BESTSELLING AUTHOR

It's Katie's 17th birthday – the dancefloor is packed, the drink is flowing and Rave-fess, the Raven's Hill School confession site, is alight with gossip.

Then a huge fight breaks out, sending guests fleeing.

When Frankie, Jess and Sorcha go back to help Katie clear up the wrecked house before her parents get home, they find more than broken bottles …

There's a body on the living room floor.

100 SUSPECTS.
1 KILLER.